The Night Singers

London Clarke

Published by London Clarke, 2024.

THE NIGHT SINGERS

First edition. May 28, 2024.

Copyright © 2024 London Clarke.

ISBN: 979-8224551446

Written by London Clarke.

For all who are caught in a trap.

If you want to find the secrets of the universe, think in terms of energy, frequency and vibration. - Nikola Tesla

1

I am not a musician. I only make my living writing about them. My whole career has been about compiling music industry articles and biographies of deceased composers, and co-writing memoirs. But my favorite part of my job is ghostwriting. I love the anonymity, knowing that I'm making someone else look or sound good, and it allows me to stand back and just let things happen.

I don't have to be in control. There's some relief in that. The secret to dealing with musicians is to keep a high but transparent wall between them and me. They tell me their story, and I write it down. They can let their egos flare, and I can maintain a distance from their emotions. It's a contract protecting everyone. The process had worked beautifully for me—until it didn't.

My safety net began to unravel when I met Riff Fall. Actually, the threads had begun to fray a few hours before that when I received a text message from my dad.

Hi, doll. I know it's been a while. I hope you're well. Give me a call when you have a chance. I'm thinking about taking a trip to Nashville to see you. There's something I need to talk to you about. It's pretty important.

I rolled my eyes and threw my head back. *A while?* I hadn't heard from my father in more than five years. Hadn't seen him in twenty. What could be so important that he needed to talk to me now? And a visit? Oh, hell no. He was the one who'd decided to cut me out of his life.

I deleted his message without responding. The last thing I needed was to be distracted by ghosts of the past right before one of the biggest initial client interviews I'd ever had.

Sitting in the designated office area of my studio condo, I pushed Dad to the back of my mind and returned to my current project notes: Riff Fall, the former lead singer of the 90s band Cry of Crows.

When Quincy, my agent and friend, first discussed the project with me, I'd experienced a rush of excitement at the prospect of meeting and working with Riff. As a teenager, I'd been a big fan of Cry of Crows. I had all their CDs and had seen them in concert. Maybe I'd even had a little crush on Riff at the time—now nearly twenty years ago.

Although I'd ghostwritten for several musicians, I'd never worked with anyone who'd been so scrutinized by the public and scandalized by the press. Since my small obsession with him all those years ago, Riff Fall's life had been filled with drama.

"And if you want to meet him in person," Quincy reminded me, "you'll have to go to the island. He won't come to the mainland."

I had that fact in my notes underlined in purple ink. *Riff Fall—forty-three-year-old agoraphobic recluse.* Rumor had it that he hadn't left his property in years.

It didn't help that the house was built on Invisible Island, a place that had earned its name because so few people knew of its existence—a fact the locals apparently relished. The island had no bridge and was only accessible by boat or ferry.

Riff and I had exchanged a few emails, but he hadn't said much about his vision for the book. Even so, he seemed to want to move forward. I had no idea what sort of person I would be dealing with or what kind of story he wanted to tell. I assumed it would be the standard musician fare: drugs, alcohol, groupies.

I'd told him that we should meet and nail down some specifics. I'd done phone calls and Zoom meetings with clients, but I preferred to meet in person if possible—at least once. From Nashville, Invisible Island was an eight-hour drive and a ferry ride. Still, I was willing. But Riff was clear—he didn't want me to come.

I wouldn't feel right about it, he'd written in one of his emails.

I wasn't sure what he meant by that, and he didn't elaborate. I decided to try and let it go. He didn't want to meet in person. I'd have to settle for video chats.

As I waited for him to appear on the screen of the Zoom meeting room, I studied old photos of Riff and the band online. I'd also watched some concert footage and music videos from 1998. Riff had been a hottie back in the day. Longish brown hair tucked behind his ears and huge, dark eyes that held a glint of crazy even then. With a chiseled jawline and perfect nose—by most standards—Riff was beautiful. Eighteen years ago, when I'd seen the band in concert, he'd been a livewire frontman. His performance style was a bit Jim Morrison-like: clutching the microphone stand with one hand, his other slung over the top of the mic itself—all while his powerful, raspy voice reverberated through the arena.

I couldn't find any current pictures of him—not since all the press died down about his missing wife—Lila, lead singer of the band Episodic Noise.

A knock at my door startled me, followed by a stab of pain. Normally, my dog Tyler would be barking. It had been a couple of weeks since he'd passed, and the stillness of my living space still unnerved me.

I checked the time on the computer. Nine o'clock. Who was knocking at my door now? Unless... maybe it was someone from the condo association stopping by to drop off a newsletter. They did that at night sometimes.

I crossed the room to the front door and looked out the peephole. No one was there. Relief flooded me. Probably a delivery driver leaving a package.

I opened the door.

A young woman stood on the other side.

Shorter than me and maybe in her twenties, she looked like she'd been standing in the rain for some time—except it wasn't raining. Her hair was plastered to her face, and her white tank dress clung to her thin body. She was covered in green sludge like she'd fallen in an algae-laden pond. Her eyes peered at me in a dark, unblinking stare.

"Hi," I said, flexing my arm to hold the door in place. "Can I help you?"

Her body jerked forward. "Listen, lissstennn," she hissed.

I braced my weight against the door more firmly. Maybe she was a tweaker who'd knocked at the wrong condo number. Were the blood vessels in her eyes broken? The whites weren't visible in the black, bulging gaze.

Shaken, I found my voice. "Do you need help? Can I call someone to help you?"

"Listennn..."

A late evening breeze blew across the threshold, causing me to shiver. Something wasn't right about this, and the longer I stood there staring at her, the more intense my reticence. "Do you need help?"

When she still didn't respond, I gave in to my instincts and shut the door. Then I stood there for several seconds—*listening*. Was she gone?

I stood on my tiptoes to look out the peephole.

Bang, bang, bang! The door shook. I jolted backward.

"What do you want?" My voice ricocheted around the entryway.

In response, a rattle vibrated from the back of her throat.

I palmed my phone from my back pocket. I could call the police. It seemed like the right thing to do when someone was insistently banging on your door. But when I looked out the peephole again, the girl was gone.

"Hello?" A voice called from inside my condo.

I jumped, but then I remembered—my Zoom meeting with Riff. *Pull it together, Callie. Get your professional persona on.* I struggled to readjust my headspace as I rushed back to my desk, where my computer waited. Riff was on the screen, sitting in front of a wall of hanging guitars and looking confused.

I leaned into the camera. "I'm sorry," I said, trying to keep my voice from shaking. "Someone was at the door." I lowered myself into the chair. "It was a little...weird. Sorry about that."

His mouth twitched into a wan smile. "No problem."

I pushed my hair back and tried to appear more settled than I felt. The encounter at the door had shaken me, thrown me off my game. I just prayed the girl—whoever she was—didn't come back. "Hi, Riff," I breathed out.

He looked at me with maple syrup-brown eyes, brought out by his tight-fitting tan T-shirt. He still had a full head of brown hair, just touching his shoulders in the style he'd always worn, though now it was streaked with gray. His jawline wasn't as defined, but otherwise, he seemed to be weathering his age pretty well.

"So, Callisto..." he remarked. "That's an unusual name."

I smiled. "Yeah, my mother was into Greek mythology. Callie, please."

He reached up and adjusted his screen, tipping it slightly. I caught sight of his arm, a well-toned bicep decorated with blue and green swirls.

"My agent recommended you, but I've also cyberstalked you a bit," he said. "You've got an impressive portfolio. You've ghostwritten for Chad Ellis and Remmy Star?" He chuckled. "How'd you get those gigs? It must've taken some coaxing to get Remmy to talk."

I pulled out my tablet and set it up with my portable keyboard so I could type without minimizing the meeting screen. "I met Remmy at a press thing, told him what I did, and he said he'd been looking for someone to write his story. First time we met up, I brought him a bottle of fifteen-year-old scotch. He was pretty talkative after two or three shots."

Riff snickered. "Now, that sounds about right. Still, the way you wrote about him—you handled the sections on his childhood well. It's the only one of your books I've read so far, but I'm a slow reader." He lifted a bandaged hand and scratched his forehead.

"What happened to your hand?"

He looked down. "Oh, punched a wall."

I raised my eyebrows.

He blinked and lowered his gaze. "Not exactly what you think. I mean, it wasn't because I was angry or anything."

That seemed likely untrue. I'd known people who'd punched walls before and it was always because they were angry. I thought about the initial news reports after Riff's wife disappeared. At one time, there'd been talk that Riff might have been involved. So, did he have a tendency toward violence? I filed the detail of his bandaged hand in my brain and decided to change the subject.

"Riff. That's obviously a stage name."

He smiled a little. "I've been called Riff since I was six years old. It's one of those—what do you call it—acronyms? My real name is Robert Isaac Franklin Fall."

"I see. Hence, Riff."

"My brother was Terrence Aaron Frederick Fall."

"Did they call him Taff?"

Riff laughed. "No, but..." He twisted a braided leather bracelet around his wrist, revealing another small black tattoo etched into the space where his palm met his wrist. "I think my mother had some lofty ideas about us kids. Thought giving us all big, long names might mean we'd end up being something fancy. Or at least fancier than quarry workers and truck drivers. And my stepfather—well, I don't think he would've been happy unless I'd turned out to be a preacher or a doctor."

"You turned out to be a rock star. That's something."

Riff shrugged. "Yeah, well, at the end of the day, it might have been better to stick with the truck driving."

I glanced down at some information about Riff I'd found online and printed out. "So, what are you thinking you'd like the focus of the story to be?"

"You're jumping right into this, aren't you?"

"I assume your time is valuable, as is mine."

He gave me a flat smile and held up his hands. "I've got nothing but time."

I, on the other hand, did not. I glanced at the clock in the lower corner of the computer. "I've got about an hour before another Zoom meeting."

He looked at his watch. "This late?"

"I'm an hour behind you—and it's another musician." I smiled. "You guys tend to keep late hours, so I've learned to do the same."

He nodded. "Okay. I get it."

I studied him. His face was South Carolina suntanned, which surprised me if he'd been holed up inside his house.

"So, how do we do this?" he asked.

I leaned toward the camera. "Well, it's pretty straightforward. First, we determine the structure—where are we going with the story? After that, you talk, I listen. If you have anything you've already written that you want me to look at, I'm happy to do that too."

He tucked a stray lock of hair behind his ear. "I've played around a little with the introduction and a chapter or two. You know, just to say why I'm writing this and all."

"I'd love to see it."

He nodded. "I'll send it to you right now."

"Great. I'll take a look at it as soon as we're finished talking." I sat back, positioned my tablet in front of me, and typed some initial thoughts while Riff tapped at his keyboard and clicked his mouse, presumably sending the intro.

Usually, at the beginning of these interviews, I had a couple of questions I used as icebreakers, but we'd somehow skirted past them. "If you don't mind, I'll ask you a few questions I ask all my clients—tailored for the individual, of course."

"Go ahead. Shoot."

I read off my notes. "Eighteen years ago, when Cry of Crows first rose to stardom, you were all over the music scene. Your photo was on the front of rock magazines. You were interviewed on MTV. People felt like they knew you. So, how would you describe yourself these days?" I poised my fingers over the keys, ready to type.

His gaze slid to the side, and his Adam's apple bobbed. "I'm the walking dead."

I hadn't expected that answer. "Sorry?"

He waved his bandaged hand. "Nah, don't listen to me. I'm just full of shit."

I cleared my throat. Okay. Moving on to question number two. "Where do you think you'd be now if you hadn't become who you are?"

"Still driving a truck, probably." Riff's eyes were unfocused. "Or I don't know. Maybe I'd be living in suburbia somewhere, married with three kids."

I couldn't picture that, but I typed it into my notes anyway.

Riff put his hands to his face and rubbed them up and down. "I think any life would be preferable to the one I've got." He pulled his hands away. "And I'm sure you're wondering—like everyone else, what's my problem? Why can't I live like a normal person?"

I did wonder that.

Grimacing, he made a noise in his throat. "I have a reason why I can't leave Belle Marsh."

"I'm sure you do." I waited. Several seconds ticked by.

"Everybody asks, see, and I don't—well, I can't tell you what the reason is, and you should know that upfront."

I shifted a little. "You can't tell me why you can't leave your house?"

"It's complicated." He sat back and looked off to the side. Then his eyes darted back to the camera. "And I know that's your job—to help me tell my story. But there are some things I can't tell you. I just...can't."

Usually, when I interviewed clients for ghostwriting projects, they wanted to tell me everything all at once. I often had to stop them, let them know we would get to this part or that part in due course. But it seemed that wouldn't be the case here.

"Okay. It's your story. There's plenty to tell without even going into the whys of your...situation. Four mega-selling albums—two of them went diamond. Cry of Crows toured all over the world and stayed on the road for unprecedented amounts of time. I think in your interview for *Rolling Stone* you talked about how the last tour almost killed you."

He sat back and groaned. "Yeah."

"Or we could start with your childhood. I've done my homework. I know you grew up as one of four kids, raised by your mom and stepdad. You probably have plenty to say about your life outside Belle Marsh."

Riff dragged his unbandaged hand across his mouth, craned his head back. "Shit. I knew this was going to happen." He shook his head. "I don't want to talk about any of that. That's all been done before. I've got nothing new to add to the sad musician's story of an abusive childhood followed by drugs and rehab." He gave a short laugh. "Obviously, I don't have the first damn idea of how to do this."

"Okay, like I said, this is your story. I'm just here to help you make it sound good. You can say or not say anything you want. We just need to figure out what story you want to tell."

Riff lifted a black mug and brought it to his lips, still staring off into space. I wondered if he'd even heard me just now. Maybe he had hearing loss. I'd met with a lot of musicians who did.

I allowed my hands to fall into my lap. "You know, this would be a lot easier if we could meet in person. As I said before, I really don't mind traveling to the island. In fact, I would prefer—"

"No." He shook his head. "No, you can't come." He looked off to the left, almost like someone was calling him. Slowly, he returned his gaze to the screen. "It's not...safe for you to come here."

I'd recently read an article about Riff, highlighting his insistence that his property was haunted or cursed or something. These claims were usually mentioned in the same paragraph that detailed his attempted suicide in 2010 and speculated that he'd lost touch with reality—or that he was covering up his crimes.

But there was no evidence that any crime had been committed. Lila Silverleaf had disappeared. They'd never found her body. The case had gone cold, and she was still listed as missing. Rumors abounded in equal parts that she'd absconded to Europe and that Riff had fed her to the sharks.

But Riff had been cleared of all charges, and I, for one, believed in the presumption of innocence when guilt could not be proven. I liked facts, not rumors. So what if he'd punched a wall? That didn't mean he was violent.

I was not afraid of Riff Fall.

My tablet had gone to sleep. I tapped a key until it blinked awake again.

Riff sat back. "I can send you photos. I can walk around, video the place..."

I grimaced. "I mean, I guess if that's the only way we can do it."

Suddenly, Riff slapped his unbandaged hand on the table. "You know, this is probably a big mistake. I shouldn't have started this. I don't know what I was thinking."

He stood, his face disappearing out of the eyeshot of the camera. Now I stared at his belt buckle.

"I'm sorry I wasted your time, Callie. It was nice meeting you."

"Riff, wait, I—"

The screen went black.

Host has ended the meeting.

I stared at the screen for a moment in disbelief, unsure if I was expecting him to reappear again. It's not like this hadn't happened before. I'd met with plenty of potential clients who wanted to write their stories, only to back out after we started talking, finding memories too painful to relive. That was fine—I respected people's decisions on whether to move forward or not. I had other ghostwriting or co-authoring jobs lined up. But now I sat with an unfamiliar pit in my stomach. I didn't like the way that ended. And for some reason, I really wanted to tell Riff's story. Maybe it was because I'd been a big fan of Cry of Crows' music. Maybe because there was something about Riff that reminded me a little of myself—all those years ago when I'd first shut everything down—all the feelings, the emotions. After my dad left me for the wolves to devour, then further humiliated me by cutting off all contact.

I too had lived in my own prison—a cell of solitary confinement that had forever changed me.

2

O kay, so that was over and hadn't gone particularly well. After the Zoom call ended, I continued to sit in front of my computer, processing the meeting. What could I have done differently? Maybe if I hadn't invited myself to the island. Even so, his reaction to the suggestion had been pretty extreme.

Shaking my head, I switched over to my email. I would have to let Quincy know that it had all fallen through. And maybe it was for the best.

In my inbox, an email from Riff stared at me. During the call, he'd sent his introduction. I could've just deleted it and moved on. But curiosity got the better of me, so I opened it and clicked on the attachment.

Fallen Star (just an idea for the title)

By Riff Fall

Introduction

There's been much speculation about my life over the past few years—from the public, media, fans, and even friends and family. I've been called everything from a "crazy hermit" to a "murderer." That's why I wanted to write this book, to tell my side of the story. To tell what happened to me and how it changed me.

There are a lot of things they don't tell you about "making it." They hand you a big black pen and show you where to sign. They tell you you're the next big thing. They tell you your life's about to change. They're not wrong about that last part.

They don't tell you you're just a pawn in their game. That at some point you'll become a nostalgic sound of the past, inevitably replaced by the *next* big thing, and that all stars burn out or fall eventually. For me, when I crashed, I was left with nothing but a bunch of demons—some were mine, some belonged to other people. I moved to Invisible Island to get away from those demons. Turns out, some demons will find you no matter where you go.

This book isn't about the band. It's not even about my life and career. It's about a choice I made that nearly destroyed me.

It's taken me several years to decide to write this book. I don't know what it will mean for me or my life, but I have to tell the truth. No matter what happens as a result. I've always hurtled headlong into fields of asteroids. Sometimes it's worth the risk to tell a cautionary tale. And if I can't save myself, maybe I can save someone else.

Riff Fall
September 2016

He'd always "hurtled headlong into fields of asteroids." It was a great line, but what did it mean?

Anyway, the intro wasn't bad. But who were "they?" I assumed music industry peeps: managers, recording company reps, entertainment attorneys, etc. I'd heard about the whole gamut of offenders from previous clients and even my dad. Riff's introduction was enough to whet my appetite for more. Except there wouldn't be more.

And what did he mean about telling the truth? Was he talking about Lila? This wasn't going to be one of those confessional books, was it? If so, I was glad he'd changed his mind. I didn't want to be a true crime writer. For that matter, I didn't really want to write about a man living in a haunted house—if that's what this was.

Anyway, I didn't believe in ghosts. Not real ghosts. If I were to define the term for myself, a ghost was an idea. An inconvenient memory. Like any memory that had to do with my dad. As far as I was concerned, our entire relationship had entered the realm of the dead. To follow that line of logic, I also didn't believe in haunted houses—only haunted people. Riff Fall was definitely haunted. I could see it in his eyes. Round, dark, and fixed—staring at me with all those memories trapped behind them.

WHEN I DIDN'T HEAR anything from Riff by the following afternoon, I phoned Quincy.

"Riff called it off."

"What?" his voice shrilled. "What do you mean he called it off?"

"He said he'd made a mistake, then ended the meeting."

"Dammit. I'll have to call his agent. See what happened."

"Soon as I mentioned going to Belle Marsh, he got all weird and left the call."

Quincy sighed. "And that was kind of the whole point of the memoir, from what I understood. He was going to do a tell-all about his experiences in that house."

"Yeah, well, I got the feeling he wasn't quite sure if he wanted to tell anything."

"That's a shame. But if the guy's a nutball, all wishy-washy and difficult, you don't want to work with him anyway."

"Yeah, I guess so. Although I've worked with nuts before." I spun around in my chair. "Anyway, after I talked to Riff last night, I had a Zoom call with Abe Brion about ghostwriting for him. He says he wants to do it. It probably won't be nearly as interesting, but if Riff is a no-go then I gotta shift my focus. Abe and I are meeting in person tomorrow."

"Sorry, Cal. I know you were excited about Riff. But at least Abe is another one in the pipeline."

Something crackled on the other end of the line.

I smiled. "You eating a PayDay?"

"Of course."

Quincy's favorite afternoon snack. Last year I'd given him a crate of the candy bars for his birthday.

"Hey, you want to grab a drink this week? There's that new wine bar in Midtown," he said.

"Yeah, that could be good. Thanks, Quince."

After I hung up, I stopped spinning in my chair and listened. For a second, I was sure I'd heard the tap of Tyler's claws on the floors. But the doorway was empty, of course. The golden-haired mutt's passing had been quickly followed by that of my goldfish Weezer—almost as if Weezer had mourned the loss of Tyler as much as I did. Without either of them there now, the studio only echoed with my footsteps instead of the scrabble of dog feet and panting.

Tyler's red leash still hung on the hook by the door, and I hadn't yet had the heart to put away his water bowl, which had dried up and collected dust.

As much as I missed his greeting whenever I came through the door, even worse was the knowledge that of my three best friends, Quincy, Tyler, and Weezer, only one was human—and still alive. I'd created a world for myself that was insular and safe, but lonely.

Maybe I should join an online dating service. Ugh. The very idea of that—constructing a profile, trying to make connections—was exhausting to consider.

I lumbered into the kitchen, my chest heavy. Maybe I should call Mom and apologize for the fight we'd had last week. But that required energy I just didn't have right now. I eyed the half-full bottle of whiskey on my kitchen counter. There was another empty bottle at the bottom of the trash. I'd pushed it all the way down—just in case my weekly house cleaner decided to take out the garbage when she came tomorrow. I contemplated pouring myself a shot. Instead, I returned to my office space, plopped down at my desk, and started sifting through the information I'd gathered on Riff. Not that it mattered now that he'd changed his mind. Shred or toss? My eye caught a glimpse of a photo I'd printed out—a shot taken during a 2002 Australian tour. Riff singing against a purple background, his dark hair covering one eye, the wrist of his right arm ringed with leather bracelets as he held up the microphone. The bottom of a tattoo peeked out of the sleeve of his black T-shirt. From what I'd seen in the Zoom meeting, he seemed to have a lot more tattoos on his arms now.

Shaking my head, I tossed the paper aside. What was my fascination with this guy? I'd be much better off spending the time researching Abe Brion's background since I was meeting with him tomorrow.

Instead, I pulled up YouTube and searched for Cry of Crows. The video for their song "Field of Sorrows" popped up—a live concert video from 1999, filmed at a packed arena in Virginia.

Riff moved across the stage, a white tank top clinging to his chest. His hair stuck to his sweaty cheeks as he clutched the microphone stand with both hands. His voice was like a clarion call—a melodic bellow over the cry of whanging guitars and drums beating out a rhythmic cadence.

> *It's not over;*
> *It's only just begun.*
> *Here we stand alone*
> *Where we once stood as one.*

His voice broke as a growl at the end of the note.

He was good. I'd forgotten how good. Riff Fall's singing was the reason so many others had emulated Cry of Crows' sound. Every garage band at that time played their songs.

I scrolled through the comments underneath the video.

Sissythomas75: *I sure miss this band. Who else is listening 20 years later?*

Metalchickboo: *Riff Fall WAS Cry of Crows. What a voice.*

FR8967: *Anyone know where he is now?*

Bleedbabybleed: *Dead.*

FR8967: *No, dude. He's still alive, that was the drummer Trey Spokane who died. The whole band fell apart after Riff left though.*

Harfna4467: *What an asshole.*

Lux4455: *Yeah, remember a couple of years ago he was investigated for the murder of his wife?*

Harfna4467: *He killed her.*

Metalchickboo*: @Harfna4467 YOU are the asshole. He did not kill his wife.*

FR8967: *Yeah, dude, Lila Silverleaf disappeared. No one knows what happened to her.*

I scrolled through the rest of the comments, mostly middle-aged men who remembered attending Cry of Crows concerts, and women who'd once been in love with Riff.

Maybe I would grab that shot of whiskey after all. Back in the kitchen, I took a glass down from the shelf, filled it with Johnnie Walker, and tossed it down my throat. Then I returned to my notes and scanned them while the whiskey burned in my chest.

-band formed in 1994 in Myrtle Beach, SC, and was originally called The Crows, but it was too close to the Black Crows, so their manager suggested they change it.

-In 2010, Riff jumped off a balcony at a hotel in Savannah, GA. Suicide attempt, assumedly. He lived but broke his hip, foot. Later that year, he moved to Invisible Island and built Belle Marsh.

-In 2011, Lila moved into Riff's house on Invisible Island. Lila and Riff married.

-Lila disappeared in 2012.

-Riff Fall was taken in for questioning about his wife's disappearance and nearly died while in police custody.

I'd forgotten about that last note—Riff had had a seizure or something while being questioned by police.

I glanced over at the pack of cigarettes sitting on my coffee table. Yeah, I was trying to cut back, but I could've really used one right then. *No, you don't need a cigarette. Only two a day, remember? Just don't think about it.*

Sighing, I turned my attention back to the computer. I'd bookmarked an article from a few years ago about Belle Marsh and the local legends surrounding it. The headline read "Former Lead Singer Now Lives Reclusive Life in Haunted House." Beneath it, a paragraph in bold elaborated. ***Two years after the tragic and mysterious disappearance of his wife, the former lead singer of one*** *of the most commercially successful bands ever—Cry of Crows—is still not talking.*

I continued to scroll down.

It's unclear as to whether his unwillingness to talk is legal or personal in nature. But in the minds of those who call Invisible Island home, the mystery of what happened to Lila Silverleaf remains a fresh wound—a blight on a small coastal community that prides itself on a simple lifestyle and remote location. Accessible only by boat, Invisible Island lies on the southernmost tip of South Carolina's coast—an island steeped in history. Part marsh, part beach, this primitive place is a mixture of forest-dwelling folks and retired property owners. The atmosphere is laid-back and low-key.

Even so, ask anyone on Invisible Island about Riff Fall and what happened at Belle Marsh, and they all have a theory.

The rest of the article was a mixture of rumor and superstition, with hardly any quotes from Riff himself.

It really was a shame he wouldn't let me write his story. I would've done a damn good job of it.

3

The following evening, I took a ride-share across town to meet with Abe Brion. It was way easier than trying to find parking. We only had a little over an hour to talk, as he was filming a video at an old warehouse in an industrial park. Abe was a nice guy—and much more willing to talk about himself than Riff. But most musicians were. I usually had far more information than I needed.

Abe's accent hinted he was trying too hard to fit into the Nashville scene by disguising his New Jersey roots. "It's like this. For me, fame was this elusive dream. I knew I could sing, knew I had talent, knew I had a future, but I just didn't realize that future was in country music, not rock. Nashville, not LA."

Every few minutes, Abe looked over his shoulder at the huge digital clock behind us, positioned there by one of the crew when we first started talking.

After an hour and a half, he checked the time and stopped right in the middle of a sentence. "Sorry. I gotta run."

Abe returned to the shoot, and I called for another ride share to take me home. As I headed outside, I dug in my purse for my pack of cigarettes. Holding the stick to my mouth, I flicked my lighter, held it to the end, and took a drag. I walked past a few crew members carrying cords and camera equipment. They moved inside, dragging the large metal door closed behind them.

It was close to ten thirty, and my ride would have to meet me outside the barriers that cordoned off the filming, so I walked down to the corner where another warehouse sat empty and dark. The app said my driver was only five minutes away, so I wouldn't have to wait in the all-too-quiet shadows for long.

I drew several long, deep drags from the cigarette and watched the smoke dissipate into the warm night air. Yeah, I was trying to quit, but right then, every little puff was a lifeline.

From twenty yards away, the warehouse where I'd met with Abe thrummed with music—a muted, throbbing sound. Then, from somewhere behind me came shuffling feet. I spun around.

A group of six emerged from the darkness. A man who looked more like a California sequoia than a human walked between two women. They strode in a line, side by side—slowly, but with purpose, their legs moving together like they marched as part of an army.

I dropped my cigarette and crushed it with my foot before returning my stare to the group.

The women had long hair of varying colors—blonde, black, green, and purple, and the male stood chest and shoulders above them. He had to have been at least six foot seven. Some women wore short dresses, some cut-off jean shorts, and others cargo pants. Their arms and legs were covered in tattoos, and as they approached silently, the green and blue swirls and lines shone under the street lamps, which began to flicker like strobe lights.

My breath caught in my throat. I glanced down the length of the street. No car lights. No one at all. I was alone, and this group kept moving closer, their eyes steady, unwavering, looking only at me.

Who were they? Gang members?

"What do you want?" I muttered—more to myself than to them.

They didn't stop. Their speed was consistent, and their feet continued to move in a synchronized rhythm as they came closer.

Now, maybe fifty feet away.

Forty-five feet away.

I backed up, heat creeping up my back, over my shoulders, into my neck.

Twenty-five feet away.

Ten feet away.

I whirled around and ran toward the barricade that blocked off the video shoot. Panting, I reached the waist-high orange and white blockade and threw one leg, then the other over it. Even though music still blared from inside the warehouse, the chain link fence just beyond the barricade had been pulled across—a lock woven through the links—blocking me from returning to the shelter.

I rattled it, a scream forming in my throat as I wrenched my neck to look behind me. They were still coming, walking like zombies toward me.

"No, please!" I shook the chains harder, but it was futile.

Bright lights cast my hands in white, and I turned to see a black sedan rolling up to the curb. My driver.

I pulled away from the fence and hurtled toward the vehicle. After jerking the door open, I fell inside. "Go!"

Unfazed by my panic, the driver flipped his mirror down and met my frantic eyes with his dark, calm ones. "Going to 59 Post Place?"

"Yes! Go! Go!" I used the flat of my palm to punch the back of his seat. He twitched his arms, clasped the steering wheel, and veered away from the curb.

The driver squinted at me in the rearview mirror, seeming to finally notice my distress. "Everything okay?"

I torqued my upper body to look out the back window. "Did you see those people? That gang?"

"What gang?"

I jabbed my finger at the back windshield. "Those people. They were coming for me. They were right th—"

My voice died as I stared at the empty street, the deserted sidewalk. There was no one. No one at all.

I twisted around again, facing forward. A squeak escaped my throat as I watched the corner disappear in the rearview mirror, and we turned onto another street. Finally, we were back on a main road. I settled. Again, the driver's wary eyes met mine in the mirror. Then he looked away. He must have thought he'd picked up a loony. A tweaker. Just what I'd thought about the girl at my door last night.

Something was wrong here. Was someone messing with me?

My phone buzzed in my hand, and I nearly took flight. Relief flooded me as I looked at the screen. Quincy. Although at that moment I would have been happy to speak to an insurance salesman.

"Hello? Quince?" I nearly shouted into the phone.

"Hey, everything okay? You sound a little keyed up."

I exhaled all the air in my lungs before explaining what had happened. "But as we were pulling away, they were gone." I jabbed my hand into my hair. "Shit. It's the first time I've felt true fight or flight since...since...oh, never mind. Anyway, it's just weird, is all. First the girl at my door last night and now this."

"What girl at the door?" Quincy's voice shrilled.

"This strange girl was banging on my door last night."

"Did you call the police?"

"No. I was in the middle of an interview with Riff Fall."

"Well, first thing's first. Are you okay?"

"Yes, I'm in a rideshare headed home."

"Do you want *me* to call the police?"

I scoffed. "No. They're not going to do anything. They'd just come out, take a report. Tell me to get a dog." The suggestion pressed a button inside of me, reminding me of Tyler's recent death and triggering a torrent of tears. I immediately sniffled and gasped, trying to regain control.

"Callie." Quincy's voice dripped with sympathy. "I've never heard you cry."

I swallowed hard. "I haven't cried in years. I mean, *years*. But I just miss Tyler so much."

Quince breathed out. "I wish I didn't live so far away, I'd come over, and—"

"No, I'm fine. I'm fine," I said, gulping back all remnants of my emotional overflow. "Really, I'm good." I laughed a little to prove my point.

"Listen, maybe I can drive out—"

"No," I said a little too loudly. "You've got Mira and the kids there." I didn't want any misunderstandings. Quince and I were friends. I didn't have many of those, and I didn't want to lose him. As much as I cared about him, Quincy sometimes had the odd affair, and I was not about to be one of them.

He cleared his throat. "You know what I think would be good for you? To get out of Nashville for a bit. And don't tell anyone where you're going."

"Like where? Where would I go?"

His tone lightened. "Well, this is why I originally called. I have some good news for you. I just got off the phone with Riff Fall's agent." He chuckled. "And guess what?"

"What?"

"For some reason, Riff's changed his mind again. He wants you to write the book."

Maybe the scare I'd just endured fueled my adrenaline, but I couldn't help but feel a whoosh of joy at the news. "Really? That's great."

"And," Quincy added, "he says he wants to talk to you in person. He says you can come to the island."

4

Riff Fall paid someone to come across Calibogue Sound once a week and bring him supplies. Abbot was an older man, probably in his sixties, blob-nosed with a protruding belly. His low-country South Carolina drawl was firmly established, and he seemed to be an expert on choppy waters and the best way to soar full speed across them. Riff had arranged for Abbot to bring me over, saving me a longer ferry ride.

"So the island's only five miles long?" I yelled to Abbot as we bumped and crashed over the wake of another boat.

"Five by three. Shaped like a feather."

I clung to the side. "What do people do here?"

"Fish. Drink. Some of the people here are in the tourist industry."

"Do you get a lot of tourists here?"

"A fair bit—especially in the summer." He pursed his lips. "We've lost a few recently, though."

I squinted against the wind. "What do you mean?"

He kept his eyes on the white-crested path in front of him. "Well, you know, kids on spring break—party a little too much and fall into the water. First-time scuba divers have a few too many at the bar before they try their hand at breathing underwater. Just last month a woman went missing from Bloodreed Point. No idea what happened to her."

"They didn't find her body?"

"Not body nor bone."

Well, that was creepy. Maybe that's what had happened to Lila Silverleaf. Maybe she'd fallen in and been washed away. I scrutinized his face. "Really?"

The edges of his mouth turned up. "Nah, I'm just messin' with ya." He chuckled.

Obviously, Abbot had a twisted sense of humor—especially since Lila had never been found.

As we dipped and rose over the waters, the sandy shore came into view along with the rooftop of Belle Marsh—an obtuse triangle. Below it, seven windows stared out at us, one of them arched in a cathedral style.

I spotted Riff in the distance—sitting among the tall grasses that sprang up in front of the house like wispy tufts of hair.

"There he is." Abbot took one hand off the wheel and extended his finger. "He's waiting for us."

"I thought he never left the house."

"He leaves the house, just not the property."

Abbot cut the motor and we slowed. The water fanned out on my side of the boat as it drew closer to the dock. White foam streamed behind us.

Abbot motioned with his head. "He's usually sitting right there when I bring him deliveries every week."

I followed his gaze. Riff stood, dusted the sand off his jeans, and walked down to the dock. Instinctively, I thrust my hands into my hair. It was a tangled mess—unavoidable when riding in an open boat with the wind nearly ripping the strands out of my head. As the boat bumped against the dock, I gathered up my small duffel bag and threw the strap over my shoulder.

"Got your groceries," Abbot called to Riff.

He hoisted a red and white cooler with wheels on the bottom, and Riff grabbed the handles and raised it onto the dock where he popped open the top and stared into it.

Abbot rattled off the list of its contents. "Got you some fish filets, two pounds of raw shrimp, and another pound of scallops, some vegetables and stuff, along with a gallon of milk and a jug of tea."

"Looks good. Thanks." Riff turned his eyes to me and held out the hand that wasn't bandaged—meant to help me out of the boat. "Hey, Callie."

"Hey." I took his hand and allowed him to pull me onto the dock. Then I readjusted the strap of my duffel bag and glanced back at Calibogue Sound. "Nice place." Spinning around, I faced the house and shielded my eyes from the afternoon sun. "That's it, huh? Belle Marsh?"

Riff craned his neck around. "Yeah, I guess from an outsider's perspective the place looks all right. I was pretty awed by it too when I first built it."

In person, Riff wasn't as tall as I'd expected. Still, he was impressive. Tanned, tattooed, muscular arms poked out of a cut-off brown T-shirt with SQUEEZE emblazoned across it. He may have been a hermit, but he obviously worked out.

He waved his bandaged hand at Abbot. "Thanks, man. See you Friday?"

Abbot saluted. "See you then."

Riff motioned me forward. "Well, come on. I reckon we might as well get this over with." Reaching over, he slid the strap of my duffel bag from my shoulder and pulled it over onto his own.

"No," I protested. "I can carry that."

"Got it." With his good hand, he reached down, grabbed the cooler's side handle, and rolled it along the dock.

As we trudged through the tall grasses, the sand working its way into the bottoms of my flip-flops, I looked around at the deserted beach. I'd never done anything like this before—stayed at the house of someone for whom I was ghostwriting. And it was a little unnerving how isolated he was here.

I took in the house's white face and seven eyes, all looking out at us from under a heavy lid. A wall of oak trees formed a backdrop behind the structure.

"I don't think I've ever seen anything like this," I said.

Riff stopped and wiped filmy sweat from his forehead. "You ever seen a church?"

"Of course I have."

He jerked his head toward the house. "Supposed to be a mixture between a church and a boat. Least that's what I asked for when I had it built. Thought I'd only use it as a vacation home, but obviously, it became a little more than that."

How had a vacation home turned into a prison?

The wind blew, whipping through the grasses, which seemed to speak—voices all whispering at once.

Riff stopped short at the front door, and I ran right into his back. Immediately, I took a step away. He blocked my passage into the house, his hand on the knob.

"Now, listen. Before we go in, there are a few things you need to know."

I raised my eyebrows. "Okay."

"There's one door in this house I keep closed. I don't go inside—ever. And you won't either. It's locked. But also... just—don't go near it."

That was strange. Was he messing with me like Abbott had? I shook my head. "I won't go in any room you don't want me to. It's your house."

His dark stare intensified. "I want you to understand this next part. You'll think it sounds crazy, but it's really important. After 11:59 at night, you do not go outside, you do not open windows, you do not open doors that lead outside. Not until morning."

Again, I searched his eyes to see if he was joking. "Why? Will I turn into a pumpkin?" Or maybe a gremlin.

His brows knitted. "I'm serious. Just don't. Okay? No matter what."

Realizing he meant it, I straightened, tossed my hair over my shoulder. "I'll probably have been in bed for an hour or more by that time. No worries."

"I'd rather you not go outside after dark at all, but definitely not after midnight."

"Okay, got it." Was he trying to protect me from staggering out into the waves of the ocean and disappearing? Or something else? On the other hand, he might have been paranoid. Probably too much partying, too many drugs over the years. Several of the musicians I'd ghostwritten for had health problems—gallbladder issues, diabetes, high blood pressure, heart disease, loss of memory. Some of them were being treated for depression and anxiety. But I suspected Riff Fall's mental status was more complicated.

He grimaced, grasped the doorknob, and cranked it. "All right then. Let's go in."

And with that, he led me inside Belle Marsh.

5

I'm not sure what I expected Belle Marsh's interior to look like, but I didn't imagine white paneled walls lined with antique armchairs and a double-height dark wood church nave ceiling in the great hall. Cathedral windows flooded the space with light. A long banquet table in the middle of the room was decorated with sculptures and glass vases and bottles of various sizes.

Arched doorways led to the other rooms, all with high ceilings and exposed beams.

The kitchen looked untouched, the white farmhouse sink spotless.

On the air, a faint smell of pine—like the whole place had been recently cleaned from top to bottom.

This didn't seem like the house of a recluse.

"Do you actually live here?"

He shrugged. "Yeah. Why?"

I held out my hands. "I mean, this looks like a model home. Or like it's still your vacation home."

Riff set the cooler down. "I try to keep things orderly. It's the only control I've got in my life."

He led me through another archway and into the next room, where framed platinum records hung on the wall behind a baby grand piano. On an adjacent wall, a collection of guitars stood like soldiers over a white couch. Riff must have been sitting here during our online meeting.

Riff motioned to the white couch facing the piano. "You can use this room to work in if you want. Sometimes, I bring my laptop in here. But while you're here, I won't bother you. By the way, I sent you a draft of another chapter to look at."

"Great. I'll read through it this afternoon." I approached the wall and looked up at the frames, my reflection and Riff's standing behind me appeared in the glass. The platinum albums shone behind the casing. The label in the center read *Cry of Crows* at the top and below it, *Night Fields*.

"This must be such a thrill," I said. "To see these on your walls and know this is your band."

"Was," Riff said. "Those were recorded years ago."

I pointed at an album and looked over my shoulder at him. "I loved this CD. Kept it on repeat."

His mouth pulled up at the corners but the smile didn't meet his eyes. "Come on. I'll show you the rest of the place."

We walked to the far end of the house, a screened-in porch with a stone fireplace, a table set (I hoped for cocktail hour)—a beige sofa and tan chair next to cathedral windows that looked out onto a rectangular pool that seemed to drop off into the sea beyond it.

"Did you bring your swimsuit?" Riff smiled.

"Uh, no."

"That's a shame. Water's perfect this time of year."

I stared out at the shimmering blue pool. "Well, I'm here to work, not swim."

Although the placid water definitely looked inviting.

There was nothing haunted or horrible about this house. So far, I hadn't seen anything scary, freaky, or macabre. Not even about Riff, except for his strange comments about going outside after midnight. I had no cold chills; no hairs were standing on end. Belle Marsh seemed like a luxurious home with intentionality infused in its construction and décor.

Riff led me through other rooms, all like something out of a magazine. Each decorative item on the walls, tables, and floors was appropriate to the house's cathedral and seafaring vessel style.

The master bedroom was on the main floor, and Riff paused by the doorway, leaned inside but didn't enter. "This is my bedroom."

I scanned the white-walled room from where I stood. Dark wood oars hung over the bed. White sheets and comforter were accented by a black and gray plaid blanket draped across the bottom. The bed looked like it had never been slept in. Nightstands on either side held a book and a generic ocean photograph on each. A large window allowed a waterfall of light into the room. A rustic wooden cross perched on the sill.

Nothing was out of place. But nothing seemed like it belonged to Riff either. Other than the albums and guitars and photos in the music room, there was nothing personal here. No photos to suggest he had a family or came from anywhere.

As we passed into the main hall again, he swept up my waiting bag and threw the strap over his shoulder.

I made a swipe for it. "Oh, I can get that." I hated it when someone else did something I could do myself. Even under the guise of politeness. Maybe I'd lived by myself too long.

Riff didn't answer but headed for the hardwood stairs. As we climbed toward the second floor, I glanced over at the stairwell wall where framed ocean paintings hung.

The landing led to a wide hallway, more hardwood floors, and a black carpet runner. Three doors on either side—presumably, guest rooms—were all closed.

Riff opened the door of the one closest to the stairwell. "Your room."

More white walls. Framed photographs of sweeping dunes and burnt sienna sunsets. An arched window filtered rays of sun and cast prisms of light on the bed's white comforter.

"I figured you'd rather have a view of the ocean than the marsh."

"It's a beautiful room." I went to the window and looked out on the ocean as it rolled in—white crests topping each incoming wave.

"Lila made sure all the beds had high-quality mattresses. That was one of her things."

I glanced down at the coffee table book on one of the nightstands. A photograph of a sand-dusted foot, the toes touching the bubbles and organic matter of sea foam. The title stretched across the front in uppercased blue letters: *The Mystique of Invisible Island*.

"I'd like to schedule a professional photographer to come in and take some photos for the book," I said.

Riff twisted his mouth, scrubbed a hand across his chin. "Let's just get through this week. One thing at a time."

I nodded. "Okay. When can we talk about the project?"

He cleared his throat, his eyes darting back and forth. "Yeah, uh, give me half an hour." He pivoted toward me again. "There's one more thing I have to show you."

I followed him into the hallway, and we marched past the closed doors of the other bedrooms to a small alcove. A high, octagonal window punctuated the space, along with a faded red Persian carpet and a small table with a lamp. A door painted a pale blue-green hid behind a pretzel-brown wicker chair—the only piece of furniture that appeared to be out of place and character with the rest of the house. Blue freezer tape ran along the top, down the sides, and even across the bottom. Another large wooden cross of the same aqua color hung, nearly camouflaged against the wood. A lot of crosses here—not to mention the one I'd seen on his wrist. Was he religious?

I pointed. "What's with the tape?"

He ignored my question. "I keep this door locked. No one ever opens it. Not even me."

"Why? What's in there?"

Riff hooked his unbandaged hand around the back of his neck, and his hair fell forward, hiding his face. "I'll tell you what I can—share what I can, but there are some things that I just can't talk about. I hope you'll respect that."

I shrugged. What choice did I have? This was his house and his book, after all. My gaze wandered over the wall to the right of the door. The paint appeared fresh and slightly brighter—ice white rather than the muted cloud shade beneath it—as though the drywall had recently been repaired.

I glanced down at his bandaged hand. "Of course I will."

6

I stood in the sand outside the screened-in porch, smoked a much-needed cigarette, and looked over the expanse of swaying grasses and the narrow beach that stretched beyond. There wasn't a soul on it. This was paradise. I might never want to leave this property either if I lived here.

Movement in the seagrass where it met the dunes caught my eye, and I focused on a person lying on their stomach. Curly red hair swished along with the reeds.

I took a long drag from my cigarette and moved toward them. This wasn't someone sunbathing. They were fully clothed.

Passed out? No, very much awake. The head popped up like a turtle's.

I stopped walking. "Hi? You all right?"

Within seconds, the body revealed itself to be a young man, who scrambled to his feet, turned, and galloped off down the beach. Odd. But most likely someone trying to get a glimpse of Riff. He probably had a lot of people wandering by his house, snapping photos.

I finished my cigarette and returned to my bedroom to call Quincy. I had told him I'd call once I was at Belle Marsh and then check in with him once a day—safety precautions. Although he was only ten years older, Quincy had been sort of a surrogate dad to me—always concerned about my welfare. He definitely cared more than my biological father.

"How are you? No gangs or stalkers there, I hope," he said once I had him on the phone.

"Not so far."

"So how's it going?"

"Hm," I exhaled through my nose. "It's interesting." I tried to keep my voice down and avoid the vents lest my conversation carry.

"Is he strange?"

"Yeah, a bit. He comes off pretty normal in general, but he's got all these rules and stuff."

"Rules? What kind of rules?"

"Like, there's this one room I can't go in. Oh, and I can't go outside after midnight."

"What?" he said, his voice rising. "Oh boy."

"But he's nice," I countered.

"Nice looking or nice?"

"Both, actually. But don't worry about the former. You know my feelings about getting involved with musicians." I lay back on the white comforter. "I kind of feel bad for him."

"You? Feel bad? The ice queen?"

"Ha-ha. Thanks, Quince."

He chuckled. "Does he know about your dad?"

"No. But I'm sure it'll come up." I decided not to mention to Quincy that my dad had recently contacted me. I didn't often share information about Trace Rowe. It wasn't a line of conversation that I enjoyed—for many reasons.

"Just be careful," Quincy reminded me. "Call me if there's any problem at all. I can have a helicopter there lickety-split."

I smiled. Quincy was a worrier. Secretly, I appreciated it. "I will."

THE HALF AN HOUR RIFF said he needed came and went while I sat on the screened-in porch with my recorder and electronic tablet. I used the time to review notes, read the chapter he'd sent me, and make suggestions. Finally, an hour later, the smell of seafood turned my head just as Riff reemerged, rolling a waiter's cart with plates of food and a bottle of wine.

"I figured you might be hungry," he said.

"Wow. Do you have a personal chef?"

He laughed. "You're looking at him."

Regardless of Riff's quirks, it was hard not to be impressed by the dinner he'd prepared. Fish, asparagus, risotto.

He moved the plate in front of me, steam rising from the grilled fish.

"I'm impressed. You're a gourmet cook," I said.

"Yeah, well, if I want decent food, I've got to make it myself, so I learned pretty fast."

We sat at the table, looking out at the ocean, watching the daylight diminish. Suddenly, we were the only two people on earth.

It felt like some Nicholas Sparks movie.

Except it was me and Riff—my client.

"There's only one main restaurant on the island, and I can't go there, so..." He refilled my glass of wine—pinot grigio. Not my usual choice, but it was what was on offer, so I drank it. Riff drank water from a wine glass, a lemon on the side.

I wanted to open up conversation about his self-imposed prison, but I sensed that I needed to ease into it, judging how reticent he'd been to tell me anything so far.

I glanced at his glass of water. "So, you don't drink."

He shook his head. "Not much. Not anymore."

I assumed his experience with alcohol was the same as so many musicians whose stories I'd written. "Too many years of partying on the road?"

He stared out at the rolling waves. "Four times in detox, three times in rehab, a couple of stabs at AA."

I jutted out my hand toward his water glass. "But you're sober now."

"Most days."

"That's more than a lot of people can say who have lived your life."

He leaned back in his chair. "For me, the key is to stop before all those good feelings start to kick in."

I smiled wryly as I thought—*then what's the point?* I was glad I'd packed that extra bottle of whiskey in my suitcase. I'd assumed Riff would have a fully stocked bar.

He continued. "Denying yourself that part—well, it sort of rewires your brain so you no longer associate it with pleasure. Alcohol, drugs—they were everything to me for a long time. Now, I can take a drink or leave it. I just can't let it take me, if you get my meaning."

"Still, it can't be easy."

"It's not." He sipped his water. "Especially on the nights I want to block out all the...memories."

I studied him. Deep grooves etched the sides of his mouth. I guessed he'd seen some things he wanted to forget.

He cleared his throat. "How did you get into ghostwriting?"

The wine was kicking in. Here came those good feelings he'd just mentioned. "My father was a musician too. A guitarist. He used to be in a band called Crashing Light in the late 80s. They were popular for a few years."

Riff lifted a candle lighter from the table, flicked it, and held the flame to the wick of the candle on the table. "I remember that band."

I hesitated. Oh, what the hell. "Trace Rowe—the guitarist—he's my dad." Cringe.

"No shit? Is he still playing?"

A sharp pain zapped below my heart. Probably a cramp. Or maybe I just needed another cigarette. Seeing the lighter now sparked the craving. "I think he still does some sessions work out in LA. I haven't been in touch with him in many years." The cramp intensified as I remembered Trace's text from the other night. The truth was, I didn't want to be in touch with him.

Riff nodded, almost like he could read my discomfort. "So, you've always been around music."

Thankful for the change of subject, I breathed in deeply and the cramp dissipated. "Always. After college, I started working for a small music publication. That's when I met Chad Ellis and he asked me to co-author his memoir for him. He passed my name along to another guy, and it just went from there."

"And you don't mind not getting any of the recognition? The fame?"

I shook my head. "Fame has never interested me."

Riff turned his water glass and drew a line through the condensation. "Lucky you." He'd removed his bandage, revealing red sores that bloomed across each of his knuckles.

I pointed. "How's the hand?"

He swept his other hand across his fingers, covering the cuts. "Yeah, it's better." He gave a nervous laugh. "Gotta stop punching those walls."

"You do that for fun, or..."

He shifted. "I lost my temper."

"I thought you said you didn't do it because you were angry."

His eyes met mine. "I lied. I didn't want you to think I was a hothead."

"Are you?"

"Not normally, no. Just sometimes all this gets to be too much, you know?" His gaze trailed past my head.

I wasn't sure what he meant by "all this," but before I could ask, a voice from the beach called out, "Hey, Riff!"

Riff waved. "Hey, Zeke."

I craned my neck around. The young man I'd seen lying in the grass earlier now stood outside the porch.

He might have been eighteen or nineteen. Tall and lanky, his face was cherubic, flushed by the sun.

Riff stood and walked to the screen. "Your mama know you're here?"

"I don't know." Zeke grinned.

Riff motioned with his head. "You run on home. It'll be dark soon. You know you can't be here after dark."

"Yes, sir. I know."

"Go on, then."

Zeke started to dash off, but then he stopped, and chugging his arms like a locomotive, he walked backward to his original spot. "Am I coming this week for lessons?"

"If you want."

Zeke saluted and blasted off again, throwing sand out from under his heels as he ran.

Riff returned to his seat across from me. "That's Zeke. I give him guitar lessons every week."

I nodded. "Oh. He's the kid I saw lying in the grass earlier. I wondered what he was doing."

Riff quirked his mouth. "Yeah, his mom's got cancer."

I grimaced. "Oh, that's too bad."

"It's terminal, I think. Zeke's been telling me about all these alternative therapies he's been researching for her." Riff flexed his fingers. "Zeke's—well, he's a little different. I mean, he seems much younger than he is—I think he's around twenty-one—but he's super-smart—like, he knows all of this scientific stuff. He'll talk your ear off about radio frequencies and electromagnetic waves."

"Ah. A budding scientist?"

"And a great guitar player."

"Even better." So, Zeke came to Belle Marsh for guitar lessons, and Riff didn't seem to mind about that. "You let him inside the house?"

He pressed his fingers against the table. "Only for an hour. Usually here on the porch or in the music room."

"Do you let anyone else in?"

"Not many. Elijah. He's a friend of mine who lives in Savannah. He comes to check on me from time to time. I got a doctor here on the island who visits me when I'm sick. Once a month my therapist travels in from Hilton Head, but we usually sit outside for our talks."

I cleared my throat. "Why did you allow me to come?"

He looked out at the water. "I don't know, Callie. I've known for a while it was time to write this book." He shrugged. "And I guess it's now or never, maybe that's why I let you come. And my agent told me a ghostwriter would be the best way to get the book written." Riff leaned back in his chair, and it creaked under his weight. "So, how do we do this—this ghostwriting thing?"

I smiled. "Well, it depends. You can continue to write out sections—like you did with your intro and chapters—give them to me to look at and suggest improvements."

He grimaced and made a sound at the back of his throat. "Everything I write sounds like crap."

"I haven't read the other chapter you sent me, but your intro wasn't crap. We should use it."

"Whatever you think."

"What I usually do is get out my recorder, or my video camera if you're not opposed. Then you talk, and I listen. I'll write up drafts of chapters for you to read and edit. If we're on the same page, no pun intended, then we move on."

He sipped his lemon water and the ice clinked against the sides of the glass. "Okay."

I dragged my recorder closer. "Do you mind if I have a cigarette first?" I motioned toward the beach. "Out there?"

"No. Go ahead."

I exited through the screen door and walked out where the seagrass and a line of reeds served as a low fence. The water swept the sand, leaving dark bruises on the beach. I tried to imagine what it was like for Riff—day in and day out—never leaving this place. It seemed like paradise now, but even the ocean might get old if it was the only thing you had to look at.

Five, six puffs were enough. Didn't want to go over my two cigarettes a day. But I'd been smoking since I was fourteen and quitting was more difficult than I thought it would be.

I turned and observed the house—the arched windows all looking at me. Was someone standing in the center window? I squinted, making sure it wasn't just sand in my eyes. No, it looked like someone—a grayish figure. Riff must be up there now. I'd better hurry back inside and get the recorder rolling before he changed his mind about talking tonight.

I carried the half-smoked cigarette with me and stalked up to the porch. Through the screen, I glimpsed Riff sitting exactly where I'd left him. In his chair, relaxed, staring out at the ocean.

"Were you just upstairs?"

Riff stood. "No. I've been right here."

A wave of discomfort coincided with the sound of the tide's roll. "I thought I saw someone standing up in the center window."

He opened the screen door and handed me a piece of sea-blue pottery. "Here, you can use this as an ashtray."

I stubbed out my cigarette against the glazed bottom of the bowl, set it on the step, and went inside. "So, is it just us here?" I knew the answer, of course.

"Just us."

Maybe I'd seen a glare off the ocean. Or maybe it was just my eyes adjusting to the salty air, coupled with the wafting smoke.

"Let's close up here and head into the music room to talk. It's getting late."

I glanced at the time on my cell phone. "It's not even eight o'clock."

He compressed his lips. "Still, it'll be dark soon."

I waited in the doorway as he pressed a button on the wall. A motor whirred, and the tan panels lowered from the ceiling, covering each of the screens, blocking out the sounds of the insects and the ocean.

"I've seen these types of things at restaurants," I said. "When it's cold out they close off the screened-in areas."

"Yep, that's where I got the idea."

I followed him into the music room where we sat on his white couch under the hanging guitars. I perched on the edge, set up the digital recorder on the coffee table, and adjusted its position. "Whenever you're ready."

He nodded. "I'm ready."

I pushed record.

Full Verbatim Transcript of Interview With Riff Fall
Notes for *Fallen Star*
9/19/16: 7:54 p.m.
Riff: So, should I just start talking?
Callie: Yes. The recorder is rolling.
Riff: Where should I start?
Callie: Why don't you tell me a little about your childhood—where you grew up? Or your first memory.
Riff: [laughs] This feels kinda like a therapy session.
Callie: It wouldn't be the first time I've heard that.
Riff: First memory. Um, let's see. Well, you know, I don't have many early memories. The farthest back I can remember I was just a boy sitting in the pew at First Springs Baptist Church. I was supposed to be lifting my heart in prayer. Instead, my heart was sliding down a black hole of sin while daydreaming about some girl or other. [laughs]

Wait. No, that's not really my first memory. My first memory was waking up from a nightmare. I think I was four or five years old. And in the dream, I was standing by the ocean looking down into the water. I expected to see my reflection, but it wasn't there. Instead, some other face was looking up at me from under the surface—it was like a—a monster of some kind but it looked human too, you know, with googly eyes and gray skin. And in the dream, I fell backward and the thing burst out of the water, grabbed my foot, and dragged me in. Then it just kept pulling me down, down, down, and there were all these other creatures floating around me that looked like the one who had my ankle. They just stayed suspended in the water and watched as this thing pulled me into the deepest part of the ocean.

Callie: That's a pretty scary dream. What did it mean to you?
Riff: Nothing then. But, um, I had that same dream years later, right before I auditioned for Cry of Crows. I remember waking up and thinking—maybe I shouldn't do this. It really rattled me, you

know? That time the dream was so vivid, so real. When I woke up, I knew I'd been holding my breath because I really needed to breathe.

Callie: But you still went to the audition.

Riff: Yeah, well, I'd just turned twenty-one, and I'd been working as a truck driver for a few months, running a route up to Philadelphia. I wasn't making a lot of money, but I was making ends meet. I had a little garage band—just a bunch of guys getting together on Saturday night, playing some cover tunes. Our bass player told me about this band he sometimes saw when he went to Myrtle Beach. He said they were looking for a singer and suggested I audition.

"They're looking to go big time, man," he told me. "They've got some producers interested in them, but their singer quit. You should go down there, give it a shot."

So, I did. I took my girlfriend to Myrtle Beach for the weekend and auditioned for the band. And they took me on. That's pretty much it.

Callie: Let's go back to your childhood for a second. I know the book isn't going to be about your early life per se, but it might play into the narrative. What was your life like at home growing up?

Riff: [pause] I was raised in the church. Sunday morning, evening, and Wednesday evening. Sometimes they were even open on Saturday too for special prayer meetings. Anytime the doors were open, my family was there. All four of us kids were lined up, told to sit quietly in the pews and no fooling around, 'cause if you did, there'd be hell to pay when we got home.

My stepdad was six foot six and he boxed, so I knew better than to test his patience. I was the middle brother and the most rebellious of the three. I probably got the majority of the whippin' since my philosophy was to commit whatever sin I was planning first and take the punishment later, so at least I got to do what I wanted. But I didn't dare try that while in church. I sat up straight and stared ahead when the minister was speaking. I looked down at my Bible when he was reading. And I closed my eyes and bowed my head when he was praying. The rest of the time, I was staring at the arched ceiling, the stained-glass window, the back of the wooden pew in front of me.

Callie: Going to church obviously influenced this house. The windows, the arched ceilings—the benches kind of look like pews too.

Riff: Yeah, I may not have loved going to church, but I loved what the church looked like. The same was true of my stepdad's fishing boat. On the off chance I got to go out on the ocean with him—usually because I was in trouble and due "a talking to"—I told myself that one day I was going to live on a boat. I loved everything about those trips—the rocking, the salty air, all the foam that floated along. And there was nothing like eating the fish we caught.

Callie: What was your mom like? Your dad?

Riff: [pause] My real dad left when I was little. Mom was a single mother, trying to raise four kids on her own. When she got so tired she couldn't do it anymore, she married my stepfather. I think that's about the size of it.

Callie: Were you happy she married him?

Riff: Initially, I mean, at first, yeah. You know, he played baseball with me, took me to games. But it didn't take long until...well, I learned different. He was the first person to teach me that people aren't always who they claim to be. [long pause] Do you hear that?

Callie: Hear what?

Riff: [long pause] Wait here. I think maybe I left a window open somewhere.

7

I stopped the recorder.

I didn't hear anything except Riff sliding a window to its base in the room next to this one. The click of a latch, the squeak of his shoes as he returned.

He strode past and stood with his back to me, staring out the window at the marshes at the rear of the property. "Damn, I didn't realize how hard this was going to be."

It had been going so well for a few minutes. He'd started talking and it seemed like we were finally getting somewhere.

"We don't have to talk about your childhood if you don't want to," I said. "I understand 'cause I really don't like talking about mine."

His voice was a low rumble. "I haven't talked about my family in a very long time."

Maybe I needed to try a different tack. The beginning of his story was difficult, but so was the ending. Maybe we needed to start from the middle. "What about the island? What drew you here?"

Riff turned and faced me. Finally, he came back to his seat. A muscle pulsed in his jaw. Then he paused and bit his lip. "I was looking for a place to escape—like, I just wanted to get away from LA and...everything. I was drawn here somehow. I was looking for a remote place, and this island kept popping up on my searches. At the time, I didn't know why. But once I visited—the nature, the beauty of the marsh and the beach—I felt like this could be a place where I could rest my mind. Refuel my body. I didn't even feel much like drinking while I was here."

"When was that?"

Riff shifted his eyes. "Um, 2010, I think. Shit, I was a mess then." He smiled a little. "That's when I first met Elijah. I was just sitting on the ground near the marsh with a notebook, looking at this big bush filled with all these white birds. I'd had this one melody bouncing around in my head all week and figured I'd try to figure out some lyrics to go with it. Then I heard someone say, 'I'd be careful sitting there.' I turned around and saw this young guy walking toward me wearing a short-sleeved button-down and jeans cut off around the knees. He came up to me and pointed at this cluster of birds. 'You looking at those birds up there? Those birds are a trick. They're bait. While you're looking at them, there's an alligator out there somewhere looking at you.'" Riff combed his fingers through his hair. "I got on my feet faster than you can imagine."

"He's the one you spoke of earlier? The kid from Savannah?"

Riff crossed his ankle over his knee. "Yeah. Well, he's not a kid anymore. He's about thirty years old now. His grandma Nona was born here—a Gullah-Geechee. She lives on the other side of the island on property that's been in their family since sharecropping days. She's a real character—full of life and great stories. And she doesn't mince any words. She'll tell you the truth. One time, she came here with Elijah when the place was first being built. I was showing her the interior decorating plans and she said the house was going to be too plain—no color." He mimicked what I assumed was meant to be her voice. "'You need some color around this place, Riff.'"

I pointed toward the ceiling. "And the door upstairs. That's definitely a splash of color. Is there a reason for the blue?"

He gave me a sidelong glance. "Haint blue. It's a superstitious thing. I'd read it would ward off evil spirits or something, but then Nona told me no one on this island uses haint blue for that purpose." He shrugged. "I left it anyway."

"Are there evil spirits in your attic?"

Riff looked down at his hand, ran his fingers over the scabs.

"Or is that one of the off-limit subjects?" I prompted.

"I guess that's right," he said.

I'd finished off most of the bottle of wine he'd left on the coffee table. Even so, I felt a little wired. I sat on the couch beside Riff, facing the door to the hallway. The hall was full of shadows, and every so often I imagined I saw something skirt by. The talk of evil spirits was making me think I saw phantoms.

"I guess I thought the island might be a place where I could escape the shitshow that had become my life." He huffed out a sardonic laugh. "I couldn't have been more wrong." He motioned toward the recorder. "I think I want to stop for the night."

"No problem." I clicked off the machine.

Riff stifled a yawn. Then he passed a hand over his face, pulling down the lower lids of his eyes. "It's late. Dark. We should pack it in tonight. You must be tired."

"Not really." I didn't want to go to bed. In a way, I wanted to keep talking, but he'd ended the information-gathering session, so there was no reason to prolong the evening.

His voice was low and raspy as he repeated, "It's late." He stood and with a groan, clasped at his lower back.

"You all right?"

"Yeah." He winced. "Old injury from jumping off the stage one night. Still bothers me now and again."

My phone buzzed and I glanced down at it. My dad's name appeared at the head of the text message. *I was hoping to come to Nashville this week. You able to get together for a cup of coffee?*

Unbelievable. I hadn't even responded to his first text. But here he was, texting me again. Why now? After all these years? What did he want?

"I can't believe it."

Riff paused. "What?"

"My dad just texted me. Wouldn't you know it? Haven't seen the guy in years and now he wants to come to Nashville and meet with me."

"Really?" Riff continued to shuffle toward the door, but then he paused and turned. "It's none of my business, but do you mind me asking why you haven't seen him in years?"

I gathered my things, forcing my mind to remain on the task at hand. My father didn't deserve the time it would take for me to text him back. "When I say years, I really mean like twenty years."

He blinked. "Wow. You'll have to tell me that story sometime—about your dad."

I shook my head. "I don't like talking about my dad."

His lips twitched a little. "I get it. I guess we've got that in common."

I followed him out into the hallway, relieved that he flicked on wall sconces as we went. The dark spaces disappeared little by little, and by the time we reached the bottom of the stairwell, the downstairs glowed.

"Well, good night." Riff's eyes flashed toward the upstairs. "I hope you sleep well. Let me know if you need anything."

My dad's text had prodded at some old, stale pain, precipitating the need for one more cigarette, and I jerked my thumb at the front door. "Actually, I think I might run out for a quick cigarette."

"No!" Riff bellowed, thrusting out his arm.

Unprepared for such a violent reaction, everything in me seized.

As he approached, his shoulders dropped. "It's dark out there. I told you—you can't—" He closed his eyes, his voice calmer. "What I mean, is smoke inside if you want."

"Why?" I kept my voice level. "I thought you said midnight." I glanced at the clock on the wall. "It's not even ten yet."

His face appeared frozen—his brow wreathed, facial muscles tense, mouth flexed and drawn. A whirring sound drew my attention to an interior security camera in the corner of the doorway. It hummed as it shifted toward us—motion-activated.

He held up a finger. "Wait a second." He disappeared down the dark hallway.

I looked around, half-expecting to see a sheeted ghost peering around the corner.

He returned seconds later, his hand extended. "Here." A small black box lay in his palm. "Ear plugs. They're military grade. Servicemen use them to block out bombs and stuff. Keep them with you. They'll offer you some protection."

"Against what?"

He exhaled. "I can't say. Just—you'll know when you need them." His face was hidden in shadows.

This was ridiculous. I felt emotionally manipulated, but I unbuckled my arms, took the box from him, and opened it. Flesh-colored cone-shaped earpieces stared back at me.

"Midnight is the worst of it," he said. "But any time after dark is still dangerous."

His eyes met mine and then skirted away. How had his life become so full of fear? A childhood phobia on steroids. Did he really believe that dangers lurked outside the door once the sun went down?

"Okay," I said in a lighter voice. "What's out there? What do you think is going to happen to me if I go out there?"

"I know what would happen."

"What?"

"Something terrible."

8

I retreated to my room, my head full of unbalanced thoughts. As I crested the landing, a black camera at the other end of the hall buzzed and rotated. The surveillance in this house was as creepy as Riff's rules.

What the hell was so dangerous that I couldn't set foot outside after dark? It was like a bad horror film where the characters were faced with clichéd rules. *Don't go upstairs. Don't go in the basement. Don't get the furry critters wet. Don't go outside after midnight.* Oh, and wait. There was one more. Don't open that blue door at the end of the hall—the one the camera was obviously protecting. Equally ridiculous was that now, of course, I wanted to open that door.

Even so, Riff seemed like a genuinely nice person. But was he delusional? Whether it was all the drugs that had wrecked his brain or the years of heavy drinking, paranoia had apparently kicked in.

Considering the consequences of spending decades as a famous musician gave way to thoughts of Dad and why my father would contact me after all these years.

Yeah, he's twenty years older than when he first decided to treat me like a pariah, but what's really changed?

Whatever it was, it didn't matter. I didn't want to talk to him.

I turned the lock on the door and scanned the interior, especially the corners, making sure there were no cameras. After all, you never could tell what sort of fetishes people had.

Satisfied there were no hidden instruments of voyeurism, I headed to the bathroom to enjoy the rainfall shower and sink with a touchless faucet. White towels, white rugs, white tile, white walls.

Everything in this place was white, eggshell, or linen. Elijah's grandmother was right. I'd never seen such a colorless palette in my life—except for the black runner rug in the hall and the weird blue taped-up door. But I assumed that's how Riff wanted it. It wasn't like he didn't have the money to change it.

White was sterile and orderly. White was the color you painted walls when you wanted to wipe out the past—like I'd done with the bright red accent wall in my condo when I moved in. But white didn't keep you from remembering. A crack or chip in the paint would reveal what the original color had been.

As I removed my pants, my eyes wandered to the inside of my leg. Nine scars—cigarette burns collected over a five-year period. The first two—my starter set I called them—were initiated by a sadistic boyfriend who enjoyed burning me. Once we broke up, I'd taken up his mantel and continued the trend because, in some ways, the physical pain overshadowed the mental anguish. I'd never told anyone about it. Each burn was a tale of repressed pain. But I was past that now. I wasn't that teenager anymore who couldn't control her emotions. I hadn't been her for a long while. I'd learned how to manage my past—the pain of my father's rejection. Thinking about it only provoked the dormant anger inside of me, and I'd worked too hard to put it to sleep. I ran my finger over the scars. They'd faded a lot. Now they were just pink swirls of waxy, raised flesh.

After my shower, I settled on the bed, propped my laptop on my thighs, and tried to pull up the internet. I'd had trouble getting reception on my phone since I'd gotten here, but now there was no Wi-Fi. When I tried to connect, the bars at the bottom disappeared, and a message conveyed that the internet was unavailable. Fortunately, I'd already downloaded the chapter Riff sent me earlier and it waited for me, minimized on my screen.

I scanned the words. Although he had labeled it as the draft of a chapter, it was more of a journal entry, starting in the middle with no real introduction to the material.

POTENTIAL CHAPTER FOR book

The band scraped together enough money to record an album. But getting a recording label wasn't easy. All the major labels passed, but we didn't lose hope and started out playing in tiny clubs. Then we played some bigger places. Maybe fifty people at a club, maybe a hundred. Mostly around Myrtle, then other towns in South Carolina, Tennessee, Georgia. That first year was wild. Me, Ricky, Trey, and Blacky, tearing up the South. It was great.

I was feeling good. I had gotten as far away from my upbringing as I could, and now I could really party.

I sucked down and snorted every drug offered to me, and I drank until I blacked out almost every night. One night at the end of the first year, I had to go to detox. By the end of the second year, I'd gone to my first rehab. I was getting into fights in bars and even with my bandmates.

It had only taken us the better part of two years to crash and burn. Trey was talking about quitting the band, maybe even moving to Atlanta to become a realtor. I wanted to go to LA, but I was too drunk and stoned to make it as far as Columbia.

Then I met Dove LaMer. And everything changed.

THE CHAPTER ENDED THERE—INCOMPLETE, but definitely some material I could work with.

After I shut down my laptop and slipped under the sheets, I switched off the light and listened for the sounds that usually lulled me to sleep. Cars, horns, stomping on the metal stairs outside my condo. But there was nothing. No noise. Dead quiet. And the glass on the windows was so heavy I couldn't even hear a muffled roll of the ocean. I tossed and turned in the dark until I finally switched on the light again and stared at the white ceiling.

I couldn't help but chuckle a little at the irony of it all. *It's too quiet to sleep.* I didn't even need Riff's earplugs.

I chuffed out air, kicked off the comforter, and readjusted my pillow. I sat up and guzzled water from the glass by my bed. Then I tried again to close my eyes. Seconds later, they fluttered open at the sound of another voice.

I sat up.

A woman's voice. Unmistakable in the quiet of the house. I got out of bed, traipsed to the door, and put my ear to the panel. The voice wasn't coming from the hallway. It sounded like it was in the room with me. Or in the bathroom. Or in the vents. Or in the walls.

"Callie." A whisper.

"Callie." Now a sing-song voice. "I know you're here, Callie."

"Callisto!" A shout.

With a gasp, I tore open the door and spilled out into the dark hallway. I ran my hand along the wall, desperate for light, my skin prickling in the cool air. When my fingers rushed over the switch, I flicked it, flooding the hall with an orange glow. Silence filled the space like smoke. No one was there. I moved along the landing and started downstairs. I wasn't sure what I would do once down there, but Riff's bedroom was on the main floor, and somehow it made me feel better to know I was closer to him—a call away. Even if I just sat on the couch in the music room all night.

My head was obviously playing tricks on me. A few times in my life I'd dreamed someone was calling my name until it woke me.

These taunting voices had to be in my head. There had to be a logical explanation. The house was just too damn quiet. Of course my ears were manufacturing sounds.

I hurried into the music room and flipped on the light. The overhead glow was reflected in the piano's black enamel and the polished wood of Riff's guitars. I scanned the dozen or so picture frames that ran the length of the back wall.

Starting at one end, I moved from frame to frame. Several photos were live concert shots of Riff with Cry of Crows—leaning into the microphone, sweat dripping from his face, his hair. Then came the photos of Riff with members of other bands. Chris Cornell from Soundgarden, Scott Stapp from Creed, Eddie Vedder from Pearl Jam. Some were even older—a photo with Riff posing alongside B.B. King holding up his beloved guitar, Lucille. Several photos must have been record producers or sound techs—men and women whose faces I didn't recognize.

I moved to the next photo. This one was different. It had been taken here in this house, in this room, with many of the same framed pictures behind them. Riff, his drummer, and Lila Silverleaf. Their arms were all locked, their faces stretched with enormous smiles. Lila was beautiful. Long black hair spilling over her shoulders and hanging nearly to waist, angular cheekbones, and aquamarine eyes. Beyond her extraordinary beauty, she'd been touted as one of the best "female lead singers" of the 20th century, which I always found offensive. Why not just say one of the best lead singers—period? Did she have to be put in a separate category from the men? I'd seen her in concert. She'd earned her status.

Tap-tap-tap. I pulled my eyes away from the photograph and turned toward the window covered by gauzy white sheers. A hazy image of a figure appeared outside. Someone was looking in.

I moved toward the window and yanked the sheers out of the way. The darkened marsh gaped back at me. No one was there.

I was hearing *and* seeing things. What was wrong with me? I could have sworn I'd seen someone standing there.

The security camera in the hallway whirred and thrummed, suggesting movement. I licked my lips; my mouth felt dry as sand.

Floorboards creaked with footsteps.

"Callie?" Riff shuffled into the doorway.

I expelled all the breath in my lungs and slumped. "Shhhit, Riff. You scared me to death."

He wore pajama bottoms and a T-shirt that looked like he'd been in an incident with wild dogs. Holes riddled the front of it and one of the shoulders hung from its seam.

He must have been asleep for a while, as he appeared groggy and squinted at me. "Everything all right? You need anything?"

I shook my head, my heart pounding in my temples. "Couldn't sleep." I pivoted toward the frames. "I was just looking at your photos."

"Oh." He continued to shamble toward me, rubbing his eyes. "My interior security system's motion detector went off."

"Yeah, I guess that was me. Sorry to wake you."

"That's all right."

We stared up at the framed memories in silence. Riff took in a long breath, and I examined him. His eyes were haunted with riptides of pain. He pointed at the photo of Lila sitting at the piano, her head thrown back and her long hair nearly touching the piano bench. "Lila and I were married by then—when she played that concert."

I lowered myself onto the white couch. "I'd love to hear about her."

Riff faced me. "What do you want to know? So much of her life was out there—on display for the world to see."

I shrugged. "Anything you want to tell me. How you met, fell in love? All I know about her is that she was your wife. Personally, I loved her music. She was an amazing singer."

"Is," he corrected.

"Is. Sorry."

He blew air from his nostrils. "I'm tired, Callie. I don't think I can do any more tonight."

"I understand. Please, I don't want to keep you up. Go to bed. We can talk tomorrow."

But he didn't go to bed. Instead, he lumbered to the stereo system on a built-in shelf and flipped it on. Strains of Lila's group, Episodic Noise, playing "Water Woman" filtered through the overhead speakers. Riff turned, his chin down as he moved back to the couch and sat beside me. "Lila was the love of my life."

I nodded. "Of course."

"She was everything I ever dreamed of—everything I ever wanted. The year we spent together...I just couldn't believe I was so lucky to be with this woman."

"What do you think happened to her?"

He covered his face with his hands and rubbed them up and down—a mannerism I was coming to understand as distinctly "Riffian." When he removed his hands, his face was red, his eyes watery. "I think she just...left. Or she was swept away."

9

Swept away? Into Calibogue Sound or the Intracoastal Waterway? He wouldn't elaborate. Still, I speculated. Maybe Lila had indulged in a few too many drinks and a midnight walk on the beach. Could she have wandered into the water? Had she left the island? Why would she leave and not tell anyone where she was? Unless she feared being found.

I went back to bed but didn't drop off to sleep until around four or five that morning when I dreamt that some distant chorus was singing my full name.

"Callisto, Callisto, Callisto!" The voices were bright and insistent like the chorus to a movement from *Carmina Burana*, and it rang in my ears even after I sat up and pawed at my eyes. It had been a vivid dream with music I could've sung upon waking. Even so, the tune dissipated within moments like vapor.

I showered, dressed, and headed out of my room, my laptop under my arm.

Thump. The noise came from the other end of the hallway. I paused and glanced over my shoulder at the blue door. What was that? It sounded like something had fallen. Or like a fist against a wall. I backtracked and the camera followed my movement, filming me as I went where I wasn't supposed to go. I looked up at the black instrument, perched in the upper corner of the ceiling, rotating like some black owl. I expected to hear Riff's voice at any moment, telling me to stop, or for alarms to go off the closer I got to the door. I reached the alcove and looked down at the brown wicker chair pushed in front of it. A board creaked and I winced. But wait. That wasn't me. That came from the other side of the door.

What was in there? And why wouldn't Riff say? Although he had claimed in several articles that Belle Marsh was haunted. But I didn't believe in ghosts.

Reaching over the chair, I ran my fingers along the blue freezer tape that sealed off the space between the panel and the jamb. There was even a piece of tape over the keyhole. Then I wrapped my hand around the knob and turned it. *It didn't take long to break one of Riff's rules.* The knob barely turned. Locked. Just like Riff said.

Several moments passed as I stood there, listening. But there were no more creaks or thumps.

Eventually, I turned and went back down the hall, and the tattling whir of the camera echoed overhead.

Downstairs it was quiet. Riff's door was shut. I returned to the screened-in porch, still boarded up from the previous night. I pressed the button on the wall and the motor hummed, lifting the panels. Cool morning air seeped in, along a humid mist that shriveled the strands of my hair. Fondling the pack of cigarettes in my pocket, I stepped out onto the sand, relishing the ocean breeze, the rush of warm wind, and the azure-blue sky—clear and cloudless.

Poking a cigarette into my mouth, I walked down the stretch of beach and held the lighter under the end while blocking the wind with my hand. Then I took in the first pleasurable breath of the day, letting the burn in my lungs replace all the tension. I walked for a little while until my cigarette was almost extinguished and a line of houses on stilts appeared in the distance. I must have been reaching the end of Riff's property line.

A young woman stood some thirty feet away. Her blonde hair raised from her head like dry seaweed tossed in the wind. Barefoot, she wore cut-off jean shorts and a midriff white T-shirt. Her legs were covered with green and blue swirls and interwoven patterns in a design reminiscent of Pacific Islander tribal tattoos.

She cocked her head at me, almost as though trying to decide whether she knew me.

I threw her a half-hearted wave, but she didn't return it.

A strange electricity radiated through my body—fearful vibes. It was time to head back. I made an about face and began to backtrack. Every few steps I craned my neck to look at the girl. She remained rooted to the spot, and even from far away, I could feel her eyes boring into me. When Belle Marsh again came into view, I looked over my shoulder once more. She was gone.

Inside, I sat on the couch, pulled my laptop onto my thighs, and checked my email. As I returned a message to Quincy, I caught sight of a piece of orange paper peeking out from under the cushions on the opposite loveseat.

I leaned forward, pinched the paper between my forefinger and thumb, and pulled it. It was a flyer for a Cry of Crows show. Faded ink displayed the date of June 18, 1998.

I tipped the cushion back, revealing that it served as a lid for a compartment under the loveseat. Several brown paper bags were filled with old, framed photographs. I lifted one. Lila smiled at the camera. It was an outdoor shot, and the sun gleamed off her dark hair and lit up the diamond quality of her eyes.

Another photograph captured Riff and Lila at a dinner function. Riff wore a black tuxedo. His hair was the same—just touching his shoulders, pushed behind his ears. His face was softer though, unlined by fear. Lila wore a gold dress with beading down the front, her hair hanging loose over her shoulders. The couple beamed, each of them raising a hand with extended pointer and pinky fingers—the devil horns flashed for the camera.

I put it back and examined the others. All the pictures were of Riff and Lila, but in the background of one of them lurked a thin girl wearing cut-off denim shorts and a peasant blouse, her arms and legs tattooed with tribal swirls. She greatly resembled the girl I'd seen on the beach. Her unsmiling face was partially blurred. A second photo looked like it had been taken the same day, and in that one, the girl stood behind him again, looking on, the same blurred-out effect masking her face.

Male voices and piano music filtered in from the hallway. Riff must be up. And was someone else here? I quickly replaced the photos, pulled down the cushion, and wandered toward the music room. I recognized the song. It was the melody for "Rebirth"—one of the slower songs off Cry of Crows' *Hall of Heartbreak* album.

I leaned against the doorframe. Riff sat at the piano, barefoot, wearing ripped jeans and a gray T-shirt. His hair hung forward, curtaining his face as he banged away. His strong wrists anchored his hands over the keys.

Riff glanced over at me and let his hands slide off. "Hey, Callie." He motioned to the side of the room hidden from my view. "This is Elijah."

I stepped into the room, and a man with mocha skin rose from an overstuffed chair and moved toward me. We met halfway and shook hands.

"The famous Elijah. I've heard so much about you."

He smiled. "Riff's just been telling me about you and the book you're helping him write."

"Trying to."

Still seated on the piano bench, Riff rested his hands on his thighs. "I thought maybe Elijah could take you on a spin around the island. Since you're here, you might want to see a little more than just this house."

"Sure. Sounds good."

Elijah nodded. "Got the golf cart outside. We can grab some lunch if you want."

Lunch meant we had a choice of three places. A seafood restaurant by the beach, a hot chicken stand by the marshes, or a tiny café nestled among live oaks.

"The café has great blueberry muffins." Elijah's grin lit up his light brown eyes. "Plus, I can introduce you to Nona. She's my grams—and the cook at the café."

We loaded into Elijah's golf cart and began a wild ride down dirt roads pockmarked with potholes that felt more like craters. One especially jarring dip caused me to groan and grip the handle attached to the roof.

Elijah laughed. "Hold on."

"Can't they pave the roads here?" My voice broke up as we careened over several more bumps.

"Nope. Locals don't want it."

I stared at his profile. "Why?"

He shrugged. "They like things the way they are. Only eleven roads on the island and just a few are paved."

We passed a sign informing us that one of the paved offshoots was private property.

Elijah pointed. "That's Bloodreed Point. Private resort, golf course, gated community."

"People who live here full time?"

"Some of 'em.

Every road we turned down was lined with thick forests of ferns and palms entangled with moss and vines. When Elijah suddenly slowed the cart and lifted his foot from the gas pedal, we rolled to a stop in the middle of the road.

I swatted at a mosquito that had adhered to my neck. "Why are we stopping?"

Elijah sat back, closed his eyes. The corners of his lips tipped. "Hear that?"

Birds. Lots of them. And nothing else.

"It's so quiet here," I said.

"Birds and insects. It's all you ever hear."

We sat staring out at the dirt road, listening to the cadence of nature. I swiped sweat from under the band of my baseball cap. Another insect buzzed by my ear and I smacked it. "This is a trippy place."

Beads of sweat lined Elijah's nose. "You either love it or you hate it."

It could be hot in Nashville in September, but this was humidity at a level I wasn't used to. Riding around in an open golf cart wasn't helping my naturally curly hair either. It probably resembled the wild shrubs in the forest by now.

Elijah bobbed his head. "This is why a lot of people come here—the peace and quiet."

"Do you think that's why Riff came?"

He chuckled. "Riff got his own reasons for being here—separate from why most come." Elijah dipped his head. "Well, when I first met Riff, he had this sort of selfishness to him, you know? He was in a big, successful band with everything at his feet. He didn't need anybody. And he was cocky."

"Like most rock stars I've met."

"Well, maybe that's so."

Elijah shifted toward me as though preparing to talk for a while. I swung a look over my shoulder. Nobody behind us. Not like we were blocking traffic.

"Riff says you're gonna write his story. Is that right?"

"I don't usually talk about that."

He sliced his hand through the air. "Don't worry. He already told me what you're doing. He's talking and you're writing."

I swatted away another swarm of gnats. "I'm ghostwriting for him. So, it's his words, his story, but I'll piece it all together in a way that makes sense and sounds good."

Elijah nodded. "I see. So he's kind of like one of those kids in high school that wants to get a good grade on the paper but doesn't actually want to write it."

"Yeah, kind of. Except this is a legit thing. Nothing shady. Contracts drawn up and all that."

He squinted down the road. "I'm glad you're here. You know, you're the first person who has stayed in that house since Lila went missing."

"He didn't really want me to come at all. I practically had to beg."

"Yeah, I know how that is." He lifted a corner of his mouth into a half-smile. "Every time I visit him, he tells me not to come inside." Elijah waved his hands and raised his voice to a higher timbre, mimicking Riff. 'It's not safe, it's not safe.'" He shot his eyes toward the sky and pursed his lips. "I'm always like, 'What're you talking about, man? You crazy.' But I've been worried about Riff. You know, he lives there all alone, never leaving the property, no interaction with anyone who's not a doctor or something. A man really could lose his mind living like that."

"Has he ever talked to you about how the agoraphobia started?"

Elijah shook his head. "Says he can't tell anyone about it."

I quirked my mouth. "Yeah, that's what he told me too."

"Riff never lets me come over after dark, and he never lets me stay long. Just like today, he always finds a way of getting me out as soon as possible."

"It's strange." But it was nice to hear that it wasn't just me.

"Riff is strange. No doubt about it. But he's still my friend."

I scratched at a nasty bite on my ankle that was already swelling and starting to itch. "I think I like it better when we're moving. The bugs don't have a chance to land on me that way."

Elijah laughed, started up the golf cart again, and we jerked forward.

Ironically, the Invisible Shack Café was impossible to miss. No bigger than a double-wide trailer, its turquoise-blue siding seemed out of place among the deep green backdrop behind it. Just like the blue door that marked the loft in Riff's house.

"Wow. That's a bright color."

"Haint blue." Elijah pressed his foot down on the golf cart's brake and turned off the ignition. "Haint—an old southern word for spirits or ghosts." He grinned. "Keeps away the evil spirits, *they* say."

"Yeah, Riff told me about that."

The seating area for the café consisted of six wrought iron tables and chairs with bright blue umbrellas positioned under live oaks dripping with moss. Most of the tables were already occupied, and as we walked by, a few people called out to Elijah, and he lifted a hand in greeting. We walked up to the trailer window, where a sandwich board listed the available foods in chalk writing.

A woman wearing an indigo-blue blouse leaned out of the window, smiling. "Hey, Elijah. You bring us a visitor today?"

"Hey, Grams, this is Callie Rowe. She's a visitor over at Belle Marsh. Riff asked me to show her around the island."

"Call me Nona." She nodded at me, but her brow crinkled. "What you doin' over at Belle Marsh?"

"I'm working with Riff on a project."

"His biography," Elijah filled in the gaps.

"Memoir," I corrected.

"His biography?" her voice trilled. "How old is he? He not dead yet, not old enough for that."

"Hard living ages you," Elijah said. "Anyway, I told Callie your place has the best food on the island."

Nona beamed. "That's for sure. Everywhere else, you get fried. Here, we don't fry nothin' except the fries." She leaned forward and lowered her voice. "She know about Belle Marsh—what happens there?"

Elijah nodded. "She knows about Riff's idiosyncrasies."

Nona straightened. "Idiosyncrasies—nothing. Riff needs deliverance from all those demons. I told him he should let me send Pastor out there—send 'em back to their watery hell."

I glanced between Elijah and Nona while flinging my hand around to disperse the insects. "Demons?" No wonder Riff was a wreck if that's what he believed.

Elijah chuckled a little and gave a quick shake of his head. "You know what he says about that, Grams."

"Oh, I know what he says—that he and God aren't on good terms. But I keep trying." She made a tsking sound as her eyes shifted back to me. "Maybe you can talk to him. He don't have to live like that. I been telling him he needs to get the curse off him."

"What curse is that?" I asked.

Her eyes ballooned. "You writing his story and you don't know?"

"I've only been here a day. He hasn't told me much yet."

Nona raised her hands to her hips. "Riff sold his soul to the devil years ago. He been trying to get free ever since."

My head was spinning. I was thankful I didn't believe in all this stuff, or I'd be heading for the mainland by now.

Three more people trailed up the ramp behind us.

Elijah cleared his throat. "All right, Grams, I think Callie is ready to eat. Like me. So, I'll have the burger. Cooked medium. Side of fries."

Elijah and I chose a table under the prehistoric-looking oak trees to consume our lunch—one of the juiciest, best-tasting burgers I'd ever eaten. I hadn't realized how hungry I was until I wolfed down the entire thing, along with every fry piled on the paper liner. I had so many questions jumping around in my mind—almost more than I had mosquitoes biting my neck, arms, ankles.

I smacked my hand against the outside of my thigh.

Elijah shook his head. "You got to get some bug spray, girl. You're gonna get eaten alive here."

I dragged a French fry through the pool of ketchup and popped it into my mouth. "So, what's all that your grams said?"

Elijah scrubbed a hand over the back of his head. "Well, you know, I just humor her. Here on the island, people got lots of ideas about things. Superstitions, curses, voodoo, and all that."

"But you don't believe in *all that*?"

He scratched the back of his neck. "Maybe I used to—a little—sometimes when I visited Grams I'd hear the stories, but I never saw anything paranormal. To me, it's all just fiction and fear. If you don't know anything different, you believe what you grow up with."

I curled my napkin around my fingers and wrenched it off again, wiping at the burger grease. "Well, your grandma's still a believer."

Elijah swiped his hand through the air. "Oh, hell yeah. She believes it all. She's a staunch, lifetime member of the Island Union Baptist Church. She's a believer to her marrow. That's never gonna change."

I liked Elijah. He seemed sensible. "Riff didn't grow up around here, yet he's completely paralyzed by...something."

Elijah rubbed his fingers over his mouth. "Yeah. I guess that's so."

I glanced back at Nona still serving people at the trailer window. "So, your grandma says he sold his soul to the devil."

"Yeah, Grams is eager to get him an exorcism or something. She's always talking about that. I tell her she needs to leave him alone." He held up his hands. "I mean, don't get me wrong. I'm not saying Riff's crazy or anything. Well..." He chuckled. "Maybe a little. But I think his mind's gotten tricked into believing what a lot of folks have told him. All this is just a coincidence. Bad things happen to people all the time. That's what it is. Maybe he's just had a little more bad stuff happening to him than most."

"Enough that he can't leave his property."

"He's working with a therapist now, so hopefully, that'll change." He spooned a bite of coleslaw into his mouth and chewed while looking off, squinting. Then he swallowed and said, "But you know, funny thing is—the island didn't change Riff. He was like that before he ever came here. Something happened to him a long time before he ever built Belle Marsh."

10

When we returned to the house that afternoon, Elijah dropped me off around the back and I entered via the door on the marsh side. Inside, the great hall echoed with the sound of acoustic guitar chords. Riff was playing a song I didn't recognize—a slow, haunting melody in a minor key. His deep, raspy voice filled the space.

I approached the door of the room slowly and stood against the wall, outside of his view. He sat on the piano bench strumming his guitar across.

So the song goes on
And so does the pain
My life has no meaning
But I feel the rain...in my heart.

He played the final chord, and I waited until the overtones finished reverberating before stepping inside. His fingers still rested on the strings, wrists limp.

"That was beautiful," I said.

Riff pushed the bench back, stood, and placed his guitar in a stand. "You're back."

"Yes."

"How was lunch?"

"It was delicious. Elijah recommended the burger."

He pursed his lips, nodding. "Good choice. Elijah brings me one of those sometimes too."

Our eyes locked. Something had changed, although I wasn't sure exactly what it was. Staring felt uncomfortable. A vaguely familiar electricity filled my veins—like an old rusty cog that hadn't turned for years.

I cleared my throat. "What was that song?"

He slanted his eyes to the floor. "Just one I've been working on. It's called 'Rain in My Heart.'" Riff hung his hands behind his neck and raised his eyes from beneath heavy brows. "I've been...well, I've been thinking about doing a solo album. But it'll be different from Cry of Crows' music—slower, more contemporary. That is if I haven't waited too long to do it. If people haven't forgotten all about me."

"People remember you."

"Yeah, as the crazy recluse living on an island." A sad smile barely reached his eyes. "I read the social media posts about me."

I wanted to tell him that after only a couple of days in his company, I didn't think he was crazy. We all had our own demons to endure—at least figuratively speaking. But the words died on my lips. It seemed too much to say then. "This book is your chance to tell the world your side of the story. Just like you said."

Riff moved back to the piano where he sank down on the bench again. "I'm not even sure why I'm doing this, Callie." His voice was hoarse. "I thought I was ready. But now I'm not sure."

"You're scared."

"Yeah. I guess you could say that." He lifted his gaze and whipped his head in the direction of the window.

I looked too.

A discordant sound rippled through the room as Riff brought his elbow down on the piano keys, dropped his head, and grasped the back of his hair.

He was obviously hurting with a pain that might never go away. Especially if Lila never turned up. I felt bad for him. But that bit was easy. It was the other part of my feelings that made me uncomfortable—the little flutter in my stomach every time we made eye contact. That had to stop. I needed to get past my schoolgirl crush from twenty years ago. Those days were long gone. Anyway, I always kept my professional life separate from my personal life. Detachment saved me. It kept me safe. It kept me breathing.

"I'm just so sick of this shit," Riff said. "She won't leave me alone."

"Who?"

Was he talking about Lila? Her memory? Several moments of silence hung heavily before Riff raised his head and lifted his elbows from the piano keys. A stray overtone carried through the room. He craned his neck, looking back at the window. Instinctively, I glanced over. Still nothing there—only the marsh in the distance and the oak branches hanging heavy with Spanish moss.

"Is someone out there?" I asked.

His face and shoulders relaxed. "No." He pushed back the bench and stood.

After speaking with Elijah, I had more of a handle on how superstition may have affected Riff. Local legend had been an easy scapegoat for whatever bad thing had happened to him.

"I guess you probably want to talk some more," he grumbled. "You want to get out your little recorder-thingy?"

I moved to the couch and fished around in my purse until I found the digital recorder, but I didn't turn it on.

Riff straddled the piano bench and exhaled a deep sigh. "What should I talk about now?"

My thumb hovered over the record button. "You said you can't tell me about it, but readers might want to know why you can't leave your property."

"Now you're sounding like Benny, my therapist."

"I've been to a few of those too—read a bunch of psychology books. We all internalize something someone told us once." I meant the superstitions he may have heard from locals or even what he'd dreamed up in his mind, but at the same time, the words were for true for me—this was something Riff and I clearly shared. "You've told me not to go near the upstairs door, warned me not to leave the house after midnight, and hinted around about 'the thing' that happened years ago that you can't talk about. But if I'm trying to help you write a tell-all about your life on this island...so far, I've only got a tell-a-little." I set the recorder on the coffee table and pressed record. "So, why *can't* you leave your property?"

Riff rolled his head toward me. "You don't know how many times I've tried to leave this place."

"What happens when you try to leave?"

"I get sick. Last time, I almost died."

I shrugged. "Could be a self-fulfilling prophecy. Psychosomatic. That's a real thing, you know."

His face slackened. "Curses are real too."

I clutched my hands and held them between my knees. "Today, when I met Elijah's grandmother at the café, she mentioned something about you selling your soul to the devil."

"She told you that?"

"Yeah. What's that about?"

He blew out air and scrubbed his hands over his face. "You want a drink?"

Full Verbatim Transcript of Interview With Riff Fall
9/20/16
5:30 p.m.

Riff: All my problems started years before I came here. [long pause][sighs] I guess, um, you could say it all started with Ricky, our guitarist. You know, no record label had picked us up, and we were all just kind of hanging out, doing different stuff, trying to save money to make a record. We'd moved out to LA, and we were all working odd jobs to keep our heads above water. I think I was working at the grocery. Trey was doing computer repair. Blacky was working at a car wash.

Callie: This was in what year?

Riff: This was like '97, I think. Ricky called me up, wanted to get together. He'd spent a week down in Laguna Beach with a music producer, Dove LaMer. Ever heard of her?

Callie: No, but I think you mentioned her in the draft of that chapter you gave me.

Riff: Ricky told me he wanted me to meet her. That she might want to help Cry of Crows do an album and might know of a label that was interested in us. Aeaea Records. So, I went down to Laguna and met Dove. She was kind of this hippy-type. She was covered in tattoos from head to toe, probably five foot two or three. Really tiny. But I mean, she'd produced some stellar albums. Um, *Streams* by the Franklin Three and November Feast's *Triad* album. So yeah, I was interested. Anyway, to make a long story short, a few weeks later, we got everyone assembled and started rehearsing, writing new songs. Then a few months later, when we had enough material, we asked Dove to produce it. And she was the best damn producer we'd ever worked with. She kept us on schedule and on budget—kept us from doing too much remixing and wasting time on overdubbing—knew how to keep the process moving forward. She had this incredible ability to cut through all the noise and see the finished product artistically and emotionally.

Callie: Was that the *Night Fields* album?

Riff: Yeah. Ended up going platinum several times. Anyway, um, as promised, Dove gave a few of the new songs to Kirka Taylor, the owner of Aeaea Records, and she loved it. She wanted to meet us. When we first met her, I think we were all a little in love with her at the time. She was tall and leggy with red hair. Kind of a Tawny Kitaen type, if you remember her from Whitesnake days.

Callie: I remember.

Riff: Anyway, we were in serious negotiations about signing with Aeaea Records, and Kirka sort of insinuated that she owned her own island somewhere out in the Atlantic and invited us all to come. In her words, she felt we'd been working really hard, and she wanted us to be totally relaxed before deciding to sign with her. Trey didn't really want to go. He kept saying, "Man, I'm telling you, there's something not right about her." But he finally agreed to go along with the group. And for the most part we were excited, you know, we were going to stay in this mansion on what we were told was a secluded island. What could go wrong?

Callie: This was a private island? Where?

Riff: At the time, we didn't have a clue. She told us she didn't want people to know where it was. It had been used as a drug drop-off point in the '70s and '80s. So we flew there on her private jet with no idea where we were going—only that it took about six hours from LA, so I figured we were somewhere on the East Coast.

Callie: Seriously? You didn't know where you were going?

Riff: Nope. We touched down on a small landing strip somewhere near the water, and then we were put in a boat and sent on a twenty-minute ride to her private dock. We all thought it was so cool. Everyone except Trey. He was really nervous the whole time. Anyway, the first night we were there, Kirka has this whole meal for us—I mean a spread. All kinds of shit. Meat, fish, vegetables, you name it. And she brings in some chef to do it all. But I don't remember much past the first course, though, because the chef laced the meat with hash, and between that and all the booze, we were all out of our minds by the end of the night.

Callie: He laced it with hash? Seriously?

Riff: Serious.

Callie: Did you know the food was drugged when you ate it?

Riff: No idea.

Callie: But you were trying to get clean, right?

Riff: Eh. I wasn't all that serious about it. All I cared about was getting a record deal. I later found out the meal was just preparation for Kirka's after-dinner entertainment plans.

Callie: Which was what?

Riff: [clears his throat] That night was weird as hell. I hardly remember any of it except at one point, Kirka started telling us she could do magic. I remember laughing about that, "Yeah, right, let's see you do some magic." She sat down beside me, looked right at me, and said something like, "Careful. I can be your biggest benefactor or your worst nightmare." If I'd been in my right mind I probably would have been like Trey—freaked out and scared as hell of her. But I was out of it, feeling all euphoric and shit. Trey was sitting in the corner, staring at his hands, and we kept trying to get him to come over and join us. He just kept saying, "I knew it. I knew we shouldn't have come here."

Anyway, the next thing I knew, there were a bunch of people sitting across from us. We didn't think any of them had been there before, but we were all so high it's hard to say.

Callie: Who were they?

Riff: Dove LaMer, two other girls, and some guy too. Anyway, [coughs] it turned into this big orgy. Totally insane. Kirka and I had sex—several times. But I just remember that at one point, while we were having sex, she started [snickers] singing.

Callie: What kind of singing?

Riff: It's so hard to explain—a sound like, like, well, I think I later described it as something that sounded like it had come out of the ocean. Once she started, I didn't ever want her to stop. Then the other women in the room started singing too. It was like we were all in a trance or something, and I felt this surge of—well, like I was high on ecstasy. Kirka asked me if I wanted to bind myself to her. I thought she meant, like, tie me up or something. And I was like, "I'm not into that." But then she said, "Do you want to be part of Aeaea Records?" And I was like, "Yeah, of course I do."

Callie: This was all while you were having sex?

Riff: Yeah [laughs]. It was crazy as shit, but when it was all over, Kirka pulled out this piece of paper, and the other women all gathered around. And suddenly it's like we're in a board room or something, but with all these naked women.

Kirka said, "If Cry of Crows agrees to sign this contract, your lives will change. You'll be free from all the scraping by—nothing will be denied you. You'll have plenty of money, fame, women—whatever you desire. And the struggle inside yourself—these notions of good and bad—they'll all be over. Do you want them to be over?" It sounded so good, what she was saying, so I was like, "Yeah, of course." I mean, I did—I wanted to be free from all the pain I was feeling inside. The years of self-torment about who I had become, the life I was living. I didn't even look around to see how the other guys were reacting. I was just going, "Where do I sign?" Then she said [clears throat] ...she said all we had to do was renounce our life as we knew it, follow her lead, and do everything she told us. "I'll make you bigger than Led Zeppelin," she said. "Bigger than the Rolling Stones."

Callie: It sounds like she was asking you to join some religion or cult.

Riff: Yeah. [coughs] Well, I didn't think she was serious. I thought it was a joke—the whole sign-your-life-away thing. You know, until she pulled out the knife.

Callie: A knife?

Riff: She pulled out this paper, rolled it out on the glass table right over top of the cocaine and shit, and told us to sign it. No lawyers, nothing. All the time this singing is going on, and the whole place is filled with it—like we're standing in a cathedral.

Callie: And you all agreed to it? You all signed it?

Riff: All except Trey. He hung back. The smart one. He kept saying, "Dude, I'm not signing nothing with my blood." So, he didn't sign it. Kirka said, "That means you'll no longer be a part of the band." He didn't care. He left that night. Someone came, transported him back to LA. But the rest of us, one by one, we all stepped forward. Signed our name and sealed it with a bloody thumbprint.

Callie: What about Trey? Did you see him again?

Riff: We left the island on Sunday night. By Monday morning, we had a new drummer. I didn't see Trey again for at least a year. He was playing with another band by then.

Callie: So this is—this is the night you supposedly sold your soul to the devil?

Riff: [long pause] That was the night I sold my soul to Kirka Taylor.

11

It wasn't like this was the first story I'd ever heard from a musician or rocker about getting involved in black magic or occult practices. Robert Johnson was a well-known legend. Rumors and stories abounded about his fateful decision at the crossroads to sell his soul in exchange for becoming a famous blues musician. Jim Morrison's relationship with witchcraft was widely speculated, along with a host of other famous bands and musicians.

But it was obvious that Kirka and her practices had profoundly affected Riff—psychologically if nothing else. And here on Invisible Island, rife with superstitions and traditions, any mention of such affiliations would be fodder for rumor and assumptions.

I sat on a beach chair with my laptop, intermittently tapping away and watching the tide roll in. I typed Kirka Taylor's name into the search engine, and she popped up right away, along with a photo. Riff wasn't wrong about her beauty—hair the color of red that you wondered if it was real or from a bottle. Gemstone eyes and cheekbones that may or may not have been purchased. In the photograph, she sat at the mixing board and looked back at the camera. The write-up said Kirka Taylor had been the owner of Aeaea Records, racking up success stories for a slew of rock and roll bands until around 2012. She only worked with producers who had the ability to make a band sound like nothing anyone had heard before. Enter Dove LaMer, who had quite a bio as well. "Mixing grunge, metal, and her own ethereal noise, Dove LaMer made legendary sounds throughout the '90s and into the early 2010s."

79

Another article talked about the bands Aeaea had worked with, but one line in particular caught my attention. "Aeaea Records set the rock charts on fire with multiple bands under its label until founder and CEO Kirka Taylor's abrupt departure from the music scene. Several of her protégés took over as Taylor was said to have retired from public life to a private island somewhere on the East Coast."

Kirka's private island.

Sand sprayed over my bare feet as Riff approached and dropped into the beach chair beside me. He handed me a bottle of beer and tipped another one to his lips.

I squinted at him. "I thought you didn't drink anymore?"

He fixed his gaze on the water. "Not often, I don't."

Fine with me. It was his life. He could do what he wanted. I turned my attention back to the information on my laptop. "Kirka Taylor retired from public life and is now living on her island?"

"That's what I hear."

"Have you heard from her? Has she tried to get in touch with you?"

He gave a quick shake of his head. "Not in a few years."

"Where is this island? Did you ever find out or—"

He pointed toward the ocean. "Somewhere off the coast of Florida, I think. I never went there again."

We sat for a while, drinking our beers in silence.

"Interesting that you ended up living on an island too," I said.

He exhaled a dark laugh. "I came here to get away from her and all the...others." He tipped back the beer, drained it, and ran his tongue along his lower lip. "But there's no escape. They never leave you alone."

"What do you mean? Who?"

Riff pushed off the chair. "I'll grab us another beer."

He'd consumed the first one in under five minutes. I watched him go and winced a little as he tripped on the steps leading up to the house. The more we talked, the more anxious and agitated he seemed to become. Was reliving these memories causing him to indulge tonight?

I finished my beer, ground the bottom of the bottle into the sand, and stared out at the ocean and the sinking sun. Much of Riff's willingness to buy into superstition and the idea that he was cursed must have started with his supposed vow to Kirka. She had a hold over him, and the fact that he'd signed a contract and sealed it with his blood must have added to the illusion that he was under her power. Riff had made some poor choices, yes, but would he have to pay for them for the rest of his days?

"Listen to that." The voice came from behind me. The guy I'd seen a couple of days ago was there again, crouching near the dunes, his red hair glowing in the late afternoon sun.

I stood. "Zeke, right?"

Zeke slowly emerged, rising from the seagrass as if coming out of the waves of the ocean.

"What am I listening for?" I asked.

He closed his eyes and held out his hands, palms up. "The vibrations."

I squinted out at the waters. "Of the ocean, you mean?"

His eyes still closed, he smiled. "It's all around. The electromagnetic frequencies. Sometimes, if you're really still, you can almost hear the frequencies cutting through the air."

I smiled, closed my eyes, and feigned concentration on the alleged vibrations.

Zeke plopped down in the sand. "Did you know that some scientists believe that diseases have their own electromagnetic frequencies?"

I shook my head. "No, I didn't know that."

He crossed his ankles. "Back in the '30s, Royal Rife was this scientist and inventor who believed you could break up microorganisms and diseases, like cancer, simply by sending radio waves of the same frequency into the body."

"Fascinating."

"Yeah, it is. He created a machine that sends out these low-frequency electromagnetic waves. The machines are for sale. You can buy them. I'm saving up for one."

Riff had said Zeke's mom had cancer. Sounded like Zeke was trying to do something to help her—even if it was unconventional. "Riff told me you were a budding scientist." I jerked my thumb toward the house. "Are you looking for Riff? He's just gone inside. He'll be right out."

"It's getting late. I should go," Zeke parroted the words I'd heard Riff say to him before.

I glanced at the sun, dropping gradually like the New Year's Eve ball in Times Square. "Yeah, but it won't be dark for a little bit. Do you live close by?"

He pointed down the length of the beach. "Over there. But only in the summer months. Most of the time we live in North Carolina. My mom wanted to stay longer this year." He flattened his mouth. "She says it might be her last time." Zeke closed his eyes. "Sometimes you can hear them before dark."

"What's that? The vibrations?"

"Listen, listen." Something about the way he spoke the words reminded me of the frightening encounter I'd had with the woman at my door in Nashville. I'd almost forgotten about her until now.

"What am I listening for?"

"Listen," he said again, swaying a little as though hearing music on the wind.

"Zeke!" The screen door banged against the side of the house as Riff nudged it with his foot. He strode toward us carrying two bottles of beer. "What are you doing?"

Zeke's eyes popped open and straightened as though responding to an army sergeant's command. "I—I was just listening, sir."

"Listening to what?" Riff kicked through the sand and held out the bottle to me. I took it, my palm slipping against the sweating glass.

"Ju-just the water music."

Riff stood beside me and swilled from his beer. "Ain't no water music. Nothing but the waves."

Zeke shook his head and grinned. "No, no, you know better than that, Riff. You know about the water music."

I studied Riff's face. His nostrils flared as he took a deep breath. "I don't know any such thing."

Zeke took a few steps forward, laughing, pointing a long finger. "No, you're teasing me, Riff. You told me you've heard it. Remember? You told me you heard it and you almost drowned and that's why I can't come around here when it's dark—"

"All right, Zeke. Time for you to go home now."

I swung my gaze back and forth between the two men. Riff looked down at his beer, his mouth moving like he was chewing on a tough piece of meat.

Zeke took another step. "But—"

"Go on. I got a lady friend here, you see. You know I told you when I got a lady friend here, you don't disturb us, right?"

My face burned. A lady friend? I almost protested that I was not Riff's "lady friend," but I had a feeling that wouldn't help Riff's purpose of diverting Zeke.

Zeke's face suddenly lit up, a smile spreading across his lips. He began to laugh as though he'd heard the funniest joke in years. "Oh, she's a *lady* friend."

Riff continued to look at his bottle. "Yep. Her name's Callie."

"Hey, Callie." Zeke waved like he was meeting me for the first time.

Biting the side of my lip, I gave a half-hearted wave.

"Now, head on out. I'll see you in the morning for your lesson," Riff said.

Zeke took one step back and then another. "Have you heard them yet?"

"Heard who?" I asked.

"The night singers."

All the playfulness drained from Riff's face. "Zeke, I'm only going to say this one time. You go on home. Right now."

"Dad doesn't hear them," Zeke said. "Neither does Mom. Just me." He again met my gaze. "But you might hear them while you're here."

Riff flung his hands out. "Go on, Zeke. Talk to you tomorrow."

Zeke continued to walk backward through the seagrass, becoming smaller and smaller until he swiveled around and took off running.

I turned to Riff. "What was that all about?"

He made a rattling sound in his throat and returned to his beach chair, straddled it, and sucked from his bottle. "Nothing. Don't worry about it."

I pursed my lips. "A lady friend?"

He didn't look up at me. "Zeke's family has one of those houses down the way. The big ones on stilts. They come here every summer. Usually, they leave before hurricane season though. I guess they're staying a little longer this year."

"But a *lady friend*, Riff? Really? What century are we in?"

"Yeah, I know." Reddish coloring bloomed in Riff's cheeks. He motioned toward me with the bottle. "Sorry about that. It was just me trying to get him to move along."

I lifted an eyebrow. "You have a lot of 'lady friends' come visit you at Belle Marsh?"

"Not hardly." His dark eyes panned across the water. Long, weathered lines seeped from the corners.

"What was Zeke talking about—the singing? The water music?"

He scoffed. "Nothing. Zeke says all kinds of nonsense."

Even so, I found myself straining to hear something more than the ocean's crashing sonata.

Riff coughed. "Sun'll be down soon. Let's go inside."

SITTING INSIDE THE screened porch, I smoked while Riff stretched out on the couch where I'd found the photos under the seats. His half-finished third beer held between his thighs, anchored at his crotch—almost obscenely. For a few moments, I thought he might be asleep. But then he inhaled sharply, tilted his head back against the chair, and looked at me under lowered lids.

"You got a boyfriend back in Nashville?"

I squirmed. "Uh, no."

"Girlfriend?"

"No."

"Ever been married?"

"No, why the twenty questions?"

He raised his hands, chuckling. "Sorry, I just—I've been talking about myself all this time, and I wanted to find out a little something about you."

My shoulders tensed. "No relationships. At least none that have gone anywhere."

He nodded. "Okay."

A few seconds ticked by. He tipped the bottle back again. I listened to the fizz of his beer as it settled.

He swiped the back of his hand across his mouth. "Sorry, I—how old are you?"

"Thirty-five."

He raised his eyebrows. "Oh, that's older than I thought."

"Thanks."

He sat up, laughing. "No, I didn't mean it like that. I was just thinking you look really young. Younger than thirty-five."

I smirked. "Maybe that's because I've avoided serious relationships."

A slow smile crept over his face. He had great lips. *Get a grip, Callie. Stop thinking like you're fifteen.* This was a job. I couldn't believe I even had to remind myself. Not to mention all his baggage. Trust me to be hot for the most inappropriate guy on the East Coast. The Byronic hero. The perfect tortured soul.

"I don't do relationships either." He held out his hands. "For obvious reasons."

"Because of Lila."

He hesitated. "Yeah. She's still out there...somewhere. And even if it wasn't for Lila, I couldn't ask anyone to live like this—or take on someone like me."

"Someone like you. You're not exactly an ogre."

Riff eyed me. "Don't forget the crazy part."

"Not everyone thinks that about you."

His gaze intensified. "What about you? Do you think I'm crazy?"

"Well...I—"

He held up a hand. "Don't answer that. I don't want to know." He reclined on the couch again. "You must've met a lot of guys like me when you visited your dad. You probably know as many people in the industry as I do. You probably even dated some of them."

A yawning pit of dread opened in my stomach. "I met a few. I never dated them."

"Smart woman. You could probably write your own memoir about your dad."

"I started one a few years ago," I said matter-of-factly. "But I've never finished it."

"You should. I bet that would be a fascinating read." His gaze wandered. "Let's see, the band Crashing Light. That was Trace Rowe, and wasn't Manny Sullivan the lead singer?"

My teeth clacked together. I nodded.

"And," he continued, "who else? Oh, yeah. Frankie Wilton was on bass, right?"

The pit in my stomach widened. "Yes."

"Yeah, I think I even had a beer with Frankie once at an after-party in Beverly Hills. He died too young. Nice guy."

I nearly snorted. Yeah, real nice guy.

"Were your mom and dad married?"

I cleared my throat. "No. My dad wasn't really in my life at all until I was around eight. My mother was between marriages, and he came to see her. That was the first time I met him. Then, I started flying to California to visit him once a year. That continued until I was fourteen." I felt my shoulders tense. "After that, I didn't really see him anymore."

Riff blinked. "Why not? What happened?"

"He was busy touring. I was busy with friends and high school. Mom remarried and we moved. There was a lot going on." It was a paltry excuse, but I couldn't even think about the real reason right then much less verbalize it. I pulled out my recorder. "Let's get back to you. Tell me about the band. I want to hear about the good times."

Riff talked an uninterrupted streak about the days when the band was at their peak and life was good—after they'd signed the contract with Aeaea Records. The recording studio, life on the road, touring overseas. Maybe it was the three beers. Or maybe he was feeling more comfortable around me, but he seemed to enjoy this part of it—reminiscing about the good times.

I noted all his mannerisms—the way he rubbed his hands over his face, the dip of his head. The timbre of his voice even. It was almost like studying someone for a role in a movie—learning their tics and tones.

"We were on the top of the world for a couple of years."

"What happened? When did things start to slip?"

"Kirka," he nearly growled. "She just wanted more and more from us. Every second of our lives were micromanaged. If my voice was flagging, there was a rock doc for that. Steroids, shots. If we were burned out or needed a break, there was a pill for that. Keep going, keep going. Keep making money for the label—for Kirka. Always for Kirka. And if she wasn't there, her minions were."

"What? Like handlers?"

"Yeah. Watchers. Making sure we fulfilled our contractual duties." His speech grew heavier as the room darkened.

"You know, it's getting late. I've got a lot of information. I think I'd like to start writing. It's going to be a late night for me."

He squinted at me with one eye. "You kicking me out?"

I laughed and stood. "No, I mean, stay if you want. I just need to get some work done."

"Sure, I'll...get out of your way." He stood, went to the box on the wall by the door, and pressed the button. The beige panels lowered, covering the screens, closing out the sounds of the ocean.

He lingered in the doorway. "Sorry if I brought up something you didn't want to—you know, about your dad—"

"It's fine."

"No, it's just sometimes, I say too much when I'm drinking." His face was partially shadowed.

I raised a hand to my hip. "Yeah, about that. I thought you always stopped drinking before getting drunk?"

His voice lowered, his face in shadows. "I don't know. Maybe—just for tonight—maybe I wanted to get drunk."

12

I wrote for three hours and managed to draft two chapters. Finally, I was too tired to keep my eyes open. I desperately wanted to talk to Quincy, but it was after midnight. Too late to call. I started writing an email to him, one I'd finish in the morning.

I left my laptop set up in the music room and went upstairs, where I collapsed on the bed and stared at the ceiling, waiting for my eyes to drift closed.

Tap-tap-tap.

My body went rigid. What was that? It was coming from overhead.

Scritch, scritch.

I turned over and folded the pillow around my ears, attempting to block out the sound. After Nona's words about demons and devils, I didn't need anything else messing with my head.

I breathed in, holding the pillow as close to my face as possible. Maybe I should grab the military-grade earplugs Riff had given me.

A few minutes later, I released the foam and let the pillow fall away. The room was quiet again.

I should've smoked one more cigarette. I usually had one before going to bed. I turned on the light, grabbed my pack off the nightstand, and carried it to the window. I unlocked the latch and dug my fingers under the edge of the sill, attempting to pry it open. No luck. It wouldn't budge and seemed to be nailed or painted shut. Uh...fire hazard, dude.

I carried the pack into the bathroom and repeated the exercise. This time, the sill shifted up—not much, maybe two inches, and then stopped, but it was enough to allow the smoke to filter out rather than gather in the confines of the bathroom.

I fumbled with my lighter, flicked it, and held the flame to the end of the cigarette. As I did, I heard...singing. I sucked in smoke and blew it out again, drawing nearer to the open window. Outside, crashing waves and the most otherworldly and mesmerizing song melded together. Deep but sonorous—like listening to a chorus in a massive cathedral. Breathtaking. Heartbreaking. I wanted to be out there where I could hear the full volume, not inside where I was only getting a small bit of it. Trapped. Imprisoned. Just like Riff.

I sank down, my back to the wall. I finished my cigarette and listened while tears streamed down my cheeks and gathered under my chin. Other than my strange breakdown the other night on the phone with Quincy, I hadn't cried in years. But there was something about this music that brought equal parts joy and devastation. Who was making this extraordinary sound?

Zeke had said something about the singing—the water music?

I could always tiptoe downstairs and exit through the porch, but the interior cameras might set off an alarm. Riff would stop me. And I would've broken one of his rules—a mortal sin—venturing out after midnight.

But the pull was strong. Sort of the way one felt when in the throes of foreplay—when you knew you had to stop but you were desperate to go on and on...

As the singing continued, I was overwhelmed with pain and anguish. It was too much. I needed relief, but I couldn't bring myself to close the window. My heart felt like it would burst. The scars on my leg screamed to burn. Finally, I clawed my way up the wall, reached for the sill, and slammed the window shut.

The singing ceased.

But the memory of it did not. And the grief inside me swelled.

13

The next morning, I awoke on the floor of the bathroom. Immediately, I pulled up the hem of my pajama shorts and inspected my scars. They stared back at me. Unchanged. I exhaled and pushed myself to my feet. My legs were shaky and pain shot through my neck from sleeping cramped between the wall and the vanity.

I rubbed at the bone near the top of my spine and lolled my head back and forth, precipitating cracks and pops. The singing from last night. I barely remembered what it sounded like now or why I'd been so desperate to hear it. It was like struggling to recall a distant dream. More importantly, I wanted to know—who had been singing?

And I distinctly remembered crying.

I dragged myself into the shower and then dressed. As I left my room, I glanced down the hallway toward the forbidden door. Then I moved toward it. The camera whirred awake, the lens following me.

Standing in front of it, I once again eyed the blue freezer tape that outlined the panel like a crime scene body drawing. Leaning forward, I pressed my ear against the door, just beside the wooden cross. Silence. A pulsing sensation pressed against the cartilage of my ear. Most likely my own blood reacting to the anticipation. I was tripping myself out—feeding into Riff's hype. Even more maddening, he wouldn't talk about it. What was in there?

Some houses were just strange. My grandmother's house always generated a weird vibe, but it was old, built in the 1800s, dressed with lace curtains and crocheted doilies on every table. An ancient radio played nothing but opera music—baritones and sopranos singing arias, duets, and choruses—the same ones repeatedly. At night, my grandfather sometimes told me ghost stories. So, with all these things combined, it was no wonder the house had given me the creeps. The power of suggestion was strong.

Downstairs, I tiptoed toward the music room where I'd left my laptop. It wasn't yet nine, and I figured Riff was still asleep. I'd continue writing and get as much down as possible before he woke and then we could continue the interviews.

When I arrived in the room, he was already there. I hoped he hadn't seen me on the monitor, snooping around the blue door. He was perched in front of my laptop, his hand under his chin and his elbow braced on the table.

His face reddened as he stood. "Oh, hey." He pointed at the screen. "It was open. I'm sorry. I couldn't help seeing what you wrote."

That was weird. Usually, my laptop locked itself after inactivity. I lunged toward the computer, wanting to block the words from his sight. Whatever he'd read hadn't been ready for reading.

He pointed at the page and laughed a little. "It's great. It really sounds like I wrote it."

I leaned forward, squinted at my words on the screen. Just the draft of the chapters—rough and unpolished—still, not terrible. But when I minimized the screen, an open email stared back at me. The one I'd started writing to Quincy last night. The words were disjointed, frenetic, and sounded more like a teenager than a professional writer.

The unsent email was in response to Quincy's from earlier in the day saying he'd not been able to reach me on my phone and wanted to know how things were going.

Quincy, Things are going—but so damn slow. Like I said before, Riff is definitely a little crazy, paranoid for sure (he's got security cameras all over the place), but holy shit he's hot. If things were different—like he wasn't a recluse with a missing wife—and if I wasn't the ice queen (as you so fondly call me)—you never know. Sparks might fly.

Oh shit.

My face flamed.

Riff cleared his throat, and I tried to drag my eyes up to his, but I couldn't bring myself to look at him as I forcibly closed my open mouth. What could I say? *Actually, I should pack up my things and leave. Right now.*

"That chapter you wrote about Kirka, about that night at her house—I mean, you don't even have the whole story yet, but you made it sound like I wrote it."

I stared hard at the opposite wall. What an absolute idiot I was. How could I have left that screen open? And why hadn't my computer gone into sleep mode, which it usually did after a few hours, requiring a password to open it?

"I'm sorry you saw that," I stammered. "Quincy is my agent—and a good friend. Sometimes I confide things in him. But that was..." I broke off. "Look, just don't snoop on my laptop. I'll send you chapters to read." I flapped my arms. "No, you know, it was my fault for leaving the laptop down here in the first place."

"Hey, Callie."

I bit my lip as I finally met his eyes.

The corners of his lips were upturned. "I'm sorry. And I shouldn't have been snooping on your laptop. My bad. But I mean, no one's written anything positive about me in a long time."

I gritted my teeth. He seemed amused by the whole thing, his eyes gleaming, suggesting he might even have been flattered.

I backed away from him. "That's a shame." I forced the rest of the words from my mouth, "Because you seem like a very decent person to me—when you're not snooping on my laptop."

He'd read the email. There was nothing to do but address it head-on.

"But I'm sorry," I blurted. "About the email. I shouldn't have...I probably had too much to drink last night. That was really unprofessional of me."

"I was a bad influence."

"No, it's—"

"It wouldn't be the first time."

A little shiver ran over me at the intensity of his stare. I looked away.

"Like I said, it's been a long time since anyone's written *anything* positive about me."

I pressed my lips together, hoping we could both forget about this quickly.

He pivoted away from me, pushing his hand through his hair. "I've got a hangover," he said. "I need water. And probably some air." He looked down at his watch. "Zeke's coming for his guitar lesson at eleven. You want to walk on the beach a little?"

"Can you? I mean, are you okay to walk around outside like that?"

"Yeah. As long as I don't leave the property."

We strolled along, and I inspected the red dots covering my arms—bug bites. I looked like I had chicken pox. The sun was already heating the sand, and the humidity crept in faster than the tide rolled out. The tall grasses swayed in the light breeze and I half-expected to see Zeke lying in them.

"I see what you mean about Zeke and his affinity for science. Yesterday I got a lesson on electromagnetic frequencies and how they might be able to cure diseases."

"Yeah, Zeke's got all kinds of wild ideas. He's applying for scholarships. He wants to go to medical school. I think his mother's sickness has spurred that idea. Not that he couldn't do it though. He's a smart kid."

I hopped over the upside-down carcass of a horseshoe crab and dodged half a dozen beached jellyfish. "What did Zeke mean when he referenced the water music?"

Riff cut his hand through the air. "Aw, who knows?"

I lifted an eyebrow. "He seemed pretty adamant about it."

"Zeke says a lot of stuff."

I hesitated, knowing how he felt about open windows after dark. "I heard some music last night."

Riff jerked his head toward me. "What music?"

"Outside. I heard singers when I opened the bathroom window to smoke."

Riff stopped walking. I stopped too.

He faced me, placed his hands on my shoulders, his eyes like coals. "Listen to me, Callie. When I say don't open any windows after midnight, I mean it. I know it doesn't make sense—at least not yet—but just trust me when I say I'm trying to protect you."

"So you'd rather me fill your upstairs with smoke."

"Yes."

I lowered my gaze to his fingers pressing into my rotator cuff.

Riff loosened his grip and then dropped his hands.

"Protect me from what?"

He didn't answer.

"Is this one of those 'you can't tell me' things?"

He exhaled and looked off down the beach. "I'll tell you everything eventually, Callie." He blinked. "Even if it kills me."

His eyes lingered on mine, but his expression was somber, melancholy even. He was so alone, so isolated here.

I watched a line of kingfishers peck the sand at the ocean's edge. "What about your family? Your brothers and sisters? Do they ever visit you?"

We resumed walking again, and Riff kicked at a tangle of seaweed. "My sisters have been here a few times, but I made them stay at one of the island cottages. My brother came once and brought my mother on a day trip from Hilton Head. Mostly, I encourage them to stay away. I don't want to drag them into my mess."

"What about your dad?"

"My real dad? Haven't talked to him since I was eighteen—and that was only one time. My stepdad—I haven't spoken to him in years." He shot me a sidelong glance. "So I'm sort of like you in that way."

I nodded. "I guess we do have that in common." Along with loneliness.

He grimaced. "Yeah, well, my stepfather's got his own demons. He was an abuser. To all of us. Beat the tar out of all us kids—and my mother. Said it was his right and for our own good. Then one day, I came home from high school and heard him beating my sister in the basement. By the time I got down there, she'd managed to get away and get out the basement door. She started running for her life. My stepfather chased her, and I went after them. But before I did, I grabbed my baseball bat. My sister ran all the way down to the pond, but he caught up and started beating her some more. He was pushing her head into the water, holding her down. I figured he was gonna kill her. I came up behind him, smacked him right between the shoulder blades with the bat. He went into the water, and I pulled my sister out. Then I told him if he ever hit her again, I'd kill him."

I glanced over at him. Even as he talked about it, his jaw tightened, making his words short and stilted. His anger swam right under the surface.

"Sounds like you made your point."

"To my knowledge, he never touched her again. I know he never hit me again. I left soon after that anyway—found some couches to sleep on at friends' places."

We strolled in silence for several paces. Fathers—they could really wreck a kid's life. "These things that happen to us in childhood are so difficult to navigate as adults. So complicated," I said.

"You said you'd started a memoir about your dad. Why haven't you ever finished it?" Riff finally asked. "You write other people's stories all the time."

I squinted ahead, wondering how long before we were off the property. "I don't know. It's easier for me to write about other people."

"Why is that?"

"Probably because I don't have any baggage with anyone else—no personal connections. Other than meeting with them to get the information, there's nothing else to it." I slung my hand toward him. "Like us. I'll interview you, go back to Nashville, then we can call or meet to collaborate on the rest of it, and I'll send drafted chapters for your input. That'll be it."

"No need to meet after that, I guess."

"Nope." I felt like I had to say that—especially after what I'd written in the email. I needed to clear the air, redraw the zones.

Riff stopped walking again. "You know, I get this feeling about you."

I looked over my shoulder at him, then turned to face him. "What's that?"

He gave me a sidelong glance. "Maybe I *am* crazy, but I can't help thinking that deep down, you're not quite as closed off as you make yourself out to be."

I suppressed a smile. "Nope. I'm just as closed off as you think. I'm even more closed off than you think."

"Hm."

I lifted one shoulder and then let it fall. "With you—this situation is...well, I don't usually spend this much time with people I ghostwrite for. I've never stayed in any of my clients' homes before. I'm usually a lot more detached."

The wind blew Riff's hair across his face, and he swept it behind his ear. "After reading what you wrote—I mean, it's like you really know me."

I knew he meant the chapters, not the email, but my cheeks simmered. Despite all attempts to keep the corners of my mouth from rising, they turned up—seemingly of their own volition.

Riff beamed. "You're smiling! This is the first time I've seen you really smile. You actually have teeth!"

Self-conscious, I covered my mouth. "I smile all the time," I muttered against my fingers.

"I haven't seen it," he said softly. "Until now. Not like that."

I strode ahead.

It was strange to have someone point out how little I smiled. But he was right. Smiling wasn't one of my easier expressions. Sometimes Quincy pointed it out too. I came across bitchy, although I didn't mean to.

I kept walking.

"Callie!" Riff called.

Realizing he no longer walked beside me, I glanced over my shoulder. He stood several yards back, where the beach met the seagrass.

"I can't go any farther than this. This is where the property ends." He pointed at a wooden stake with a light pink ribbon that fluttered from the top. "This is the boundary."

With a sense of defeat and sadness, I walked back to him, the wind blowing my hair into my mouth. The boundary marker was a reminder of his limitations. Riff would never leave this place. He was as stranded on Invisible Island as if he'd been shipwrecked.

14

When we got back to Belle Marsh, Zeke was waiting by the door to the screened-in porch. He held a guitar case in one hand and swept his other arm through the air in wide arcs, beaming as we approached. "I told you I could be on time, Riff. And today, I am."

Riff opened the door. "You are. You're early."

"Is that bad?"

"Nope."

Zeke put a foot on the steps and pivoted toward me. "Hello, lady friend."

"Callie, remember?" I followed him up the steps and inside.

"Are you going to watch my lesson?"

"I don't know, Zeke. I have work to do."

He glanced over his shoulder at me as Riff led him to the music room. "Oh, please. You might be the only audience I ever have."

Riff paused at the door. "You're welcome to sit in."

Why not? What was an hour of my life to make the kid happy? Plus, it would give me an opportunity to watch Riff at work since this too was a part of his life.

Riff and Zeke settled into chairs side-by-side and Zeke unpacked his guitar—a red Fender that he plugged into the amp and immediately began strumming. Even though I didn't play myself, I'd learned a fair bit about instruments over the years. An unavoidable side effect of hanging out with musicians. They all loved to talk about their instruments.

Riff grabbed the neck of his Miami blue Fender and balanced it on his lap. "Okay, let's hear the song we were working on last week. You been practicing that one? The Led Zeppelin one?"

"The Immigrant Song." Zeke positioned his hand.

Riff reached over and nudged one of his fingers. "First finger, fret two of the E string."

Zeke launched into the loping rhythm of the bluesy rock song.

"Down, down, up," Riff instructed. "Use your pinky on the D string."

Riff was right about Zeke's abilities. He was a natural and seemed to take Riff's every direction with ease, shifting hand positions as needed.

"What do you want to learn next?" Riff asked after they'd played through several Led Zeppelin, Soundgarden, and Cry of Crows songs.

Zeke rested his hand on the top of the guitar. "What about that song you wrote for your wife? 'In the End.' Wasn't that the name of it?"

Riff's face clouded. "Why that one? It's a slow one—you said you don't like the slow songs."

Zeke shrugged, his eyes turning toward me. "I think she'd like it."

Until now I'd been silently observing, only nodding occasionally to signal agreement with Riff's praise of Zeke's playing.

"Why do you think I would like it?"

Zeke fluttered his eyelids. "'Cause it's all about *lurve*." He overemphasized the word.

Riff cleared his throat, a tiny smile pulling at the corners of his lips.

I wrinkled my nose. "What makes you think I want to hear a song about love?"

Zeke rolled his eyes. "Well, because." He snorted. "Obviously." His eyes darted between me and Riff. Was he saying he thought there was something between us? Was there something between us? No, that wasn't a possibility. Even if there was some rogue attraction on my part. As for him, well, I was probably the only female he'd seen for a while that wasn't related to him or over sixty-five.

But the controls were firmly in place: His wife was missing; I didn't do romantic affairs.

"You know, Zeke, Riff and I just have a professional relationship," I said.

Riff nodded. "Yeah, we're just friends."

Zeke rolled his eyes again. "Uh-huh. Yeah, right. *A lady friend.*" He resumed strumming chords.

Riff lifted his eyebrows and shrugged. "All right. Let's do the song if it'll make you happy." He pointed at the neck of Zeke's guitar. "D minor."

Zeke shook his head. "No, I want you to play it."

Riff dropped his arm. "Why me? This is your guitar lesson."

"You always play the songs before you teach them to me."

Riff hesitated. Then, with lowered eyes, he sawed a finger under his nose and his brows deepened. "All right." He positioned his hand over the strings.

He began to play a tune that had no lyrics, only notes that depicted heartbreak and loss. The song started slowly, transitioned with arpeggiated chords, and then moved to a faster rhythm toward the end.

As he strummed the last diminished chord, Zeke and I clapped. It was perfect. A song that hinted at uncertainty—his love for Lila hanging in the throbbing overtones of an unresolved chord.

Riff set his guitar to the side and stood. "Be right back."

I watched him go, noting the emotion etched on his forehead.

Once he was out of the room, Zeke turned toward me. "He wrote that for her."

"I know."

"He really loved her."

"I know. He still does."

Zeke's eyes met mine and held them. "She probably walked into the sea."

I cocked my head. "Walked into the sea? What do you mean?"

He thumped his hand against the strings of his guitar and a harmonic echo sounded. "I've read all about it. You hear the singing and walk right into the water like you're strolling down the street."

I thought about the music I'd heard last night—a sound I could no longer remember. "Have *you* heard the singing?"

Zeke stared up at the ceiling. "I've heard 'em, and I've seen 'em. One of 'em came to the door one night. I didn't let her in though. I hear they stalk you before they kill you." His face tightened.

My skin prickled. I tried to make sense of his words. Who were *they*?

"Yeah. I didn't tell my parents though. And shhhh..." He put his finger to his mouth, his eyes darting toward the hallway. "Don't tell Riff. He warned me, and I stay in at night 'cause I know what'll happen if I don't." Zeke pointed at the ceiling. "But I can see them from my window. It looks right out at the ocean. One time, two of the women stood down below. They were calling me, but I didn't come out."

"Women? Who? Who are they?"

Zeke didn't blink. "The night singers."

Riff returned, his eyes red and watery. He pinched the bridge of his nose. "I think that's all we have time for today, Zeke."

Zeke dutifully stood and replaced his guitar in its case. "Next week? Same time?"

Riff nodded. "God willin' and Calibogue Sound don't rise."

15

Later that night, Riff and I sat at the dining room table, which stretched practically eight feet long—like something one would expect in a medieval banquet hall. WE shared a corner at one end, our voices echoing against the vaulted ceiling.

Riff had cooked spaghetti Bolognese with penne noodles and a mixed green salad. We'd barely spoken while eating, both of us seemingly focused on our food. Once I'd eaten every bite and finally came up for air, I sat back with a satisfied groan. "That was awesome, Riff."

He leaned forward, his elbows on the table. "You know, if you ever decide to write that memoir—about your dad—I'm interested in reading it."

Jarred by his sudden change of subject, I shook my head. "I don't think I'll ever finish it." Why was he so interested, anyway?

"Why's that?" he asked.

"I got to a certain point and then got stuck—I couldn't go any further. I didn't ever mean for anyone to read it. It's highly personal. And it's not any good."

How else could I explain it? Riff had been a rock star and lived in that scene. He knew what went on. Some of what I'd written was about my dad, but some of it was about what had happened to me. Riff was the last person I wanted to read all of that. He'd think I was stupid or naive for putting myself in that type of situation and letting myself be taken advantage of. Because, even now, I thought those things about myself. My father had pushed me away because of what had happened.

I toyed with a decorative ball sitting in a wooden tray on the table. "Early on in my career, I did a memoir for this woman who'd married a con man. When the truth came out, and she finally understood what her husband had done, it crushed her, you know? It shook the earth from under her feet. It made her distrust everyone and everything she knew until then; it made her doubt herself."

A vertical line formed between Riff's brows.

"But she felt she had to get her story out there. It was as much to warn other women as it was to put order to her own thoughts. She wrote it for catharsis—like self-therapy, if you understand my meaning."

"I do."

I suspected he did. It was why he was writing his story too, after all. "But when the book came out, she didn't get the response she was expecting. People castigated her, saying how could she be so stupid? How could she not have known? What sort of idiot marries a man after knowing him only a few weeks? She deserved what she got, and so on and so on."

The line between his eyebrows deepened. "So, you're afraid that might happen to you?"

"I guess I am." I trailed the tines of my fork through the remnants of meat sauce on my plate. "Aren't you?"

Riff balled up his napkin and placed it on the table. "I got different reasons for wanting my story out there." His gaze drifted across the room. "You know, people will think whatever they want to think. Look at all the articles written about me. I'm this caveman living on a deserted island."

"That's a much more interesting story than the truth."

Riff nodded. "You're judged by a different standard when you're in the public eye."

"I never wanted to be in the public eye. That's why I'm a ghostwriter."

"I get it. I do."

He kicked off his flip-flops and stretched out his legs under the table, his foot pushing against mine. Accidentally, I assumed.

"I remember when the police came to arrest me," he said. "After Lila disappeared."

I grappled under my seat for my digital recorder. I'd learned to carry it with me. I never knew when he might launch into a story unprompted. I set it on the table. "May I?"

He nodded.

I switched it on. "How long after she disappeared?"

"Maybe two months later? They transported me to Bluffton in a police boat. Held me overnight until my attorney could get in to see me, but by then I was so sick I couldn't talk. The police thought I was faking it." He took a deep breath and then slowly released it. "But while I was in the interrogation room, this one cop—Detective Forbes—says to me, 'I always hated assholes like you. You think you're better than everyone else. You think you'll get away with murdering your wife and throwing her body in the ocean. I've seen it before.'" Riff's eyes met mine. "And that hurt, you know? I've never seen myself as above anyone else. I was born right here in South Carolina just like he was. I grew up with a little bit of nothing. I was a truck driver. I was thankful for everything I had. And at that time..." His Adam's apple bobbed. "I couldn't imagine life without Lila." Riff tipped his head to the side, his voice lowering to a growl. "'Rock stars are just scum,' the cop said to me. And then he said, 'And I can tell you're even lower than scum.' He really thought I'd killed her. Right about then, I actually felt like scum." Riff's eyes skimmed the ceiling. "Tell you the truth, Callie, I don't think I've ever stopped feeling like scum."

I sipped my wine. "When did you last try to leave the island?"

"About three months ago."

"What happened?"

"Same thing that's happened every time I've tried to leave." He stared at his empty plate. "The first time, I was in a boat going toward Hilton Head when the boat just flipped—like a dolphin jumping out of the water or something. The driver and I were thrown out, and I smacked my head. Coast Guard had to rescue us both." He scrubbed his hand across his heavy stubble. "The second time was with the police when they arrested me. I actually made it to the mainland before I came down with a fever. Elijah got me back to Belle Marsh just in time. Turned out to be bacterial meningitis. Cleared up as soon as I got back and the doctor saw me." He turned his eyes toward the ceiling. "The last time, I tried to go to Savannah with Elijah, and as soon as we got off the boat, I stepped onto the dock and had a grand mal seizure. Took three grown men to hold me down and stop me from flailing."

"Had you had seizures before?"

"Never."

"Have you had any seizures since?"

"Nope."

Riff lowered his eyes again and settled them on me. The moment seemed to freeze, our stares locked. He rose from his chair and came toward me. Reflexively, I stood too, my defenses on full alert, preparing me to push him away. The way he was looking at me...was he going to try to kiss me? I couldn't let that happen. But I didn't push him away, and he didn't kiss me. Instead, he took my hand.

"Thank you," he said.

"For what?"

"For coming here. I know I didn't want you to, but I'm glad you did. You've really listened to me. I still haven't given you all the info you need, still haven't told you everything, but I promise..." His words sounded like a plea. "I promise I will. Before it's all over."

Then he sauntered out of the room like he had all the time in the world.

I closed my eyes and sat down again. And there I remained for some time—motionless, breathless, and fishing through all the feelings floating in my brain for one I could identify.

16

I didn't sleep a wink that night, and I knew Riff didn't either. I heard him downstairs in the music room, playing one of his guitars and several old albums.

Nerves had set in. I was leaving Friday. And I was having all these *feelings*. For Riff, about my dad, about the memoir I'd started so many years ago. In truth, I'd only ever written one chapter—the only one that mattered as far as I was concerned. It was the chapter of my life that changed me forever and irreparably damaged my relationship with my father.

Sitting on the edge of the bed, I dialed Quincy's number. As I listened to the ringtone, I had no idea what I was going to say. 'Help me? What's happening to me? Why am I feeling like this?'

In the end, the phone went to voicemail and I left a message.

"Hi, Quincy. Um, it's Callie. Just calling to check in. If you have a chance tomorrow, give me a ring. Thanks."

I woke my laptop and pulled it onto my thighs. Then, I clicked on a folder I'd entitled OLD STUFF. Within, I found the chapter I'd written some five years before. Taking a deep breath, I read it.

THE LAST TIME I SAW my father, I was fourteen—just a month away from my fifteenth birthday. My mother and grandparents had finally allowed me to fly to California on my own to spend a week with him, and I was thrilled. However, I hardly saw him the whole time I was there; he was always at band practice, sleeping, or on the phone with his manager, publicist, or producer. So, I sat alone by his pool most of the time.

One night, his band, Crashing Light was playing at the Troubadour. One of the major perks of being Trace Rowe's daughter was that I got front row seats (not like there were any seats and not like anyone actually sat during a Crashing Light show), and for an hour or two, I thought my life couldn't be better.

I was proud to see my father up there on the stage, wielding his guitar, flipping it over his shoulder, and throwing his foot up on the small amplifier at the front when he did his solo. The women pushed and shoved toward the stage, reaching up to touch his boot like he was Jesus or something.

But the lead singer was the one I was most interested in. Manny Sullivan. Manny flailed his long blond hair around as he sang, and I just melted. During one song, the crowd pressed forward, more women frantic to touch his hand as he squatted during one of the ballads and reached out to us. I pushed too, suddenly fueled by the hysteria, desperate to connect with him.

I reached up, standing on the tips of my toes, and braced my other hand against someone else's back. I was just able to touch the tips of his fingers. Something like electricity radiated through my wrist and up my arm. Magic.

Later that night, my dad invited the band members to his house along with some other women I didn't know. I guessed they were groupies by the way they were hanging all over the band members. They all drank beer, and I was clearly expected to do the same as I was handed a bottle not too long after we sat down on the sectional sofa. The night went on like you'd expect—there was drinking, the men and women smoked, but all the while, my eyes were glued to Manny. He was beautiful. His voice was low and sexy, and he had these piercing sky-blue eyes. I just wanted to touch him, to run my fingers through his hair or down his smooth, tanned chest. But Manny only had eyes for the busty woman who sat on his lap for most of the night. I didn't have a chance.

Even so, every time I turned my head, the bassist, Frankie, was staring at me. He had tattoos that ran up his neck, and I didn't particularly like his look, but I got a little thrill every time I saw his eyes making their way up my legs and wandering over my hips. It made me think maybe I wasn't completely unattractive. Maybe men could find me desirable. Maybe sometime in my life, a man might want me. Even if it wasn't Manny Sullivan.

"Want another one?" Frankie motioned to the almost empty bottle I was clutching in my hands.

I shrugged. "Sure."

He got up from the couch, went to the kitchen, and brought me back a beer. Something about him making that special trip to the kitchen made me warm up to him a little. And then, we talked.

It seemed like we talked for a long time, but later I realized it was only a few minutes. Everyone, including my dad and his girlfriend, began to slip off. I was left alone with Frankie.

It didn't take long for him to take the beer out of my hand and set it on the coffee table amid empty bottles and full ashtrays. Then he put his hand on my leg, and he kissed me.

It was the first time anyone had kissed me. I didn't know what to do. My mouth felt like it didn't belong to me as he pressed his lips against mine, forced his tongue into my mouth. I just tried to let him do what he wanted, but it felt like I was doing it all wrong.

Finally, he pulled away.

"Wanna do some coke?" He scooted to the edge of the couch, his knees against the glass coffee table. Then he shook out two lines of white powder and rolled up a dollar bill.

"No, thanks."

"Sure? It'll make you feel good."

I watched him snort the two lines. He leaned back on the couch and wiped his nose. Then, staring at me, he unbuttoned his jeans.

I froze. My heart felt like it might explode as he grabbed my hand and put it between his legs. I didn't want to touch him. I didn't want to do this. The two beers had made me tired, and I wanted to go to bed and sleep.

"No." I yanked my hand away. "My dad's in the other room."

Now he stood and slid his jeans off altogether. "So? What do you think he's doing? He won't know or care."

The words rang like an alarm bell in my head. Was that true? My dad really wouldn't care that his bandmate was doing this to me? What if I screamed? What if I cried out?

But I didn't. I only struggled a little in the beginning.

"Is this your first time?" he murmured against my ear.

"Yes," I whimpered, hoping that might stop him. It didn't. And I stopped fighting him. Once he had my panties off, it seemed futile. It was done. I endured it, telling myself I should enjoy it. This was a member of a famous LA rock band—how many other girls got a chance like this? The important thing was someone wanted me.

When he was finished, he immediately pulled his jeans back on. "Hey, maybe don't tell anyone, okay? This'll be our secret?" Then he cuffed my chin and slunk out the door.

I sat in the dark, feeling the shadows creeping around me, pawing at me, whispering that this was how things would be from now on. Overhead, the air conditioning pumped out cold air, chilling my bare legs. I scrambled to find my panties under the glass coffee table. Then I slipped them back on, pulled down my dress, sat on the edge of the couch, and finished drinking my beer.

Frankie died of an overdose a year later.

And my father never asked me to visit again.

Riff had said he wanted to read it. Who better to understand this situation than him? And anyway, after Friday, I'd probably never see him again.

I skimmed through the chapter again before I attached it to an email and hit SEND.

17

As soon as my senses bloomed the next morning, I remembered what I had done. Had I really sent that chapter to Riff? Every day I was here I did something dumber than the last. I could only pray he hadn't yet read it, and if not, I'd beg him not to. Why I'd been inspired to send it I didn't know. I hadn't even been drinking much. No one needed to know that stuff about me.

I again resolved to recover my dignity. Following my nose to the kitchen, I made my way downstairs. The smell of bacon and butter was unmistakable, but my stomach was in knots and food was the last thing on my mind. As I emerged in the kitchen, Riff's back was to me as he tended a crackling frying pan.

"Do you like eggs?"

"Sure," I answered in a monotone. "But I'm really not that hungry." There was a first for everything.

"I'm making omelets."

"Great."

He shoved the spatula under the yellow disc in the cast iron skillet and flipped it over. Next to the stove, a wooden cutting board and knife sat scattered with diced onions and red pepper.

"I've arranged for Elijah to take you to an early dinner, and you can hear a band from Hilton Head play. They're good. The Glory Days. 80s rock."

I sat with this information for a few seconds. Why the hell was he arranging for me to go off with Elijah? Was he trying to get me out of the house? He'd probably read the chapter and was as embarrassed as I was. This was all starting to piss me off. It was like I was a teenager again, passing notes that I didn't want anyone else to see.

I leaned against the counter, reached over, stole a sliver of red pepper from the cutting board, and popped it into my mouth. "You know, what I really want to do is what I came to do. Write your story."

He glanced over, his eyebrow arched. "We can do that too."

"When?"

"Today. Or maybe when you come back from dinner with Elijah."

I made a sound of frustration deep in my throat. "I don't need to go to dinner with Elijah."

"I just figured you wouldn't want to hang out here with me all day, and Elijah's a nice guy and—"

"I don't mean to sound rude, but I'm writing your story, not Elijah's."

Riff turned off the stove and tossed the stainless-steel spatula onto the counter. It clattered and skittered to the backsplash.

"So don't go then." His voice dripped with irritation.

Why is he getting mad? I stood by, debating what to do as Riff loudly set out plates, banging them against the granite countertop. Maybe I should go to dinner with Elijah. Maybe I should be grilling him for answers about Riff. He'd been forthcoming with me when we'd talked the other day.

Riff handed me the plate with the omelet and stormed off, leaving me to dine alone.

I was amazed at my ability to eat even in the middle of turmoil. I'd think I wasn't hungry and then clear a plate like I hadn't eaten in a week. The omelet was good—just the right amount of seasoning and flavor. I hadn't expected otherwise since everything Riff had cooked had been excellent.

Afterward, I went to find him. I figured it was best to clear the air between us if there was to be any more work accomplished before I left. And I needed to address the chapter I'd sent. He hadn't mentioned it, so maybe he hadn't read it, and there was time to tell him to delete it. I checked all the usual places—the music room, the porch, the beach. No sign of him.

I passed through the breezeway that connected the hallway with the utility room—the alcove where the monitors lived. I scanned them quickly, looking for Riff. On the screens in front of me, grainy, black-and-white footage showed the upstairs and every door in the house, including the front, the back, and the screened-in porch, where the door stood wide open. Riff must have gone out and left it ajar.

The camera tracking the upstairs hallway caught my attention. Maybe an insect or a fiber waving in the lens of the camera. But something else began to swell into view. It wasn't a fiber—it was hair. The top of a head crowned, followed by the flat of a forehead, eyebrows, eyes.

Someone was looking into the upstairs camera—and right at me.

Music crashed from somewhere down the hall. Lila Silverleaf's voice soared through the cathedral ceiling, accompanied by a driving beat and searing guitars. I staggered backward into the hallway and then jogged into the music room, calling out, "Riff! There's someone up—"

The music room was empty. The stereo system was alight, flashing, the music blaring from the speakers.

No one was in the room. But there was someone upstairs.

My heart pounding, I dashed for the nearest exit—the screened-in porch, where the door swung back and forth on its hinges. I hurtled through it and jumped down the three steps into the sand. Riff was jogging toward me, wearing shorts and a sweat-stained T-shirt.

"Hey," he huffed out air. "Sorry. I went for a run."

Words suddenly seemed insufficient. I pointed toward the roof and whispered, "I saw someone. Inside. Upstairs."

Riff's eyes flashed and he sprang up the steps and through the open door. I followed. The music from Episodic Noise blared, filling the house with a thrashing beat and Lila's soaring voice. I caught up with Riff near the stairwell and glimpsed the bottoms of his shoes as he rocketed upstairs. Seconds later, boards squeaked and doors banged. He must have been walking from one end of the hall to the other.

I waited at the base of the steps and held my breath, expecting to hear yelling, a scuffle.

But a minute or two later, Riff returned down the stairs, panting. "There's no one up there." He swallowed hard and bent at the waist. "I checked every room." Then he straightened, his eyes meeting mine before shifting toward the music room. "Are you playing that?"

"No, I thought you were."

Again, he shot forward and I trailed behind, worrying my lower lip, my mind filled with the image I'd seen on the upstairs camera. "I promise you I saw something on the screen."

But no one was in the music room either.

Riff strode over to the stereo and smacked the power button with the pad of his hand, silencing Lila's voice. Then he swung back to me. "How long has this been playing?"

I shrugged. "A few minutes."

"You really didn't put this on?"

"No."

Wordlessly, he lunged past me and out the door.

More frustrated than scared, I moved toward the staircase again, determined to search the upstairs myself for any sign of the woman on the monitor. Like Riff, I found nothing. Then I stood in front of the taped-up door...and listened.

But all was silent.

18

That afternoon, Elijah and I sat at the bar sipping mojitos and listening to the band on the stage play their rendition of Journey's "Faithfully." Behind them, a dock stretched over calm waters and a blazing sun. In the distance, sailboats cruised toward land and Jet Skis skimmed across the surface, leaving a trail of white foam in their wake.

Elijah was good company. In contrast to Riff's brooding demeanor, he was easy to be with, glib and relaxed. He turned, his eyes partially shielded by the visor of an orange and purple Clemson ball cap.

"You getting everything you need from my man Riff?"

I made a noise in my throat that sounded a little like the one Riff so often made. "It's like getting juice from a pomegranate. There are all these protective layers and it's one seed at a time."

Elijah chuckled. "He's not easy, is he?"

"But I think I've got his tone, his speech patterns, sentence structures down." I touched a finger to the side of my temple. "I can hear his voice in my head now."

He wheezed out a laugh. "Well, that's scary as shit."

I smiled. "It's kinda like a song—or an earwig."

We watched the band for a few minutes until they reached a set break. The musicians mopped their foreheads with paper napkins and picked up plastic cups filled with gold beverages.

"I have news," said Elijah.

"What news?"

"I got hired on at Pierson and Judd—a law firm in Savannah. I start next Monday."

I held up my drink. "That deserves a toast. Congratulations. Elijah, that's wonderful."

He bumped his plastic cup against mine and grinned. "Thanks. I'm pretty excited about it."

"I'm excited for you."

He pinched his straw and pinned the soggy mint leaves to the bottom of his cup. "Of course, this means that I won't be coming to the island as much. Won't have as much free time. Grams'll be disappointed."

"So will Riff."

He nodded. "Yeah, I thought about that too." He nudged me in the arm. "You should come visit me in Savannah. It's beautiful."

"Yeah, maybe one day." I picked through the discarded tails of my fried shrimp and found one remaining French fry to pop into my mouth. Then I pushed away the red plastic basket and its grease-soaked liner paper. Nona was right—nothing on the menu at this place that wasn't fried. "What do you think it would take to get Riff to leave the island? Even for a day?"

Elijah ballooned his eyes. "A lot. To be honest, I'm not seeing it happen."

As I chewed, I focused on a passing yacht. "I really want to help him, Elijah. I feel like there must be some way to shift his brain so he's not so fearful of leaving."

Elijah stacked his empty basket on mine. "Where do you want him to go?"

I shrugged. "Anywhere. I just feel bad for him, you know?" I toyed with the edge of the napkin that had been resting on my lap for most of the meal. "Even though I hope my instincts aren't wrong. Because I still have a lot of questions about the guy."

"Like what?"

"Like, is he telling the truth? Or is he just leading me down some garden trail away from it?"

Elijah pursed his lips. "So you're not one of those mercenary writers that doesn't care who their subject matter is as long as the check rolls in?"

"I care. I care that justice is done for the sake of the victims. I don't want to contribute to a lie."

"What if he is? Lying?"

I folded my hand under my chin. "Do you think he's lying?"

Elijah shook his head. "For what it's worth, I believe Riff believes everything he says."

"Spoken like a true defense attorney."

"Look, all I know is ever since Lila disappeared, he's stayed within the boundaries of those property markers. I saw what happened the last time he tried to leave—the seizure. That really scared him. Shit, it scared me."

"Don't you think it could all be a psychosomatic reaction to Lila's disappearance?"

"I do."

I agitated my straw against the ice in my empty cup. "It's been hard getting him to talk about Lila."

"Yeah, he doesn't like talking about her." He patted the top of the bar. "I'm going to grab us another round."

While Elijah fought for the overwhelmed bartender's attention, I sat back, feeling loose and relaxed. I replayed what had happened earlier in the day—the top of the woman's head in the video, the Episodic Noise music playing on the stereo. Those things happened. I hadn't imagined them. But I'd checked the upstairs myself and found no one. What was going on in that place? There was so much Riff wasn't telling me.

Finally managing to flag down the bartender, Elijah ordered us fresh mojitos and slid cash across the weathered wood of the bar.

Elijah was a nice guy. A really nice guy. And maybe I could confide in him.

He shifted my drink in front of me.

"Thank you." I passed a hand through my hair and pulled out several tangled blonde strands. "You know, something weird happened today. It's really kind of messed with me."

Elijah rested his head on his fist. "What happened?"

I quickly filled him in on what I'd seen, heard. "And Riff checked the house, said there was no one there, and then just went about his business like nothing happened."

He whistled. "Okay, so that is weird."

"Thank you. Yeah, I thought so too." I huffed out a breath. "And then I heard this music the other night—from my window. It wasn't like anything I've heard before, but it was mesmerizing. Otherworldly. But when I told Riff about it, he had a fit." I put the straw to my lips and swallowed the sweet, minty drink.

"So what's your verdict?" Elijah asked.

"I'm starting to think Riff's house really is haunted."

The lines on Elijah's forehead deepened as his eyes scanned the partiers around us. "Sounds like those water witches Grams used to talk about."

"Water witches?"

"Yeah, she used to tell us these stories when we were kids to scare us into being good. You know, like if you don't eat all your collards, you might hear the water witches singing tonight."

"What about them? What are they?"

He wrenched his mouth to the side. "Well, you'd probably have to ask her for the whole story, but the way she used to tell it, there were these women—half-human, half-demon that lived on the beach. Their favorite thing to do was suck little children into the sea. They'd draw them with their singing, then they'd take them down under the waters—never to be seen again. You know, like everything else, it's just a bunch of fairy tales and superstition."

Zeke had mentioned "the night singers" and "water music." It sure seemed like a lot of people believed this stuff. But then, I couldn't deny that I heard the singing.

Elijah shook his cup and the ice rattled against the sides. "What did Riff say about it?"

I huffed out a laugh. "After he scolded me and told me never to open my window again after dark?"

"Kinda like what he told me about takin' you out tonight." He fisted one hand and beat it against his flattened palm while exaggerating his voice. "She has to be back before dark. Promise you'll bring her back before then."

I rolled my eyes. "Oh geez. He really said that?"

"Yep." He swiped his hand through the air. "I was like, 'All right, Dad.' But hey look, I can tell he really likes you, and..." He stopped, looked down. "Nah. I'm not going to say it."

"Say what?"

He shook his head. "Nope, nope. Not saying it."

"Come on. Tell me."

"I'm just saying that you're the first woman since Lila he's had in that house. That's a big deal for him."

"Well, if he wanted me to write his story then we had to meet. And due to the situation, there was only one place that was going to happen."

Elijah smiled. "Still, he's real protective of you."

I waved my hand dismissively. "Oh please. You know him better than I do. You know he's like that with everyone." Anyway, I didn't want to think about Riff and whether he had any feelings for me. Or the fact that I might have some for him. "What do *you* think happened to Lila?"

He wadded up a napkin and tossed it into one of the empty plastic baskets. "You know, I don't like saying it, but *I* think she's dead. To be honest, I think Riff thinks she's dead too. I think he knows she's dead."

My breath caught. "How would he know that for sure?"

Elijah shrugged. "Like I said, Riff's my friend. I'm a lawyer. And I don't have bad thoughts about Riff. I just feel like he *knows*—like maybe it's just one of those things you sense when you been married to someone. Maybe you just know when they've left the earth—even if you haven't seen it."

I'd consumed my second mojito much faster than my first, and the rum was really hitting me. My head was swimmy.

"You know," Elijah said. "There's this old, abandoned place here on the island. Used to be a resort. Folks say the water witches live there."

"Really? You ever been there?"

Elijah sputtered his lips. "I used to work there in the summer. That was when the place was up and running and *fine*. Lots of folks coming there to play golf, havin' parties. I mean, that place was nice."

I poured an ice cube into my mouth and let it melt under my tongue. "Did you ever see any water witches?"

He turned his head. "Nah, nah. We saw a bunch of rich people gettin' married and then drunk at the receptions. That's all we ever saw. Wasn't till about 2011 the place went all to shit." He raised his eyebrows. "Plenty of people in these parts say that place has a Gullah curse on it. That they see the devil's messengers in the windows looking out." Elijah bugged his eyes and cupped his hands around them. "They say they eat people at night or some shit like that." He coughed out a laugh.

I squinted. "Can you take me there—to the resort?"

"Why do you wanna go there?"

"Seems like local folklore is going to be a big part of Riff's story. Might as well see it firsthand."

Elijah adjusted his baseball hat, pulling it low over his eyes. "Well, okay, then. Come on. Let's go."

PEOPLE ON INVISIBLE Island seemingly had no problem with drinking and driving golf carts. Several groups we passed on the dirt roads held up their cans of beer or tipped a solo cup as a greeting.

"I guess there aren't any cops around here pulling people over for DUIs," I said as we bounced through a pothole.

Elijah threw his head back and laughed.

I took that as a no.

The trail to the resort was the bumpiest, most uneven road I'd been on so far. I clutched the armrest as Elijah swerved to avoid craters. We took a sharp right down an overgrown path, and a sandy trail stretched ahead of us, zigzagging through tangles of vines, fans of ferns, and Spanish moss casting shadows as it hung from every oak tree. The wheels on the golf cart whirred as foliage fronds slapped the spokes like a box fan with plastic strips tied to the grates.

I hadn't seen a house anywhere along this route. The salt in the air was strong. We were nearing the ocean. As we turned down a paved road, green marsh lay to one side of it accompanied by a huge bush full of white tittering birds. This must have been the place Riff told me about—where he'd first met Elijah.

A rooftop peeked through the trees. Then a sign, green with mildew, peered out of overgrown vines as though it had been hiding: "Invisible Island Resort." So this was the abandoned resort. The structure and all its surroundings were engulfed in unkempt foliage, overgrown trees, and untamed weeds—a property gone wild. An iron fence stretched in front of us, vines woven and rusted into the spires. A heavy overhang of moss swung from hovering oaks, creating a curtain to the entrance. The wind and waves provided the setting's soundtrack.

Elijah stopped the cart.

An animal foraged in the ground a few feet away. A squirrel? The tail was reminiscent of one, but the brown-black coat, white nose, and long body made me question.

"What is that?"

"Fox squirrel," Elijah said. "You probably don't have them in Nashville."

"Definitely not."

Elijah jabbed a finger toward the wall of moss. "Right through there," he whispered. "That's where the water witches live." He chuckled.

"That place used to rock and roll," came a voice from behind us.

I turned around to see a man sitting in his golf cart holding a can of beer. His eyes were shaded by mirrored sunglasses and his longish gray hair poked out from under a baseball cap.

"Hey, Milton," Elijah said.

The man nodded. "Elijah. What's going on?"

Elijah pressed his foot down on the brake. "Just showing my friend around. She wanted to come by the old resort."

Using his can, the man pointed toward the ruined monstrosity. "You shoulda seen it back in the day. That place used to rock *and* roll."

Some of the windows were boarded, others were left open, and the broken panes formed large, sharp fangs.

"What happened to it?" I asked. "Why is it abandoned?"

The man shifted and his golf cart squeaked under his weight. "Well, there was some bad business in that place—eventually went bankrupt in 2011. But back in the day—music there every night, every room filled, I mean, we were doing weddings on Wednesday."

He motioned his head toward Elijah. "You remember, right? You were working there some, weren't you?"

Elijah nodded. "I do. I was."

It was obvious the place had once been impressive. Two sets of steps led up to the plantation-style main building. But the entrance and both wings that flanked it were in decay—the yellow paint peeling. Several black shutters had fallen off or were hanging by one rusted hinge.

I turned back to the man swilling his beer. "Did you work there too?"

"Yeah, I used to do HVAC maintenance for them—me and my brother handled the resort." He pointed the can behind him at a community of small beach cottages painted pink, blue, and green. "And those too."

Some of the cottages seemed to be in decent shape, only they were boarded up like the resort. "Why hasn't anyone bought these places—or the resort—and tried to refurbish it?"

"Too expensive. Plus, it's totally ransacked inside. Graffiti everywhere. Squatters and vagrants been in and out of the place. This whole part of the island feels like a ghost town these days. But let me tell you, back in the day, that place used to rock and roll." He crushed his empty can in his hand.

I eyed Milton's cooler sitting in the back of his golf cart. No doubt he had a few more cans in there.

"I hear the place is inhabited by water witches." I raised an eyebrow at Elijah while testing this local's appetite for superstition.

Milton cocked his head. "Water witches? What the hell are they?" He laughed, a chesty sound that soon turned into a cough. "Well, I reckon people will come up with all kinds of crazy. They're just some vagrants that stay in there from time to time. Or kids. No water witches that I know of." He chuckled again, released the brake on his golf cart, and without even a "see you later" or a "goodbye," he shot off down the lane.

I twisted around to look at Elijah. "You want to walk back there?"

Elijah shook his head. "Nah, nah, nah. I been in there before, remember? Anyway, they got a fence up now and don't want anyone going in there. And I don't need to go looking for no water witches today."

"Oh, come on." I raised an eyebrow. "I thought you weren't superstitious."

"Superstitious? Why do I need to go crawling through all that mess? I'm not trying to get a bunch of ticks and chigger bites and poison ivy. Nah. I'm perfectly happy to sit right back here and spectate."

I directed my eyes toward the moss cascade blocking the entrance. "Mind if I take a peek?"

Elijah made a "pshh" sound. "I think you're crazy but go ahead if that's what you want. I'll be staying right here."

I stepped out of the golf cart and took long strides over the clinging grasses and vines that grabbed for my ankles. I stood in front of the iron fence and pushed my hands into the tacky tendrils of the moss, attempting to part it enough to see what lay beyond.

"You know that moss is full of chiggers, right?" Elijah called out to me.

I ignored his comment, too hell-bent on spying on what it covered. I already had a million bug bites. What were a few more? But there was so much of the moss. Once I pulled a handful away, another slid forward in its place. Determined, I tried again, shoving both my arms further into it and then pulling back my shoulders like I was doing the butterfly stroke.

Once a creamy yellow, the resort's exterior paint was chipped, faded, and green in places from mold and plant life. Graffiti had been sprayed across the second-floor balcony: *Death lives here.*

The low-hanging limbs of the live oaks created a canopy, immersing the place in a gloaming, even though it was still broad daylight.

I wiggled the loose fence, and as I tinkered with a crusty latch draped over two spires, the iron gave way, opening with a hoarse squawk. Disentangling a vine from my sock, I stepped across the overgrowth.

"Hey, hey, what are you doing?" Elijah called after me. "Nah, nah, don't do that, Callie. Don't go in there."

I held up my pointer finger, signaling I would only be a moment.

Elijah climbed out of the golf cart and took a few steps. "Come on, Callie. Don't do this to me. If you disappear in that place, I'm not comin' after you."

"Don't worry. I'll be fine. I'll only be a sec."

Elijah continued to protest as I waded through the weeds, the damp darkness of the trees enveloping me. What was I looking for? I didn't know. Some sign that the water witches were real? That the local folklore had some teeth? Or maybe that Riff's fears were founded after all?

"Callie, come on! Riff's gonna kill me!" Elijah's muffled voice came from the other side of the moss screen.

"I'll be right there," I called to him. I progressed around the back, where a full view of the ocean extended beyond the derelict lawn. The air tingled in my nostrils and the lulling sound of the water swelled. I stopped at the first window I came to, braced my fingers on the ledge, stood on my tiptoes, and looked in. As I'd suspected, the inside was dark, everything in shadows. I lowered my heels and sidestepped to the next window.

Must have been the dining room at one time. A wine glass lay on its side on a white linen table, red juice encrusted on the glass and staining the tablecloth like a bloodspot. Perfectly positioned silverware flanked a dinner plate. It was as though the dining guest simply stood up and walked away. As I wound through more impossible weeds, I looked out at the waves in the distance. A gazebo stood like a Grecian temple just before the property dipped toward the beach. Probably where the weddings used to "rock and roll." I pictured brides in white dresses with bridesmaids wearing ocean-blue regalia. A sense of loss and grief hung over the place like a fog. Dreams gone to seed.

I walked as far down toward the shore as I dared. Erosion had taken much of the safe boundary, leaving a steep drop from the lawn to the beach. But people must have walked here quite a bit. The weeds were plentiful but many were downtrodden and passable. A large bug ran over my sandal, prompting me to do an involuntary kick-line move and sending a wave of shudders over me.

Somewhere in the recesses of my auditory consciousness, I heard Elijah calling.

I stalked away from the shore and worked my way back to the abandoned inn. Putting my hand against the mildewed siding, I stood on a clump of cement and again peered in. This room was dark, but a greenish light illuminated what looked like moving water. It was an indoor swimming pool—rancid and algae-ridden, covered in the sludge of neglect and decay.

I blinked, straining my eyes against the darkness in the room. Across the pool, someone was there. I pressed my forehead against the dirty pane. A head, shoulders, waist and hips were silhouetted in the green light. Water streamed over the female's shoulders and down her arms. Dark tattoos stretched from her neck to her wrists. They emblazoned her abdomen and curled around her legs like clothing. Her coppery hair was plastered to her shoulders in wet ropes. She stepped into the light, staring at me with wide, hollow, algae-green eyes.

A gasp tore from my throat as I catapulted away from the window, lost my balance, and toppled off the cement block onto my back, blasting the air out of my lungs. I scrambled to my feet. Embarrassed to have been the equivalent of a peeping Tom, I ducked down and ran past all the broken and boarded-up windows, falling once more on a tangle of weeds before rounding the side of the resort. Then, I plunged through the moss curtain and the open gate to where Elijah stood by the golf cart.

His mouth hung open. "What happened? Did you see one of them?"

I clambered into the golf cart. "I saw something. Let's go."

Elijah climbed into the driver's seat, released the brake, and floored it, quickly reaching maximum golf cart speed of fifteen miles per hour.

"Was it a water witch?" His voice broke with laughter.

I smacked his arm. "I'm not sure that I didn't just have a mild heart attack. It was a woman. Naked. She looked human to me." I dusted bits of moss from my arms and shoulders.

"Naked? You saw a naked woman in there?" Elijah jerked the wheel and veered the cart toward the ditch. "Hold on, girl. We going back."

This time I punched his bicep. "Stop it. That was so embarrassing."

He cackled. "You saw—of all things—you saw a naked woman in the abandoned resort."

"Her whole body was covered in tattoos. I only saw her for a second. In the room with the indoor pool."

"Indoor pool? Shit. I forgot they had an indoor pool there. There was someone swimming in that? That thing must be a nasty son of a bitch. Rancid. Who'd want to swim in that?"

I hung my head forward and tousled my hair, hoping none of the moss chiggers had nestled in.

The image of the woman's green eyes pulsed in my head along with her tattoos. I wasn't a tattoo expert, but they looked the same as the ones on the woman from the beach. Or were these types of tattoos an island trend. "Hey, are green and blue swirly tattoos a thing around here?"

He glanced over at me. "A what?"

With my finger, I drew a circular figure in the air. "You know, like a swirl—green and blue tattoos. Like what Riff has on his arms."

Elijah raised his eyebrows. "I don't know. I haven't seen 'em on anyone but Riff. Maybe he started a trend."

"Never mind. I thought I saw the same ones on the girl in the resort just now."

Elijah steered the cart around a curve. "Damn, girl," he said. "Look, if some naked woman follows me home from that place, and I gotta fight her off, I'm holding you responsible." He howled with laughter again and smacked his palm against the top of the steering wheel. "Anyway," he gasped. "What were you trying to find there in all that mess.?"

"I don't know. I just wanted to see what it looked like in there."

"Nah," he said, still trying to catch his breath from laughing. "Tell the truth. You were looking for the water witches."

I shook my head. "I don't know. I mean, after you said that, maybe I was. Riff's guitar student Zeke was talking about water music and the singing women. He told me a similar story that your grams told you—about them luring people into the water..."

Elijah tried to suppress more laughter and snorted.

It all seemed comical. Like Milton said, vagrants had probably taken up residence in the resort. That woman was probably just one of the vandals, not a water witch. Ridiculous.

Elijah shook his head. "Don't go telling Riff I let you go in there. He'll kill me."

We turned off the blissfully paved stretch and were soon back on a primitive route through jungle and swamp.

Most likely all these superstitions and stories were just that, with nothing more to them. But there was something different about this island—the remoteness, the crude and undeveloped landscape, the untamed land—maybe this really was where the wild things were.

19

The sun was still high when Elijah drove me back to Belle Marsh. I climbed out of the golf cart. "Thanks for dinner. Are you coming in?"

He seemed to consider for a moment but then shook his head. "Nah, I'll go on. I'm thinking about heading over to the lighthouse tonight and watching the sun go down. This may be my last trip to the island for a while—with the new job and everything."

I headed around the side of the house, planning to smoke a cigarette on the beach, but I spotted Riff in the pool, gliding from end to end. Storm clouds whispered in the distance, dark gray billows of smoke that blew across the sky. Elijah's trip to the lighthouse might be spoiled by incoming weather.

"Looks like rain," I called out.

Riff drifted to the shallow end and stood. Water cascaded down his upper body, over his bare chest. It was the first time I'd seen all his tattoos—the ones that glistened on his upper biceps, on his back. He raked his wet hair away from his face and waded toward me. "Sure you don't want to come in for a swim?"

I raised and lowered my hands, motioning to my T-shirt and cargo pants. "What? In this?"

Riff smiled. "Why not?"

"No, I'm good." Even though my legs were on fire from bug bites and possibly poison ivy. The chlorine might offer some relief.

He grabbed a white and gray-striped towel from the ground and flung it around his shoulders.

I sank onto a beach chair, the canvas almost too hot to sit on, and inspected the red welts that encircled my ankles.

Water dripped on my arm as Riff moved by me dropped into the chair beside mine. "How was dinner?"

"Fried."

He nodded. "You didn't have the deviled crab, then."

"I don't even know what that is."

"It's good."

"I prefer your cooking."

He bit his lip, suppressing a grin.

I fixed my gaze on the ripples in the pool. "Apparently, Elijah just got a job in Savannah at a law firm."

"Oh yeah? Good for him." Droplets made a leisurely trek from his temples to his chin and he toweled them away. "That should keep him out of trouble."

"Elijah's a nice guy. I enjoyed talking to him."

"Did you? I thought you two might hit it off."

"Whoa-whoa-whoa." I held up a hand. "Is that what all that was about? You making me go to dinner with him? You were setting me up?"

He shrugged. "I wasn't setting you up. Elijah asked if you'd go to dinner with him. I think he was half-joking, but you didn't protest, so..."

"Oh, well, thanks." I exhaled a dark laugh and shook my head. "Look, first of all, I'm way too old for Elijah. Second of all, I'm here to do a job. And third, like I said, I don't do relationships." I could feel myself pulling back into my hard shell, my mind reeling in disbelief that we were having this conversation. "And I can get my own dates."

Riff chuckled. "Okay, okay. But at least he's not a musician, right?"

He stood and ran the towel across his chest, putting me in direct eyeshot of his abs that looked like they had come off a human loom.

I crossed my arms. "I don't care. I don't need anyone. Musician or otherwise."

"Oh, come on, Callie. Everyone needs someone."

"Even you?" I shot back at him.

His face tensed, but his eyes dipped to my legs. "You are covered in bites."

I scratched my ankle. "I asked Elijah to show me the abandoned house—where the water witches supposedly live."

Sorry, Elijah.

Riff's brow crinkled. "How do you know about that?"

I hurtled on. "Elijah told me about it. Said it was where he used to work. Anyway, I asked him to take me there. That's where I got all the bites."

Riff looked out at the pool, his lip curling. "He shouldn't have taken you there."

"I was just curious."

"Cats have died for less, Callie. Curiosity, you know."

I ignored his concern. "Well, it was pretty creepy. I saw someone inside. A woman." I pointed at his arm. "She had tattoos like yours."

"You shouldn't have gone there, Callie." His voice held the tone of dads when chiding their kids.

"Why?"

Anger flashed in his eyes. "It's not safe. Don't do that again. It's dangerous."

I stood and moved toward the pool. "I've tried to follow all your rules about not going out after dark and not opening the upstairs door. But just because you're a prisoner here doesn't mean I have to be one too. And I wanted to see the place."

A muscle pulsed in his jaw.

"Do you know who that woman is?"

"Yeah, she's—she's not good."

"Tell me."

His voice dropped to nearly a whisper. "I...can't."

I exhaled through my nose. Of course he couldn't. I kicked off my sandals and lowered myself to the side of the pool, putting in one leg and then the other. An involuntary sound of relief escaped my throat. I looked back at Riff, still standing, holding his towel, looking down at me.

I felt bad about what I'd said but couldn't bring myself to say I was sorry. Instead, I stared at my legs—pale beneath the surface, little bubbles clinging to my skin as I swished my feet.

The heat from Riff's body radiated into my side as he sat on the edge next to me and plunged his legs into the water. The damp skin of his arm brushed against mine.

Something electric, animal, magnetic charged through me—like those vibrations Zeke had spoken of. I didn't want it, but I couldn't help it. In the few days I'd spent with Riff, I'd become attached. We'd shared something intimate—an exchange of information that neither of us had ever told anyone else. It felt almost sexual.

"Callie."

I looked at him.

"I'm sorry. I didn't mean to be a prick. I just...feel responsible for guests in my house. For their safety."

I kicked my leg and sent a ripple across the pool. "I know."

He cleared his throat. "And there's something else I should tell you. I read your chapter."

His words jarred me, knocked the wind from my lungs. I'd known that he might have. I'd just hoped he hadn't.

"I—I'm so sorry," he said.

"It happened a very long time ago."

"Yeah, but what Frankie did was criminal. I've never been one to wish ill on anyone, but I'm glad he's dead. Otherwise, I'd have to kill him. I'm just surprised your father didn't."

"I didn't tell him."

"Why?"

"I was too embarrassed. But somehow he must have known. He sent me home right after. Never invited me back to LA again. We barely spoke after that."

"What?" his voice softened. "You were just a kid."

"I think he figured that if he acknowledged what happened, it might mess up the band—everything he'd worked so hard for." I choked down the bitterness. "A few years later, my mother called to see if I could go out to stay with him in the summer since she and her new husband were going on a honeymoon. She had him on speaker phone and I was standing in the hall—heard the whole thing."

"What did he say?"

I gave a quick jerk of my head, recalling the weight of the shame. "He said he didn't think it was a good idea. That the last time I was there, I'd gotten 'a little wild.' Crashing Light was recording in the studio then. He couldn't watch me and keep me out of trouble. It was like I was punished for something his bandmate did to me." I squeezed my eyes shut. "I'd never said one word to my mother about what happened. So you can imagine the conversations that phone call spawned. Mom was sure I was sleeping with every boy in my school." I laughed a little. "I was so humiliated. I hadn't been with anyone since Frankie. I didn't want to. I didn't want another man to use me like that. Ever."

"Son of a bitch," he muttered under his breath.

"I mean in college, that all changed. I started thinking maybe I'd just use men before they used me. But sex always signaled the end of the relationship."

"Shit, Callie. I'm so sorry."

I swallowed hard. I'd literally never talked about this with anyone ever. Now, receiving words of sympathy was almost too much.

Riff lowered his head. "I wish I could say he was just one asshole musician who took advantage of a young girl, but we both know that's a lie. You know yourself the business is rife with assholes like Frankie. Worse even than Frankie."

"Yeah, I know."

"I think you should finish it. The memoir. I think you owe it to yourself."

"Maybe someday," I replied vaguely.

Riff kicked his legs too and sent water skirting across the pool.

"You still planning to leave Friday?" Riff asked.

"Yes."

He cleared his throat. "So I've got one more day with you."

I knocked my ankles together under the water. "Yes. One more day to get me the information I need." I forced myself to look up at him. The water reflected in his eyes.

Riff's shifted his gaze past the pool toward the ocean. "I know I'm not an easy subject, Callie."

"Easy is not a word I'd ever use to describe you, no." Something thick stuck in my throat, and I ground my larynx to make it dissipate. "But I'm glad you let me come here. I only hope this visit hasn't inconvenienced you."

He chuckled—a dark sound. "Inconvenience me? Oh yeah, you might've interrupted that Caribbean cruise I was planning on taking. Or the busy tour schedule I've got these days."

He was bitter. I understood.

"I'm more worried about how this affects you," he said.

I shifted my eyes from his. "There's got to be help for you. Surely, you don't have to keep living like this."

He bowed his head, a tight smile stretching his cheeks. "It's been a long time for me...since I've had hope of living a different way."

Time must have seemed relentless for him. Days and nights never-ending. Unless he met someone willing to live here with him. There were women who would. At least for a while. Just not me.

"For what it's worth, I've enjoyed my time with you, Riff. Not just because I'm writing your story. You seem like a good guy."

He ran a hand over his chin.

Thunder rolled in the distance, and drops of rain dotted my cheeks.

Riff stood. "Storm's blowing in. We'd better head back to the house."

He reached out a hand and I grabbed it, allowing him to pull me to my feet.

I yanked my packet of cigarettes from the pocket of my cargo pants and quickly lit one. When we reached the door to the screened-in porch, I paused to finish it.

"Sometimes I wish I still smoked," Riff said.

Blowing smoke out of the side of my mouth, I laughed. "It's never too late to take it up again." I held out my cigarette to him.

He shook his head. "No, I don't. Not anymore." He wagged a finger at me. "And you shouldn't either."

As I took a drag, I stared at his lips. Full, reddened by the sun. Drops of water still rested on his collarbone, his chest. I wanted to reach up and clear them from his skin, slide my hand across his shoulders, and trace the mermaid tattoo that ran the length of his arm. I wanted to touch him. I wanted to kiss him.

He's not your boyfriend, Callie.

No. Of course he wasn't. That I even had to remind myself of the fact jarred me, and for a moment, time seemed to stop. I watched his chest rise and fall. His round, dark eyes bored into mine. It was nearly unbearable.

"You really don't have any regard for your own safety, do you?" he said.

I shrugged. "Whatever happens, happens."

"I don't like feeling like I'm the one endangering you."

"You seem to have a lot of rules for yourself."

His face didn't change. "The funny thing is, I could say the same about you."

He was right.

Thunder churned overhead.

Riff turned away. I breathed out, closed my eyes, felt the heat of the cigarette between my fingers, and hastily put it between my lips, willing the moment to pass. It did.

Riff grabbed his white T-shirt hanging on the wooden railing and pulled it over his head. The dampness of his skin shown through the material, revealing the outlines of the tattoos underneath.

I stubbed out the cigarette out in the pottery ashtray on the step. I needed to get back to business, remember why I was there. "I want to hear more about what happened—after you signed the contract with Aeaea Records."

Riff waited on the top step, suspended between inside and outside. His face clouded again. "Come inside when you're ready."

Full Verbatim Interview With Riff Fall
9/21/16
8:30 p.m.

Riff: We signed the contract, and after the weekend was over, the band went back to LA. That day I was hungover as hell and already starting to feel the beginnings of regret creeping in. I just wanted to be alone, go off and lick my wounds. Figure out what I'd done. And I was so bummed that Trey had left the band.

Callie: How was everyone else in the band feeling?

Riff: Most of the guys were psyched about signing with Aeaea. You know, they were excited about the new album. We'd done this amazing record with Dove LaMer, and we were playing like never before, producing sounds like never before. But Trey. It was a real loss. A good drummer is hard to find. The others knew it too. The new guy—Cole. He was an all-right drummer, but he was like—he just didn't gel with the rest of us, you know? He was part of Dove and Kirka's crowd. And I just had this feeling...like, something really bad was going to happen.

Callie: Because of him?

Riff: Yeah, partly, but a lot of my fears had to do with what I'd signed. I mean, I didn't really know what I'd signed. I told myself it was probably just a standard contract. But honestly, in the beginning, I didn't put a lot of stock in what I'd said or done that night when I'd been out of my mind. We all talked a lot of shit when we were drunk and high.

Callie: You didn't get a copy of the contract?

Riff: Not then, no. I don't know, maybe it was my background—growing up in church or whatever—but I just knew something bad had happened. I couldn't explain it then, but I felt this huge shift...inside myself and all around me. I tried to lay low for several days. I went back to my apartment, watched TV, ate cans of Spaghetti-Os, and drank booze. Just trying to drown out all the feels, you know. Kirka left a bunch of messages for me. First, they were nice, just checking up on you—that kind of thing. But I knew then that everything was different, and it scared me.

Then, one night, [coughs] I went to a party in Laurel Canyon. I was walking alone down this road toward the house, and I felt something behind me. So, I turned, and there were these two women following me. I didn't think anything about it at first, but as I kept walking and they kept following, I finally stopped and was like, "What do you want? An autograph or something?"

They stopped walking too. They just stood there, staring at me and not saying a word.

And then [clears throat], then it was just like, weird as hell. I turned my head. And so did they. I scratched my face, and they did the same. They were mimicking me. Pissed me off.

They followed me to the party. Everywhere in the house I went they were there. But they weren't hanging out with anyone else. They were just silently lurking. I'd be talking to people from other bands, managers, producers, and over their shoulder, I'd see these two weird girls just staring at me. I'd move to another room and they'd be standing in the corner watching me.

Finally, I went outside by the pool, and I was talking to this guy, Anjou, who was working on our upcoming tour details, and I realized the girls weren't there. I was like, finally. I've ditched them. I just figured they were groupies or something. But I asked the guy about them. "Have you seen those two girls just hanging around here? They don't seem to belong here."

Anjou looked at me like I'd just asked him if he knew where I could get some weed. "Two girls?" He started laughing. "In case you haven't noticed, there are a *few* girls here."

I felt stupid then—because, of course, the place was filled with women everywhere you looked. No one had seen anything or anyone out of the ordinary. So, I ended up checking out of there soon after.

Since I was leaving so early, there was no one else around. And I walked back down that same dark road. When I reached my car, there they were again—the two girls standing across the road—on the sidewalk—just watching me.

So I shouted at them, "What do you want?"

They didn't answer. I got really creeped out then. I jumped in my car and sped out of there. When I looked in my rearview mirror, they were still standing on the sidewalk. I drove like a madman back to my apartment, swilling whisky out of my flask, sweating, blaring music, trying to get away from them. I knew Kirka had sent them.

Callie: How did you know?

Riff: I just had this sense. So when I got back to my place, I parked my car and just sat there for about ten minutes, smoking a cigarette, trying to calm down. Finally, I got out and started walking toward the building. [claps hands together] *Bam*. There they were—standing by the stairwell, waiting for me, watching me. Then they started walking toward me. I stopped. They stopped. But I was like, how did they get back here so fast? It was impossible. I couldn't get away from them. Finally, I started walking again and so did they until we were standing right up against each other. I could smell them. This weird moldy algae smell. Then I just flipped out. I screamed in their faces, told them to get the hell away from me, that I'd call security, the police, whatever. But they didn't care. Somehow I got by them, went into my apartment, locked the door.

Callie: Did they try to get in?

Riff: All night. They knocked and shook the doorknob. But when I went to open the door, no one was there. I called Kirka. I was like, "Did you do this? Are they with you?" I knew they were.

Callie: [a long pause] So, what did she say?

Riff: She said... [scoffs] I'll never forget what she said. She was like, "Yes, Robert"—she always called me Robert—"They're there to remind you." And I was like, remind me of what? And she goes, "That you are no longer your own person. I own you. I have control."

20

That night, after Riff went to bed, I stayed in the music room to write. Surrounded by all the framed photos, I played back the recordings. The ones from tonight were different from the others. He'd talked more, told me more than before. The details were finally coming together about what might have led to his agoraphobia. But there were still so many missing pieces.

I hit rewind on the recorder and listened to Riff's voice.

"After that, I started seeing the two women everywhere—after concerts backstage. Outside bars when I'd stumble out at one in the morning. They were constantly outside my apartment, waiting, watching.

And um, well, after that, all kinds of weird shit started to happen. At first, I thought I was just paranoid, but I'd hear pots and pans clanging at night. I'd come out in the morning and the oven would be on. Then I started seeing them at night. In my bedroom—just standing there watching me while I slept. I mean, it was seriously driving me crazy. Then I realized the lock on my back door was broken. They were just walking in like they owned the place."

A sound in the background of the recording caught my attention—a high-pitched, melodic sound. "Ah-ah." Two notes on a chromatic scale. Had music been playing when we'd talked? In the grainy background of the recording was a faint, beautiful, and haunting sound, like the cry of whales beneath the waters. I rewound the recording and played it again. It was reminiscent of the sonorous singing I'd heard through the cracked window. And like before, I couldn't stop listening to it.

Tears filled my eyes. This strange music brought emotions to me I hadn't felt in years. Indescribable pain, shame, loneliness, and fear. My chest constricted. I could barely draw in a breath.

I shut off the recorder and pressed my fingers to my eyelids, attempting to clear my mind of the images the music had spun. An overwhelming longing to feel physical pain assaulted me. This wasn't a new sensation but a familiar wave of need that threatened to overtake me. But I'd successfully fought the urge for years.

Get it together, Callie. Back to work mode.

Shuffling feet drew my attention to the doorway.

Riff came into the room, his eyes wide and deep with dreams. "Have you been up all this time?"

I nodded. "Yeah. You?"

"Couldn't sleep."

He sank onto the couch beside me as if we were old friends hanging out. But the music lingered in the recesses of my mind like a scent.

"How can you stand it?" I asked.

"Stand what?"

"Being here—all alone, all the time."

Riff pressed his back against the couch like he was trying to crack it. His voice was soft. "What choice do I have?"

I looked down at the sleeve of green and blue swirls that twisted over his arms, ending near the base of his palms. I lifted his wrist, turning it to see his inner forearm.

"I don't remember getting most of them," he offered. "I was blacked out when Kirka's tattoo artist inked me."

"I keep seeing these," I said. "The woman in the resort—she had them too. They looked just like this."

He rested his hands on his thighs. "They're common designs, I guess."

Or maybe I'd just looked at Riff's tattoos so much that they'd become as recognizable as my cigarette burn marks.

I focused on the small black cross at the base of his palm and placed my fingertip against it. "This."

"That one I remember. I got that after I realized what had happened—what I'd done by signing the contract." He blinked, long eyelashes temporarily masking the pain. "I guess I wanted to try and reverse it. Thought putting a cross on my body might somehow protect me from all this."

That would explain the cross in his bedroom and the one on the door of the forbidden room—protection.

"But to answer your question," he said. "There are some days that I don't think I can stand it. Those days, I think about jumping on the boat with Abbot and heading for Hilton Head." He shook his head and his hair slid out from behind his ear, hiding the side of his face to the tip of his nose. "But then I remember I've tried that before. There's no escape from this."

LATER, IN THE EARLY hours of the morning, I awoke from a sound sleep. At first, I wasn't sure what had woken me and I lay there, my eyelids fluttering.

Then I heard it.

"Ah-ah." Two notes produced by a female voice—a chromatic progression—just like on the recording. My heart jolted into action. I sat up and scanned my eyes around in the darkness and strained my ears to listen. The notes sounded close—as though sung from the bathroom.

Had I left the bathroom window open after smoking my before-bed cigarette?

Ah-ah. Again, the same two notes from a descending scale.

Then—

Tap, tap, tap.

Three slow taps sounded on the windowpane to the right of the bed. I switched on the bedside lamp.

Tap, tap, tap.

I stared hard at the dark panes of glass, horror washing over me. I was twenty feet from the ground. No one could be standing at my window knocking.

Tap, tap, tap.

I scrambled out of bed and rushed to the window. Outside, the beach stretched before me, barely visible except for a motion-activated exterior light that shone like a beacon across the sand and over the tufts of seagrass. Maybe something had been caught on the windowsill and had blown repeatedly against the glass.

The exterior lighting blinked intermittently, picking up speed until its rhythm was like a strobe. The lamp in my bedroom began to flash in time with the outdoor light. Was something going on with the electrical wiring in the house?

Tap, tap, tap. Tap, tap, tap.

Through the panes, a moonlight-pale face with luminous eyes stared back at me.

It was like looking at an exotic fish in an aquarium. The woman seemed suspended in midair, her hair swirling around her, her mouth open. She was singing.

I spun around and lunged for the bedroom door, tearing it open and spilling out into the hall. The wall sconces pulsed just as the lamp in my room had done. My chest pounding, I bolted downstairs, swung myself around the banister, and headed for the front door. I had to see if anyone was outside, floating in front of my window.

As I flipped the locks and yanked the door open, a shrill sound sliced the air. An alarm. Holding my finger to one of my ears, I padded outside onto the sand and ran toward the side of the house.

"Callie!" Riff's voice echoed behind me.

I jogged around the corner. The beach was empty and dark. The exterior light only came on again once I entered its detection zone. The seagrasses shivered in the wind. Above me, light streamed from my window.

"Callie, what are you doing?" Riff roared.

I whirled to face him. "I saw something." I thrust out my finger. "She was floating on the other side of my window."

Riff hesitated, his body rigid, his eyes roaming the grasses beyond. Then his heavy brows lowered. Grabbing my arm just below my elbow, he tugged, pulling me toward the house.

"Riff, she was there. I saw her." I dug my heels into the sand, attempting to ward off his strength, but my bare feet slid as he towed me along. "She was there, I'm telling you. It may have been the same one I saw on the security camera, but then she—"

I broke off. Music. It seemed to be coming up from the ocean, echoing like a chorus in a cathedral. Otherworldly, almost angelic voices soared over the blare of the alarm. *Water music.*

"Listen to that," I whispered. I dropped my weight, my butt skidding on the ground even as Riff tugged me. I was determined to hear it.

"Don't listen to it, Callie." Riff's voice broke under the strain.

He crouched down, put his hands against the sides of my head, pressed against the soft tissue of my ears, and closed off the sound, lifting me by my head from my crouched position. I grabbed his wrists and attempted to pull them away.

Riff forced me to move forward, walking me back into the house, his hands still holding my ears shut. I stumbled over the threshold, and he released me before slamming the door and twisting the lock.

The alarm still screamed, and he strode toward an electronic panel on an adjacent wall. He jabbed his finger against the keypad.

Mercifully, the shrieking ceased.

Riff threw his back against the wall and stared down at me, his chest and shoulders heaving. His voice was a growl. "Damn it, Callie! You could have been killed. Why weren't you wearing your earplugs?"

"Someone was outside my window," I panted.

Sweat coated his neck and the indention at the base of his throat. I could see in his eyes that he believed me.

"You know who it is, don't you?" I said. "Why won't you tell me? If you're so concerned about me, why won't you—"

He broke away from the wall.

"I don't understand..."

Yanking out his earplugs, Riff walked past me through the great hall.

My mind was packed with questions, and I trailed behind him. "Where is the singing coming from, Riff?" My voice echoed in the high rafters. The sides of my face still tingled from his hands, and I rubbed the hot skin of my cheeks. "What is it? The music—the singing?"

Riff pushed a hand through his hair. "I'm sorry I was so rough with you. But you can't listen to that music."

"I've already listened to it."

He moved his hands over his face, tenting them over his mouth and nose.

"Tell me," I insisted.

He dropped his hands, and his face seemed to melt as he exhaled. "It's—it's something evil. Those things are—are evil."

My brow furrowed. "What are they?"

Shaking his head, he paced, speaking in a low mutter to himself. "No, no, I'm not ready yet."

I watched him and waited, my body still trembling with adrenaline. Not ready for what?

Riff jutted out his bottom teeth and clamped them over his top lip. Then he looked past me, his mouth drawing into a hard line. When he spoke, his voice was rough. "You ever heard of sirens?"

"Sirens."

"Yes."

I blinked. "I read *The Odyssey* in college. Are you talking about the women who sang and lured sailors to their deaths?"

Riff nodded, his eyes round and almost childlike.

With a sinking feeling in my stomach, I lowered my head. "Are you telling me that's what I've been hearing? Sirens?"

The water witches.

Riff hesitated, then nodded again. "That's what you're hearing, Callie."

I inhaled slowly. "Riff, I believe your story about Kirka and the group of Manson-esque sisters who followed you around to make sure you were keeping your promises or whatever. But you'll forgive me if I'm having trouble believing those voices came from some mythological creatures that live in the ocean."

His mouth pressed together. "They don't live in the ocean. They lure people into the ocean. And they're not mythological and they're nothing like the ones you read about in Homer. They're vicious, demonic creatures that walk around this earth looking for someone to devour."

How could I believe this story without feeling like I was starting to lose my mind? Still, I couldn't deny what I'd seen and heard. "I just..."

Riff took my hand and closed it inside his own. To reassure me or to find strength for himself? "This is the most important part of the story, Callie." He breathed hard. "And no matter what happens to me, I hope you'll still write the book, tell others about it. Even if you don't believe me, I hope you'll give others like me the opportunity to know the truth." He lowered his head, his hair covering his face.

I swallowed. "What truth?"

I couldn't make heads or tails of what I'd just experienced. I didn't believe in ghosts. So, how could I believe in sirens?

Full Verbatim Transcription of Interview With Riff Fall
9/22/16
2:32 a.m.

Riff: I hadn't really understood what I was getting myself into when I signed that contract. I lived with the terms for years, but I was still doing my own thing, trying to cut corners and most of the time, I stayed drunk or high. And I kept myself away from Kirka and her watchers as much as possible.

But the touring schedule was running me into the ground. My voice was shot, my body was shot, my mental state was impaired. Deep down inside, well, I just wanted it all to end. I didn't want to live under Kirka's thumb anymore. And whenever I was drunk or high, I talked a lot. I got really loud and I started blabbing, complaining about how I was a slave to Kirka and the record label. Rod—our manager—and Ricky would try to tell me to shut up, remember that part of our terms was to keep quiet about them. Anyway, I guess word was getting around—back to her that I was unhappy with the arrangement.

Then, one night in 2010, I'd been drinking whiskey for three days nonstop and couldn't even think straight. We played a club in Savannah and after, apparently, I went back to the hotel and passed out. Sometime in the early morning, there was a knock at the door. Like so often happened, no one was there, so I got back in bed. Then I heard it—outside—the singing. I went to the balcony, opened the curtains, and on the other side of the sliding glass door leading to the balcony stood this girl. She was dripping with water like she'd just come out of the ocean and staring at me with eyes that seemed just as deep. She looked just like the women who'd been following me around the past few months, but she was singing—this voice was coming out of her. I knew what that meant.

Callie: Had you heard it before—the singing?

Riff: Oh, yeah. Kirka and the others used their song to keep us in line. Whenever they wanted us to do something, say something specific to the media, they would sing, put us in a trance of sorts—they could pretty much get us to do whatever they wanted then. So when I saw this girl on the balcony that night and heard her singing, I knew I was screwed.

Callie: How did she get on your balcony?

Riff: Well, that was the thing. I was on the sixth floor of the hotel, and while I was staring at her through the glass, I was trying to figure out how the hell she got up there. The hotel was on the riverfront and directly below was the swimming pool. I thought I was hallucinating—at first. When I opened the sliding glass door and went out on the balcony, she was still singing, and I asked her who she was, how she got up there. She told me she was there to warn me—that I wasn't taking the contract seriously. Kirka had shown me mercy because she liked me, this girl said. But ultimately, I was dispensable. No one would miss me. Cry of Crows would have another lead singer in a heartbeat, and all of this would end for me. My life would end. She said that Kirka would tear me apart along with everyone I'd ever cared about.

Callie: Who did you think they were—these women?

Riff: There were men too. [pause] I saw them as my handlers. Demons—now I know that's what they were. Demons masquerading as humans. Later, I'd come to call them sirens.

[banging sound]

Callie: Riff, someone's banging on the window.

Riff: It's them. They don't want you here. They hate that I'm telling you all this. It's their warning.

Callie: What kind of warning?

Riff: Don't you get it? By telling you my story, I'm breaking the silence. I'm breaching the contract.

[banging continues]

Callie: Do you want to stop? Should we stop?

Riff: No. No, it's time. It's time for me to tell the truth.

[banging continues]

Riff: [raising his voice] Anyway, so I'm on the balcony, and all the time this singing is going on, echoing through the place like we're standing in a cathedral or something. And then this girl says, "What's it going to be, Robert? Make your choice." Well, I mean, I didn't feel like I had a choice. I just said, "Yeah, yeah, whatever. Tell Kirka I'll be cool." And then, this girl, she climbs onto the balcony railing and says, "Here's your first test." She looks down at the pool six stories below us and says, "Jump." And I'm like—what? Yeah. I look down there and see the pool is filled with all these women, all of them singing like a chorus. And this girl's singing the words into my ear. "Jump, Robert. Go to them!" So I climbed over the railing, and I'm standing there, feeling like I'm about to kill myself, but like I said, the music—it did something to my mind—put me in a trance or something. Then, I jumped.

Callie: [clears throat] So, I've heard about that incident—the media said you'd tried to kill yourself by jumping off a hotel balcony.

Riff: Yeah, and I had to let them believe that. I'd sworn not to tell anyone about that night. By some miracle, I survived—because it wasn't like I was standing on a diving board looking straight down into the water. The pool was a ways out from the overhang. I had to launch myself. I landed in the water, but from six stories up, it was like hitting concrete. I broke my foot and my hip—injured my back.

Callie: It's a wonder you didn't die. [pause] But that injury you mentioned to me earlier. The one you said you got from jumping off a stage.

Riff: It was actually from that night. I mean, I couldn't walk on my own for nearly a year after that. The band—we had to cancel the rest of our tour. During that time, a constant stream of these watcher women pounded on my door every night for months. They forced me to come out to them—in a wheelchair at first, then on crutches, following them through the streets of my neighborhood like a madman, doing whatever crazy shit they asked me to do.

Callie: Like what?

Riff: All kinds of—well, they tested me. Asked me to roll down a hill in my wheelchair, walk down the train tracks on crutches. Most of it was just humiliating—like hazing kind of stuff. Just to show that I was back on board, so to speak. But I was addicted to painkillers by then. So, a lot of the time, if I was hurting myself, I didn't even feel it.

Callie: How long did this go on?

Riff: About six months in, the watcher visits stopped. But then Kirka showed up one night at my house. I hadn't seen her since this all started.

Callie: How did you feel when you saw her?

Riff: Actually, I was scared. When I opened the door and saw her face—I almost pissed myself.

Callie: What did she want?

Riff: What she always wanted. Control. She told me she'd brought in a songwriter to work with the band on a new album.

Callie: Which album was this?

Riff: Our last one. *The Descent.*

Callie: That album had a totally different sound from your others, but I remember playing it over and over again—in my car, in the house, on my iPod.

Riff: [nods] Reviewers said it was addictive and hypnotic. But not one of those songs sounds anything like what Ricky and I originally intended. It was all Kirka's interpretation. It wasn't enough that she had control over my life, my mind. She wanted every part of me. My music, my body, my soul. [stops] And she required so damn much from me—physically.

Callie: Sex?

Riff: [dark laugh] Yeah, you could say that. Sex with Kirka was—well, she was insatiable. She wanted control in the bedroom too. I think she maybe wanted me to love her, but I came to hate her. I guess that was the one thing she couldn't control—my heart.

Callie: What did your bandmates think? Was she having sex with them too?

Riff: No, and she didn't want me talking to them about it. She said she didn't want it to mess with our relationship as a band. So, I kept it from them as much as possible, which wasn't that hard because I was sort of embarrassed about the whole thing, you know? It was like I was her sex slave or something. So, even though they figured I was sleeping with her, I don't think they knew the extent of the arrangement. Ricky might have signed the contract, but I think, like me, he was coming to regret it. He mentioned to me one day that he thought Kirka was a little "stalkerish," but other than that, we didn't talk about it.

Callie: How long did that go on?

Riff: Forever—it felt like. We recorded *The Descent*, then went out on the road again. By the time we got off that tour, *The Descent* had gone platinum. Then we toured with Episodic Noise. That's when I met Lila.

Callie: How did that go down with Kirka?

Riff: You know, it was strange, but she actually left me alone during that time. I guess I'd proved my loyalty to her well enough by then.

Callie: What about Lila? How did you two even happen during all of this?

Riff: Yeah, well, I'd tried to keep my distance from Lila other than what fraternizing was expected—you know, being on tour with her band. I thought she was gorgeous, and she sang like an angel, but I didn't want to drag her into my shit. About halfway through the tour, Kirka stopped showing up. I don't know what happened—if she found someone else to feed on or whatever, but...well, I mean, for a little while it was awesome. It was like this weight had been lifted. I had some freedom again, and I started hanging out more with Lila after shows.

But when that tour ended, I was so burnt. I just wanted to crawl off somewhere and be alone. I didn't want to be anywhere near LA, so I sold my place and headed east to Invisible Island. I just wanted to get as far away from the West Coast as I could.

Callie: Almost like you thought getting away from the West Coast could somehow free you from Kirka?

Riff: Yeah, I was drawn to this place from the first time I visited. I had peace, you know, and I wanted to feel that again.

Callie: So that's when you built Belle Marsh?

Riff: Yeah. Little did I know that Kirka's entourage was vast. These beings—they're everywhere. They travel by water or by land. They'll find you no matter where you go. Turns out there was already a flock of them here. They're like carnies—the traveling carnivals that go to all the beach towns to hit up the tourists. The sirens—they love to prey on the tourists. Check out the stats of how many people go missing without a trace from tourist trap destinations. It's not a coincidence. [exhales] So, I built Belle Marsh as a refuge, a place to escape all the craziness that had become my life. And you're right. Maybe deep down, I thought I could escape Kirka too. I was wrong about that.

[banging in background stops]

Callie: It stopped.

Riff: Yep. [long pause] But sometimes the silence is scarier.

21

Now it made sense why Riff hadn't wanted to tell me or anyone else the reasons behind his self-imposed exile and imprisonment at Belle Marsh. Whether Kirka's threats had teeth behind them or not, he believed that they did and that she would use her power to kill him and everyone he loved. He'd sworn silence. But now he'd talked.

Riff sat on the couch in the music room, clasping his shaking hands between his knees. It had taken a lot out of him to tell me all this, and now, obviously he was scared.

I moved from my chair and sat beside him. When I put my hand on his arm, he flinched.

His damp eyes were fixed on the floor, but they had a wild look like a highly strung horse. "I've wanted so damn much to be free of these things, Callie."

When he finally turned his eyes to meet mine, I glimpsed a haunted emptiness in them. Riff had weathered too many storms. Dark crescents ringed his eyes like shadows, along with the desolation, the weight of countless sleepless nights, and the invisible barrier of anguish. He'd carried this burden too long. And yet, there was an undeniable resilience. We'd both survived our trials, not without injuries, but we were still breathing.

"I want to help you," I said.

He leaned back, rested his head against the back of the couch, a wan smile on his lips. "You are."

"No, I mean really help you. There's got to be a way. You signed a contract with Kirka. There's a way out of every contract—a loophole, something."

He reached up and tucked his hand under my hair, between my neck and shoulder. "Thank you for caring. But I'm pretty sure there's only one way out of this."

I knew what he meant, and his words chilled me. I shook my head. "No, no. Don't even think that."

"It's too late. I told you. If I've learned one thing from Kirka over the years, it's that she doesn't go back on her word."

"There's always another way. You should talk to a lawyer." I sat up a little straighter as the idea came to me. "Elijah! If you just told him about this, showed him the contract. You have a copy, don't you?"

He scoffed. "It's an air-tight contract, Callie. I signed it in my blood."

"No, I don't believe that. There has to be a way."

"The only way for any of this to mean anything is to help others avoid the same trap. I decided several months ago that I was going to do this—tell my story, knowing that I would die as a result, but hoping it could save others."

"I want you to save yourself, Riff. Kirka's not even in the business anymore. She's retired to her island, right?"

His stare was cavernous. "Kirka's always in the business. Even if she's retired from the industry, she's still controlling her minions, passing on her heinous tricks to others." He shook his head. "She's not really human, Callie. None of them are."

LATER THAT MORNING, I scoured the internet for information about "water witches" on the island or people going missing. But I only found a small local story about a man who had jumped from a dock late one night and never resurfaced. I could see nothing about people mysteriously walking into the water or disappearing without a trace. Nothing about local police investigating. Elijah had said Nona knew a lot about the island and the superstitions that abounded. Maybe she was the one to talk to.

While Riff was in the shower, I called Elijah and asked if his grandmother would see me.

I knew Riff didn't think there was any help for him, but I couldn't believe the situation was hopeless. Under the ruse that I wanted to explore more of the island, I asked if I could use his golf cart—rusted with disuse and covered with cobwebs but still operational. "As long as you're back well before it gets dark." A condition that had started to sound like a mantra.

After plugging Nona's address into my phone's GPS, I drove across the island to a small cream-colored house sheltered under a bridge of live oaks and palmettos. I stepped on the brake, my eyes drawn to the woman standing in the doorway—a little more stooped than I remembered her.

"I just made blueberry muffins," she said. "They're still hot."

We sat in her oven-warm kitchen, the air heavy with the scent of steaming blueberries and sugar. The two of us just fit at the square table that was pushed into the corner and cluttered with leftover berries, measuring cups clouded with flour, and crisscrossed wooden spoons.

I cut into my blueberry muffin and watched the steam rise from the middle. "I was hoping you'd talk a little about the local superstitions."

She hacked at the stick of butter and pushed a cube into the center of her muffin. "Mm-hm."

I popped a chunk into my mouth and bit down. Berries squirted across my tongue. "What about these..." I hesitated, almost too embarrassed to say the word. "Sirens?"

Nona cut her muffin into fourths before taking a bite herself. She chewed and swallowed before answering. "They demon witches of the water," Nona said. "Some call 'em sirens, I guess."

I took another bite of muffin and considered how to question her about something that seemed so outrageous. "So, if one were being tormented by one of these...water witches, how would one go about getting rid of them?"

Nona pursed her lips. "Well, now. That's not so easy. You don't get rid of something that's been around for thousands of years. And they everywhere. They walk around looking just like beautiful people—because they're half-human. They occupy a human body. But what lives inside them—what that thing looks like in its natural state? Mm-mm." She shook her head. "They're monsters with talons, feathers—part bird, part demon fire." She lifted an eyebrow. "And they know things. Since the beginning of the earth, they know what's happened. And if you listen to their songs, they'll tell you things you never wanted to know. They'll offer powers you never wanted to have. They make you feel things you never wanted to feel."

Nona passed two paper napkins my way. "But they can look just like you or me. And they can go all sorts of places. Sirens—as you call 'em—are travelers. They go by waterways mostly. Some say ghosts can't cross water, but water witches can."

I shivered, remembering the woman's vacant eyes staring at me from the other side of my window—suspended in the air as though she floated in water. "I think I saw one outside my window last night."

Nona nodded. "Mm-hm. They probably trying to scare you—warn you off." She raised her gray eyebrows. "Or, maybe they just want to lure you out, drag you down into the depths of the water. That's what they do—they feed and live on the energy and flesh of humans."

I pulled a face. "They eat people?"

"Some say they do," Nona said. "Some say they eat your mind away—make it so you don't know anything anymore, can't make any decisions. Others say they turn humans into creatures just like them." She shrugged. "They can't reproduce like humans so they have to bring some humans in to teach and keep their evil going, I guess. Doesn't matter. Death is death. And the sirens are very close with Death." She held up a finger. "But sometimes, one of 'em fall in love with a human, and instead of killing them, they take them to their lair. They all different. But they only sing at night—most dangerous after midnight—and they can't cross through a locked door."

Ah. That was why Riff was so adamant that I should not go outside after dark or near the blue door at the end of the upstairs hallway. "They can't cross through a locked door?"

"Nope. That's why I stay inside at night here—and never venture out after midnight."

I slanted my eyes to the window and watched a black and blue lizard move like quicksilver over the panes before disappearing.

"You know, I looked for stories about people disappearing from the island, but I couldn't find anything."

"Usually it happens out on the open water, where it's easy to say someone drowned. Mostly, they use the island as one of their hideouts. Like I say, they travelers."

I swiped the napkin across my lips. "Do you know how to stop these things?"

"I know how to keep 'em away from me."

"How?"

Nona exhaled through her nostrils. "Are you a religious woman, Callie?"

"No. Not really."

"Some people around here get help from preachers or witch doctors." She waved her hand in the air as though swatting away flies. "I can handle 'em without all that. But once you've contracted with them, once you've agreed to their demands like Riff has..." She tsked. "Well, then that's a whole other problem."

Wait. Riff said he hadn't told anyone but me about the contract. "How did you know about that—the contract?"

She quirked her mouth. "I put it together in my own mind. Elijah told me some things, but he don't believe, you know. But I know how these hags do their thing. They grab prey as they can get it—like a shark. They don't usually follow people around in broad daylight—not unless they feel that person belong to them." She nodded. "Riff belong to them."

I finished my blueberry muffin and wadded up the paper baking cup. "Even though I've heard them myself, seen them, to tell you the truth, Nona, I've had a difficult time believing these creatures are real."

"They are real, I promise you." She crossed her arms. "Down by that old, abandoned resort, you'll see 'em. That place, built on cursed land as it was, been empty for years now. But the water witches think of it as their own. They got a good view from there of people wandering the beach, taking their boats out on the water."

Most likely the naked woman I'd seen in the basement of the resort hadn't been a vagrant. I'd been kidding myself to believe that.

I scooted my chair away from the table and met Nona's eyes. "Have they ever bothered you?"

She moved her mouth as though she tasted her answer. "I came face to face with the old hag some five years ago. She come knockin' at my door, rattling, trying to call me outside to listen to her squallin.'"

"What did you do?"

She sat back, crossed her arms over her chest, and the smallest of smiles tipped her lips. "She didn't like me singin' my spirituals. That's for sure."

Then Nona began to sing, her voice low and throaty as she thumped her hand on the tabletop for rhythm.

The day is comin' when we'll all sing together,
We'll fall on our knees in the presence of the Lawd,
Hab mercy on me, Lawd, Oh Lawd.

She clasped her hands together and chuckled. "Oh Lawd, you never see a demon fly away so fast."

I couldn't help but smile just a little at Nona's obvious pleasure with her siren-slaying weapon.

Her eyebrows joined. "Like I said, you don't just get rid of 'em. Riff—they know him now. As long as he lives, they'll keep trying to take him. You better off if you live somewhere without water nearby though." She held up a finger. "Oh, and here, take this."

She went to a cabinet and took down a clear plastic bottle the size of a container of cooking oil. "This here is holy water—blessed by the Reverend Alberto Jones. They come too close to you, squirt 'em with this. They don't like that at all."

I fought off the sense of dread blooming in my chest as I took the water from Nona. I really didn't want to come close enough to one to have to squirt them.

"Thank you."

Her knees cracked as she sat down again. "But the main thing to remember is—don't ever listen to their singing."

22

Back at Belle Marsh, I placed Nona's bottle of holy water on the coffee table in the music room. After my talk with her, it was time to delve a little deeper into this subject. If these things were real—and based on my own experience I was forced to believe they might be—and if they were everywhere like Nona said and really as dangerous as Riff thought, then someone besides Homer had to have written about them. Sitting on the couch, I set up my laptop, pulled up a browser, and typed in "siren."

As a child, my mother had read to me from Homer's 8th-century epic poems *The Odyssey* and *The Iliad*, and I distinctly remembered the stories about the sirens and how Odysseus's men were turned into swine at Circe's behest. The legends had been right up there with fairy tales—a fun bedtime yarn.

Scanning the screen of my laptop, I scrolled past the links for alarms and television shows and movies. The dictionary definition: a woman men find they are unable to resist; a vamp. The synonyms included temptress, seducer, beguiler, sexpot. All traditional associations.

Next came the academic articles about Circe and the women who lured sailors to their deaths by singing music so beautiful and enchanting that the men ran their boats aground. Odysseus was so terrified of this happening to him and his crew that he bid them all stuff their ears with wax and tie him to the mast of the ship so he could not throw himself overboard. Just as Riff had taken to wearing military-grade earplugs and shut himself in his house.

Whole literary analyses were dedicated to Circe—the leader of the sirens, a sorceress deemed both good and bad, depending on the scholar. Greek pronunciation of her name was a hard K and a long e—Keerkee. *Kirka.*

The second revelation followed swiftly. Aeaea Records. Aeaea—the name of Circe's island in *The Odyssey.* Of course. Why hadn't I caught these things before?

As I continued to scroll, another link caught my eye: "Anatomy of a Siren" by Horace K. Jennings.

I scanned its contents. Like so many writings on the sirens, it began with Homer's take on the women. Apparently, Homer never described the appearance of the sirens. Instead, the 3rd-century poet Apollonius of Rhodes suggested the siren was half-woman, half-bird. In circa 77-79 AD, author, Roman army commander, naturalist, and scientific expert Pliny the Elder wrote of the creatures in his *Naturalis Historia* in a chapter called "Fabulous Birds," claiming that "they charm men by their song, and having lulled them to sleep, tear them to pieces." Although he said he didn't believe the creatures were real, he made a confusing statement that maybe they existed in India.

The article went on to say that these creatures might have once been common in the Mediterranean and, through extraordinary environmental adaptability, had evolved into something that could dive so deep in the waters that no one would find them while also being equally comfortable on land. Although they traveled by water and were known to stay close to such a source, they were ectothermic and depended on environmental light sources for heat. Hence, sirens chose to live and travel in areas of the world that were generally warm.

Unfortunately, when I checked out Horace K. Jennings's bio online, I was disappointed to find that he was also dead. So much for contacting him.

AFTER DINNER THAT NIGHT, Riff and I sat in the music room, and I told him about my meeting with Nona. I held up the plastic bottle she'd given me. "Holy water. Water-witch weaponry, she said. Maybe if you keep this with you, you could set foot off the property."

He swept his hand across his forehead. "Look, I appreciate you trying to help me, Callie. But..." He shook his head.

I bit my lip, broaching the next subject carefully. "I just want you to know I believe you."

Riff inhaled slowly, nodding. "Thank you."

"And I believe there's a way to fight this."

He was silent.

"You have to have some hope, Riff."

He looked down at his hands. "I've been living under a hopeful delusion for a long time. The hope that Lila might..." He broke off.

"What about Lila?"

His face changed again, tightened around the edges as he sat back against the couch. "For years, I've hoped and prayed that she would turn up somewhere. Like, maybe she really did just run away. I kept thinking maybe someone would spot her in some obscure place—New Mexico, Arizona. But now? I just don't hold out much hope anymore."

"So what are you saying? That the sirens got her?"

"I can't even think about that possibility."

But I thought about it. She had disappeared without a trace. The possibility was strong that was exactly what had happened to her.

"We still haven't talked about her," I said.

A sigh trickled from his throat.

"You plan to include her in your story, right?"

His voice was gravelly. "Yes, I have to. She's the reason I'm still here."

I sat back. "Tell me, then. What drew you to her?"

Riff rubbed his hands over his face. "Well, to start, she was—is—gorgeous. But I mean, she's beautiful inside too. During the whole shitshow of my life, she was there for me. As a friend, you know?" A small smile crept over his face. "After the first few weeks of our tour together, I knew I loved her. I mean, I just knew it. And I think she knew it too. We clicked. Really clicked. But I didn't touch her. Didn't try to kiss her. Nothing. Not until she came to visit me here on the island, and then I think I might have held her hand once in the golf cart on our way to the restaurant. And that was because, well, you know, this place gets hella dark at night. No streetlights, no sounds but the insects and the night animals."

"Yeah." I rolled my eyes. "Tell me about it."

"Lila slept in the room you're in now. We stayed separate for the first week she was here. It was almost like we were trying to fight the feelings we had. We watched movies, played music, and ate lunch on the beach. We got really close, told each other all sorts of stuff. And we spent every day together. We even wrote a few songs together during that time." He chewed at the side of his mouth. "But the more time we spent together, the more something grew between us." Riff rubbed his hands up and down his jeans. "I guess I finally tried to kiss her or something, and Lila didn't want to screw up our friendship. She knew how things ended in situations like ours. But then one night, we were out on the beach, and I was looking at her, she was looking at me, and it just sort of happened." He laughed a little. "I'd always thought having sex on the beach would suck—you know, with the sand getting everywhere and all that. I know what I'm going to say next is so cliched, but I guess we just couldn't fight it anymore. It was like magic between us. Sand and all."

"Was REO Speedwagon playing?"

Riff looked up at me. "Huh?"

"Never mind. I'm sorry. That was dumb."

He chuckled. "Oh, I get it. Yeah, like we couldn't fight the feeling."

"Sorry. My little attempt at humor."

"Yeah, anyway, we got married. Just a little ceremony here on the island, closed to the media and the public. After that, for a time, we were living as close to paradise as we could get."

"What did Kirka say?"

His face clouded. "Kirka." Riff scrubbed his forefinger under his nose. "For a while, she didn't say or do anything. But months later, she sent her minions here. The watchers. Maybe they were already here before, I don't know." He compressed his mouth and shook his head. "And I was so damn weak."

I sat forward. "Weak how?"

"One night, when Lila was in New York recording a new album with Episodic Noise. I sat up really late—drinking as usual. Anyway, it was sometime after midnight. I went for a walk on the beach. I sometimes did that before going to sleep. The floodlights were on outside, but I kept strolling along until I was off the property and in a dark area. Anyway, I came across this woman sitting at the edge of the water, singing. When I approached her, she got up and stood there, just kind of looking at me. I said hello to her, asked if she was okay." He swept a hand through his hair. "She told me she was waiting for some people. I started to move on, but she caught up to me. She had these amazing eyes, you know. They glowed in the dark. Then I saw her tattoos. I knew then what she was. She had the mark of the sirens."

"But not *only* them." I pointed to his arm. "You have them too."

He looked down at the curving lines. "You get these once they consider you their property. It's part of a ritual. In my case, every time it happened, I got so drunk I blacked out. Don't remember any of it." He traced the blue ink to his wrist. "This is meant to be an ocean wave. It's on my forearm to mean creativity. The ocean is symbolic of life and change. Kirka said it was meant to give protection from the gods." He quirked his mouth. "Whatever that means."

"So what happened with the girl on the beach?"

"Yeah, anyway," he continued. "She said, 'Hey, aren't you that singer?' And I said yeah, told her my name. She said her name was Silla. Her friends never showed up. So we started talking—we talked for a long time.."

"What did you talk about?"

"I don't know. That's the crazy part of it. I don't remember one damn thing we talked about. Couldn't tell you. But...well, I ended up having sex with her."

His words disturbed me. Maybe it was empathy for Lila. Or maybe it was frustration with how easily he'd given in to this random woman. "But you knew she was a watcher—a siren—sent by Kirka."

His face twitched. "I knew. But that was the thing—I knew and yet when she started singing, I just fell right into her hands. Without any way to stop my ears, without the earplugs, I was defenseless. The next thing I knew, we were on the sand and she had my pants down and she was on top of me. We were just going for it. I woke up the next morning. She was gone, but I was sprawled out on the sand—my business exposed to the world and everything." He grimaced. "She could have easily killed me then. At the time, I didn't know why she hadn't."

"Why did Kirka send this girl? Why not come herself?"

"I think it was strategic. If Kirka had come, I could've chalked up my behavior to the contract. Instead, I didn't have that as my fallback. Kirka sent this woman to remind me she could still get to me. Kirka made sure there were plenty of people in place to keep me where I am."

My eyes wandered back to the pictures on the wall. "Did Lila find out?"

Riff coughed. "Yeah, she did. But not right away. We were going back and forth to New York then. Lila and her band were in the recording studio, and I'd gone with her at first. Until Silla started showing up at our hotel room at night, knocking on the door. There was nothing I could do."

"Did you let her in?"

He dipped his head. "Yeah. A lot of the time Lila wasn't around. She was recording or meeting with producers or something. So yeah, I let her in. Or I met her out somewhere." He held up his arm. "It's how I got so many of these damn tattoos. Silla was Kirka's tattoo artist. They'd get me drunk, I'd black out, and I'd wake up with another one of these." He brushed his arm over his bicep. "Now I just wish I could get rid of them."

"How long were you in New York?"

"A couple of weeks. Then we came back to the island and I figured it was all over."

It was hard for me to believe that Kirka had given up so easily after spending so much time reminding him that she was still in control. I wasn't sure how it worked in the supernatural realm, but in the natural, obsessions didn't die that quickly. "You really never heard from her again?"

He huffed out air. "Nope. But I still hear 'em. Sometimes I even think I hear 'em inside the house." He rubbed his scraped knuckles. "That's how I ended up with this. I thought I heard one of them upstairs, near the door. I reacted and threw a punch. But of course it went into the wall." He looked up at me. "See? I really am crazy."

"You've been through a lot."

I tucked my legs under me and moved closer until my knees touched the side of his thigh. "Look, you were terrified to tell me all this. Terrified that you would die if you did. But you haven't died. You're still sitting here right in front of me."

He continued to stare down at his contused hand, using the finger of his other hand to trace the scrapes. "After Lila found out about Silla, I told her almost everything. I told her that I'd signed a bad contract with Kirka, Aeaea Records...I told her they owned me."

"How did she react?"

"She was freaked out. She'd known others in the business who had gone down a similar path. Lila wanted us to get some help. She wanted us to go talk to a lawyer, someone who could maybe get me out of the contract." Riff shook his head. "But I knew what would happen if we did that. I couldn't risk it."

"You never told her what Kirka was?"

"No. And anyway, after I talked to Lila, the trouble really started. The sirens, they knew what I'd tried to do, and they were so pissed."

Just as they'd been angry that I was here, trying to tell Riff's story. "How did they know?"

He shrugged. "I don't know. But they knew. They always know. Not long after that, Lila disappeared. The record company dropped us for breach of contract—not that I was surprised. Not that I cared either. Actually, I was relieved. I don't know that Ricky and Blacky were too happy with me though."

I exhaled, turned off the recorder, and clasped my hands to keep from pushing his hair behind his ear, touching his face. This whole debacle had slipped so miserably far from being professional that I wasn't sure I could ever get it back.

"Riff."

He met my eyes out of the corner of his, and the energy around me exploded with a blazing intensity. Was he feeling any of it? I had no idea other than the fact that our gaze held—interminably, it felt.

"I want to help you," I said, my voice nearly a whisper. "In any way I can."

"You are helping me," he returned, his voice as low as mine.

I knew what he meant. I was helping him by putting his words down on paper, getting the truth out for the world to see. "I can do more."

He closed his eyes and exhaled softly through his nose. "No, you can't."

I continued, "Look, I'm pretty much alone in the world. No relationships, no kids. I know you're worried about protecting everyone, but I'm willing to take a risk. To help you."

Riff focused his eyes on something across the room. "If only I was as unselfish as you seem to think I am, Callie." He swerved his eyes back to mine. "Truth is, I'm a coward."

I shook my head. "No, I don't believe that—"

Riff twisted and reached for me. His hands grasped my face, and his mouth smothered my words. Flooded with shock, I wrapped my arms around his neck, and his hands moved to the back of my thighs. He turned me, pulling my body under his until my knees were on either side of his hips. I met his every kiss with open-mouthed enthusiasm. His skin tasted like salt and sun, and his body was warm and heavy against mine.

I couldn't remember feeling anything like this for anyone, and even though the words ran like a jumbotron in my mind—*this is the end of everything*—I countered the announcement with my own rationale. *Maybe I'm not the ice queen after all.*

But even as the passion between us swelled, something felt off. His mouth was bruising, his hands gripped my face. His desire quickly seemed to morph into a violent hunger that stopped me from responding. I felt his arms and abdomen tense, and he pushed up, raising his face inches above me. "Oh, shit, Callie. I'm sorry. I don't know what I was thinking." Breathing hard, he pressed his forehead against mine. "I can't. I can't."

Of course he couldn't. There was still Lila...

A stab of confusion—familiar as the rain now falling on the roof—jabbed at my insides.

Riff sat up and pinched his eyes shut. "See? What did I tell you? I'm just as much of an asshole as any other musician." He shot his hand through his hair. "I can't offer you anything, Callie."

I sat up too and clasped my fingers so tightly that the tips turned white. "It doesn't matter. I don't need anything."

He lowered his eyes. "You deserve everything."

His words touched some part of me that had never seen the light of day.

We sat in silence for several minutes. Finally, he stood. Before he left the room, he reached down, grabbed my hand, and squeezed it. It felt like a goodbye.

I DASHED INTO MY BEDROOM and closed the door behind me. Then, I swept my pack of cigarettes off the nightstand, poured one into my hand, and popped the end into my mouth. While lighting it, I moved into the bathroom, lowered my cargo pants, and inspected the circles on my inner thighs. Tonight, my scars called out to me. I longed to sear one of them—to feel that momentary and perfect pain that drowned out everything else. *No. It's been years. You can't start that again. It took too long to stop it.*

In the past, with every failed relationship, every rejection, the pain had centered me, allowed me to move past it. Right then, I felt something I hadn't felt in a long time. The kind of pain that came from caring. *Don't waste flesh on a fleeting feeling.*

Shuddering all the air from my lungs, I took long drags from the cigarette and dropped it into the toilet.

It was no longer possible to deny it. Something strange was going on here. As hard as it was for me to believe in all these paranormal happenings, something wasn't right. I hadn't felt like myself since coming here. Now, I was falling for a man who was being stalked by something that was supposed to be mythological. And I was even beginning to believe.

When I returned to the bed, my phone beeped with a text. Finally, some cell phone reception. I picked it up and looked at the message. My dad. I held my breath as I opened the text. It was a photo—brown and grainy—circa 1989. An eight-year-old girl with wild blonde curls stood next to a man with long, sandy hair dressed in a jean jacket and a T-shirt that advertised a diner. In the background, the golden spires of the Disneyland castle bloomed with its pink and blue turrets. Me and my dad, the first time I'd ever visited him. He'd taken me to Disneyland.

In the photo, I was beaming—and the emotion from that day rushed back to me. I'd been so thrilled to meet my father finally. In my young mind, he was bigger than life, bigger than Disneyland. All my years of yearning for a dad were forgotten—my dreams fulfilled. A few years later, those dreams would be dashed—all the good memories tainted by one night.

I clicked off my phone. Why did he want to reconnect? Why now when it was too late? My heart was stone. Sending text messages and a photo wasn't going to change that.

23

Daylight finally came—a relief after tossing and turning all night, plagued by images of visits to my father over the six years that preceded the event with Frankie. I hadn't thought about our good times together in ages—the time we'd packed up and spent a weekend in Monterey seal and dolphin watching. Once, we'd gone for a week to the Grand Canyon. Or there was that first time he'd ever introduced me to his bandmates and made sure I was in the front row at the concert. Those were the days of awe—when I couldn't wait for my yearly visit. What would the next time be like? What would we do? Where would we go?

And then that had all ended.

Like a zombie, I rose and dressed as quietly as I could. Heaviness in my chest was the only physical barometer by which I could measure my emotions. This was the day I was leaving Invisible Island. It shouldn't have bothered me, but it did. I'd become too attached to Riff. Being isolated on the island with this man had done weird things to my head.

Quickly, I stepped back into the room, grabbed my bag, swung the strap over my shoulder, and hurried toward the stairs.

On my final pass through Belle Marsh, I glanced again into the music room, the framed photos hanging on the wall. Over the last few days, I'd memorized them. I panned my gaze over to the side table where the plastic bottle of holy water sat. Maybe Riff would never need it. Maybe it would become another conversational piece in a room full of many such things.

I trekked toward the front entrance and met Riff in the hall. I stopped, my heart in my throat. He was wearing the same clothes as last night, his hair unruly, his salt and pepper stubble starting to look like a full-on beard.

Why did I feel like I was going to cry? I hated this. I'd been blissfully numb for years and now I was an emotional shipwreck.

Riff smiled. "I've called Abbot. He should be here within the hour. Do you want some breakfast?"

"No, thanks. Actually, I think I'll wait by the dock. I need a cigarette."

Riff's face was inscrutable as he stepped out of my way, and I tried not to look back at him.

"Callie?"

I stopped at the door.

He came toward me, slipped his fingers under the strap of the duffel bag, and slid it from my shoulder. "I'll walk down with you."

I allowed the strap to glide off my arm and onto his. Then, we walked side by side toward the dock, my shoulders and back stiff. I stared down the length of the beach, noting how quiet, how solitary it was. No boats on the water. It was almost like it was only us here on the island. No water witches, no curses, just two people who'd spent a few days together and formed a connection—and maybe, well, you never knew what might happen. Except we weren't those two people.

When we reached the dock, the sun beamed down on my face, coaxing sweat from my hairline and lower back.

Riff hung his hands behind his neck. "Callie, I say this with well-meaning intent. Don't come back here. We can send chapters back and forth like we've been doing. Don't put yourself at risk again."

I stared at the water flowing under the dock. Last night's physical encounter replayed through my mind, and a sigh slipped from my throat. Abbot would arrive any minute. Soon, I'd hear the whir of the motor. This torture would be over.

"I'm sorry," Riff said. "I'm sorry I'm such a messed-up bastard. You deserve a lot more. If circumstances were different..."

"Stop." I shook my head, willing him not to say anything else.

He scratched the scabs on his knuckles. "I really enjoyed having you here. I liked your company. Maybe a little too much."

I watched the water for signs of Abbot's boat. My heart panged like it had the night Tyler died.

Riff continued. "I still feel like a married man, you know?"

"I know, and it's fine."

A faint buzz sounded in the distance as Abbot's boat sped toward the dock.

I squinted up at Riff. "My dad wants to see me. He keeps texting me. I've been ignoring his messages, but...I don't know."

"Maybe you should see him."

"Maybe. It's just a lot to think about."

Riff anchored his tongue firmly between his lips and turned his attention to Abbot's approach.

Suddenly eager to be in that boat, I moved toward the edge of the dock. When I reached it, I looked back once—my gaze fixed on Belle Marsh and the upstairs window. It was empty.

"Take care of yourself, Callie," Riff called out. "I'll be in touch."

ON THE BOAT SPEEDING toward Bluffton, my breathing normalized, my heart rate slowed, but my thoughts still raced.

If I decided to meet my father, how would it go? Would we meet at a restaurant? Or would he come to my place? For so long he'd been dead to me. Most people didn't even know he was my father. If I was ever asked, my answer was always the same. "I don't talk about Trace Rowe."

Except I had told Riff. I'd shared everything that had happened, which had anchored the subject of my father at the forefront of my mind.

As I watched the island disappear, I breathed a sigh of relief. I could handle everything from my home office now. Riff was right—there was no need to return.

I had escaped before anything serious happened between us. I could forget a kiss or two. I'd call Quincy from the car. Oh, how I wanted to speak to him, tell him everything that had happened. Tell him how messed up my head had been while I was on the island.

I moved to the seat closest to Abbot, raising my voice over the din of the motor.

"You'll take care of Riff, won't you, Abbot? Check in on him? Make sure he's okay?"

Abbot pointed at his ear and shook his head. "Can't hear you. Forgot my hearing aid today."

When we reached the mainland, Abbot helped me out of the boat with my duffel bag.

"Thanks." Hoisting my bag, I started to pivot away from him.

He cleared his throat. "A lot of people say a lot of things about Riff, but his life is none of their business."

I nodded, wondering why he was telling me this. "I know that."

He looked back at his boat. "No reason for you to come back here. You leave him alone now. I love Riff like a son. I'd do anything for him. Anything to protect him, make sure he's not moving in a direction he shouldn't."

My mouth dropped open. "I'm not—"

"He doesn't know what he's doing," Abbot said. "I'm trying to keep that boy alive. He doesn't need you here messing with his head, making him think things can be different. Making him say things he shouldn't. Things can't be different for him—not now, not ever. If you know what's best for you, you'll steer clear."

Abbot's stare—an icy squint—sent a cold bolt of realization through me as I recalled Riff's words. *"Kirka made sure there were plenty of people in place to keep me where I am."*

Was Abbot one of those people?

I backed away.

As if to reiterate his point, he called after me. "There's nothing here for you. There's nothing you can do for him. Nothing at all."

I turned and hustled toward the shuttle that would take me to my car, my heart thumping. Suddenly, I was back in the headspace of a fourteen-year-old—an annoying groupie rather than a professional writer. Tamping down my bruised ego, I climbed onto the shuttle.

Half an hour later, I was safely settled behind the wheel of my car. I turned on the ignition. Lila Silverleaf's soaring voice blared through the speakers. I quickly hit the off button.

I had a long drive ahead of me, and all I wanted was silence.

24

I'd missed the sounds of cars honking, drunk people yelling at each other, country music clanging from the honky-tonk down the street. City sounds drowned out all the noise in my head—the voices formed out of thin air.

On my first night back, I slept like a newborn puppy—waking only once to go to the bathroom, then back to bed until noon the next day. No dreams, no voices. In many ways, it was like none of it had ever happened. Except, I had a desk full of notes, photographs, and scribblings that said otherwise.

I shuffled into the kitchen and poured a bowl of cereal, splattered some milk over the flakes, and carried it into the living room. As I shoveled breakfast into my mouth, I checked my messages. Quincy had texted.

Checking to see how you're doing. Call me when you have a chance.

I dropped my gaze to the next name.

Trace

My heart stuttered.

Hey. Hoping you'll return my calls or at least text me. I'd really like to come out to Nashville to see you. I've got some pretty important stuff to talk to you about.

When was this sent? What date? Thursday. The delivery must have been delayed with the poor phone reception I'd had on the island. An apology was the only thing Trace Rowe could say that would mean anything, and even that would be too little too late.

My fingers shook as I typed the words back to him. *Let me think about it.*

It was a start. At least I was acknowledging him, not blowing him off. I *would* think about it. But for now, I wanted to focus on Riff's book without the distraction of dredging up old emotions about my dad.

Once it was all over, I might meet with him if he really wanted to trek out to Nashville. Maybe I could finally get some closure on that chapter of my life.

QUINCY AND I MET IN Midtown at a new wine bar called Corked. Quincy moved his wine glass in circles, allowing the cabernet to climb the sides. Deep rings hung under his eyes, making the blue of his irises stand out.

"Have you gotten any sleep?" I asked.

He stifled a yawn. "No. Perils of having a six-week-old."

"You're getting too old for this, you know."

He scoffed. "Tell Lissa that. I told her this is absolutely the last one. I'm getting snipped next month."

I drew back. "Really?"

"Oh, yeah. Not risking another accident after a night of margaritas."

Quincy seemed to have sprouted gray hairs overnight. Or maybe he'd been coloring his hair all along and I just hadn't known.

He eyed me through narrowed slits. "Honestly, kiddo, you don't look so hot yourself."

I rubbed my hands up and down my face, suddenly aware it was the same mannerism Riff used all the time. Still, it seemed to fit my state of mind. "I slept last night. Before that—not for the last week."

He lifted his glass to his nose and inhaled. "So, do you think he did it? Killed her?"

I furrowed my brow. "What? No. No way. Riff's a nice guy."

"Did you sleep with him?"

My mouth dropped open. "That may be the most offensive question you've ever asked me."

He shrugged, unfazed. "Did you?"

"No."

"Good girl." He swilled his wine.

Now I really was offended, even though part of me cringed with guilt. I had kissed Riff, and I'd certainly contemplated the prospect of sleeping with him. Still, keeping up professional appearances in front of my agent—and more importantly, my friend—was of the utmost importance. "When have I ever slept with a client, Quincy? Seriously."

He coughed. "Well, if you have, you haven't told me."

"That's because I haven't."

He shrugged again. "I don't know. I've felt like this was a different sort of project for you. You told me several times that you had a thing for the guy back in the day."

"Back in the day." I drew in a mouthful of chardonnay and swallowed. "When I was a teenager. What kind of person do you think I am, Quincy?"

"How's the book going?"

I dragged my eyes back to his. "Fine. I've got a lot of good material, but I hope to get more from him. I was thinking about going back to the island, but..."

Quincy raised his eyebrows. "You sure you're not sleeping with him?"

Rolling my eyes, I finished my wine and stood. "Thanks for the drink, Quince."

He held out his hands. "Hold on, hold on. Don't go yet. I'm sorry. You know I'm just kidding."

I wasn't normally sensitive, but I didn't want to joke about Riff. "I know. I've got a lot of stuff to do."

The teasing smile slipped from his face. "Come on. At least stay while I finish my wine."

I lowered myself into the seat.

He leaned forward, corralling his glass with his hands. "So, what's his deal? What's the angle?"

I stared at the yellow napkin under my glass and debated telling him about Kirka, Riff's contract, the singing I'd heard while on the island. I needed to tell someone about the craziness that Riff had shared with me and what I'd experienced.

On the other hand, Quincy was no-nonsense, and I was pretty sure he'd tell me to get a grip. He'd say the week I'd spent on Invisible Island affected my judgment and sanity.

I shook my head. "Not sure yet."

He drew his head back. "You're not sure? I figured you'd already have this in the works."

"I do. I am—working on it. It's not that, it's just..." I traced the yellow napkin's edge. "Riff's story is kind of—" I wriggled my mouth. "Fantastical."

"In what sense?" He pointed at his temple. "You mean because he's unwell?"

"It's not that." What did I have to lose? I might as well tell him. If Quincy thought it was all madness, no one else would believe it. I met his eyes. "Years ago, when Riff and Cry of Crows got started in the business, they signed a bad contract."

Quincy snorted. "What musician hasn't? Did you see what George Michael and Prince went through?"

I chewed at my lip before forging ahead. "I mean, this was a *really* bad contract, like, the band members basically signed their lives away. Their souls." I took a deep breath. "Have you ever heard of Kirka Taylor? She was a music producer and CEO of Aeaea Records until around 2012."

"No, you know I don't keep track of all the music industry names."

"Kirka Taylor was in charge of their label. But before they signed the contract, she drugged them."

Quincy swiped a hand across his mouth. "Wow."

"Yeah. I haven't seen this contract, but apparently, they didn't really know what they were signing. It gave Kirka access to every area of their lives. She controlled their every move."

Quincy quirked his mouth and lifted his glass. "Hate to tell you, but this isn't that uncommon."

I stared at him. "Yeah, but I think Kirka was a little...extra. Riff says that she wasn't entirely human."

Quincy drained his glass.

Should I just say it? "Riff says that Kirka and her associates are—well, he thinks they're sirens." I cringed.

He didn't blink.

"I know. It sounds crazy, but some strange things happened to me on the island, Quince. I even talked to some locals who confirmed his story, and I think...well, I think I believe him." I braced myself for the blast.

Quincy sat back. His Adam's apple bobbed. "And you're planning on putting this in the book?"

"I don't know yet."

He covered his eyes. "Holy sh—have you talked to any of his former bandmates? Didn't you tell me two of them are still alive?"

I nodded, surprised at his calm reaction. "Yeah, I think Ricky's still playing music out in LA, and I don't know about Blacky. I tried to call both. Neither have responded. I think Riff mentioned that Blacky had changed his name and left the music business altogether." I cocked my head. "Why aren't you laughing or making fun of me or saying it's ridiculous?"

Quincy poured himself another glass of wine. "Because...strangely, this is the second time I've heard that term this week. Sirens." He shook his head. "I also heard it from a Nashville musician I'm representing. He's writing an autobiography too. But this word—siren—was in the treatment he sent over. When I read it, I was like—uh, no. You can't write about that."

I felt my mouth drop open. "Who? Who is it?"

He eyed me regretfully. "Sorry, kiddo. You know I can't tell you that."

A thread of hope welled in me. "You couldn't even ask him if he'd consider talking to me? We don't have to meet in person. I could just chat with him over the phone."

Quincy's eyebrows knitted together. "So, you believed Riff's story? About the sirens?"

"I did."

"What are we talking about here? Mermaids or just a bunch of singing women?"

"I don't know what they are." I could tell Quincy Riff's theories and Nona's stories, but it would all sound like hearsay and superstition. I *really* wanted to talk to Quincy's client.

"Please." I held his eyes for a few seconds longer. "I would appreciate it if you'd ask your client—see if he'll talk to me."

He nodded. "I'll try, kiddo. All right? Listen, call me later, okay? I'm worried about you."

25

At home, I perched on the couch, flipped on the television, and watched a few seconds of the midday news before switching to my streaming apps. I rechecked my phone, hoping Riff might have texted. He hadn't.

Instead, there was another run-on text from my dad.

Thanks for at least thinking about it, doll. I know there's a lot to talk about a lot to say so let me know what you decide

I tossed the phone on the couch beside me, picked up the remote, and clicked the icon for StreamandGo. I scrolled through the new programming in the documentaries, my favorite thing to watch. As I skated through true crime and serial killer selections, my eye caught the familiar band logo for Episodic Noise. The new documentary was out. What timing.

As I hovered my thumb over the play button, the preview ran one of their most famous songs, "Under the Waves." Video footage of Lila SilverLeaf and a voiceover from one of her bandmates played.

"Lila was the heart of Episodic Noise. After she disappeared, none of us knew where to go." Concert shots showed Lila at the piano. Then, the film cut to the band at the Grammy Awards.

The preview ended. I watched it again. Finally, I clicked the play button to roll the whole thing.

The documentary highlighted Lila and the guitarist—the only two original band members who had stuck together through the years of touring and shifting sounds. It delved into their childhoods, showing old videos of each playing instruments as children—Lila's piano recitals and battles of the bands in high school.

An hour and a half in, the mood of the documentary shifted. Photos of Riff filled the screen. My stomach dropped. Even seeing his face again addled me. Had it only been two days since we'd kissed? Quincy had read me like a book. He knew me too well.

When the documentary finished, I sat for a few minutes, thinking. Maybe after Lila found out about Riff's infidelity, she'd been so broken up that she left. But would she have left everything? Her career? Maybe if she was afraid for her life. Riff had said he'd told her about the contract and Kirka but not the sirens. On the other hand, Zeke seemed to think she'd been coaxed into the sea. I'd heard those voices and knew how powerful they could be.

Next to me, my phone lit up with a call from Quincy.

Crunching something and smacking his lips, Quincy told me he'd spoken with his client. "He's willing to talk to you."

"He is?" I moved across the room to my computer. "That's great, Quincy. Really great. Thanks so much for asking him. Where? When? Can you tell me his name now?"

Quincy continued to chew. "I've got his number. You set up the meeting and all that. I'm out of it now. It's Wally Lux."

Wally Lux. A fuzzy, vaguely familiar name. A quick search on the internet revealed that he was an older bluegrass musician who often played the Opry and Ryman Auditorium. Certainly not a big name anymore, but he'd been successful in his day.

"Look, the guy's in his late seventies now, so keep that in mind when you talk to him."

"What are you saying? He's senile or something?"

"No, but he's had some health problems."

"I see."

"I hope you get what you need."

Me too. Even so, it was hard to imagine white-haired Wally entering into a blood bond with sirens.

I disconnected the call with Quincy and dialed the number he'd given me for Wally Lux. I expected to get his voicemail, but he answered.

"Hi Wally, I'm Callisto Rowe. I'm a friend of Quincy's and—"

"Yeah, I know who you are." Wally's voice shook.

"Oh, good."

"The bear," he said.

"Excuse me?"

"I remember Callisto from the Greek myth. Hera turned Callisto into a bear because she'd messed around with her man, Zeus."

I laughed. "You and my mother could have been great friends."

He chuckled a little, but it was a dark sound. "I've had to learn a lot about mythology over the last several decades."

"So you know why I'm calling."

"Yes," he said. "I know. You want to meet."

"Or we can talk now on the phone."

"No, I'd rather meet. Why don't you come my way? There's a diner called Rosie's just outside the city before you reach Brentwood. It gets real crowded around lunchtime, and I have some doctors to see at two. So let's say four? We'll beat the dinner crowd."

"I appreciate you talking to me."

"Gotta talk to someone," he said in a low voice.

ON MY DRIVE TO THE diner the following afternoon, I called Riff. I hadn't gotten a text from him since I first returned from the island, and I was starting to worry. The phone went straight to his voicemail. I didn't leave a message. Maybe after everything that had happened the other night, he was hesitant to talk to me. I couldn't blame him.

The diner was located at the bottom of a high-rise hotel, not far from the interstate. The chalkboard sign told me to seat myself, so I found a booth and felt it buckle beneath me as I slid across the blue vinyl. The diner was old—the counter full of truckers and people who'd probably been eating there since its inception. Maybe the food was good, or the locale was nostalgic and historic, but the place looked like it hadn't been properly cleaned in a few years. Dust and dirt particles caked the booth's base and a grease veneer shellacked the laminated menus.

The server asked if I'd like to order anything while I waited, and I quickly scanned the menu for alcohol.

"Do you have any beer or anything?"

She pushed her pen into place above her ear. "Sorry, sweetie. We recently lost our liquor license and can't serve alcohol."

I could taste my disappointment. "That's too bad. I could use a drink."

"Me too," she said.

My eyes trailed above her head to a white and red sign: No smoking.

Well, crap.

I stared at the thin gray lines drawn where the woman's eyebrows should be. "I guess I'll just get a black coffee."

She nodded and her tennis shoes squeaked as she pivoted and walked away.

Through the dirty tear-streaked window beside me, I glimpsed a truck stop across the street. Truckers dropped from their rigs and walked stiff-legged to the gas pumps. Bending to the right and the left, they stretched their backs after a long haul. This would have been Riff's lot had he not become a rock star. He could have lived his life—maybe in suburbia with the three kids he mentioned when I first talked to him. He wouldn't have been under the threat of these creatures. Of course, I wouldn't have met him. And that might have been for the best.

It was a relief when Wally finally arrived and swung into the booth opposite me.

He wore a bandana around his forehead, and his crown was covered with a closely cropped stubble of gray hair.

He shrugged out of his leather jacket. "I know. I look like a member of a motorcycle gang." He motioned to the red cloth around his head. "Please excuse this, but I had some cancerous lesions on my head." The corners of his eyes crinkled as he smiled. "A side effect of being mostly bald and out in the sun too much, I expect."

He reached across the table to shake my hand. I felt his fingers against my palm, calloused and slightly bent as though he might have arthritis. A tattoo of a black panther on his forearm. No green or blue swirls.

"I'm sorry."

He raised his eyebrows. "What, that I'm bald?"

"About the lesions."

"Oh, yeah, well, those are the least of my worries right now." His voice shook as badly as I remembered from our brief phone call.

The server finally arrived and set a stainless-steel carafe of coffee and a smaller one of cream in front of us before taking a pad of paper out of the front of her apron that looked like it had been in the back room since this place opened. She flipped to a fresh yellow page.

Wally ordered a hamburger. For once, I wasn't hungry. I looked at their desserts—desperate for something with chocolate. Chocolate was the only thing that would keep me from wanting a cigarette. New York-style cheesecake or apple pie were the choices. I ordered the cheesecake.

"Oh, and can you drizzle some chocolate on that?" I asked. "If you have some Hershey's syrup or something?"

Her eyes rested on me. Then she nodded and moved toward the kitchen.

The corner of Wally's lips turned up.

"Everything's better with chocolate," I said.

"I agree."

I tapped my fingers on the tabletop. "I assume you know what I want to talk about."

Wally nodded and poured cream into his coffee. Then he lifted a half-bent metal spoon and stirred. "Quincy said we have a shared interest." He looked up at me with pale blue eyes. "The singing stalkers."

Singing stalkers. Water witches. Night singers. Sirens. "How long have they been following you?"

Wally let out a stream of air, his eyes turning toward the ceiling. "Let's see. I guess it's been about forty years now."

"Forty years?"

"Yeah, that's when they first came knocking at my door all hours of the night." He let his spoon clatter into the saucer. "It started long before that, of course. The real beginning of the story goes back some fifty years when I signed with a record label."

Sounded familiar. His story was similar to Riff's. Wally had played clubs around Nashville with a bunch of "pickers" when he was approached by a record label who presented him with a contract, which he'd signed without fully understanding what he was agreeing to.

"I saw all that money. That was it, really. I mean, this woman was promising me the moon *and* the sun. She told me I'd be bigger than Johnny Cash, Merle Haggard, and Tammy Wynette." He shook his head, chuckled.

"What was her name?"

"Her name was Love Carisi. She was part owner of a record label nobody had ever heard of at the time. Goddess Records."

So, not Kirka Taylor.

"And I'll be honest, it was the 60s, and I was smoking a fair bit of funny stuff, and I was pretty entranced by this woman. I mean, there was just something about her. Long black hair and these bright green eyes." He formed his hands like goggles around his eyes. "She was something. You've heard people say they felt bewitched when they did this or that. Well, that's how I felt after my first few encounters with Love. I'd do anything she asked. Including signing that contract."

Wally's story sounded just like Riff's. Seductress drew him in, promised him the world. Obviously, Kirka Taylor wasn't the only siren doing business.

"When did you realize what you'd signed?"

He grimaced and rubbed the cloth on his head. "It took a few years. 'Cause at first, it was just like she said. I was playing the Opry, travelin', tourin', selling tons of albums, and making lots of money. But just a few years in, I woke up one day and realized I hadn't had one thought that was my own. My life wasn't my life. The record label owned me." He leaned forward, folded his hands together, and practically whispered. "I could hardly take a shit without these people telling me which toilet to use. I'll bet it was the same for your friend. The person Quincy said you were writing about."

I'd already decided to leave my experience with Riff out of the equation and not reveal his identity. "Yes, my client told me a similar story to yours."

He nodded. "They're all the same. I've come across others in my years who have endured the fate. Most of 'em ain't alive no more."

I sat back and allowed my hands to fall into my lap. "How have you stayed alive?"

His gaze slid to the side. "Well, like I said, a few years in, I figured out what was what, knew I'd made a huge mistake. And then I went to a lawyer to see how I could get out of that contract."

The server arrived and set my cheesecake in front of me. I looked down at the red drizzle—like someone had opened an artery all over my dessert.

"I guess they didn't have chocolate," Wally said.

I tamped down a wave of irritation as I pushed the plate away. "So, what did the lawyer say?"

"Well, he was a smart man. A savvy man. He'd been in the industry a long-ass time. Said he'd seen contracts like this before. And there were ways to get out of them, but there was one problem."

"What was that?" I held my breath.

"No matter which way we used to squeeze out of it, he'd never seen anyone who'd signed a contract like this who was ever completely free."

I exhaled. "So, are you saying there's no way out of this for anyone? Ever?" I put my elbows on the table and my chin on my clasped hands. "I don't accept that there's no way out of this. There has to be."

He sat back. "The lawyer told me he could technically get me out of the contract, but in his experience, it was only *really* null and void if one of the parties died. And usually, that was the contracted party."

My insides plummeted. I'd longed to hear something from Wally that would offer a thread of hope. He made it sound as hopeless as Riff had.

Wally took a bite of his burger and chewed, darting his eyes around the diner. "So, I told him to do what he could. First, he tried to renegotiate the contract with the record label. They wouldn't budge. Then, we offered money to buy me out of the contract, but they're not interested in money. I mean, they are, but what they're really interested in is having complete and utter control. They don't just want you to give them money of your own free will. No, they want to steal it. That's what makes them happy. Love Carisi had one goal for me, and it wasn't for me to be bigger than Merle Haggard. No, her goal was to destroy me."

I shook my head. It didn't make sense. "But why?"

"They're predators, ma'am. Plain and simple. Why does a bully go beat on someone half his size? Why does a hawk grab smaller birds? It's just what they do."

"What did you do?"

"Only thing I could do. I breached the contract. I gave up music altogether, moved to Maine, holed up in a fishing village, and worked a lobster boat."

Wally's gaze slid toward the window. The truck stop's lights cast neon shapes onto the glass. More truckers poured into the diner and filtered up to the counter.

Wally finished his burger, wiped his fingers on his napkin. "But then one day, I saw this girl peering in my window."

A chill sliced through me.

Wally pretended like he was opening an imaginary door. "I walked outside, asked her what she was doing, what she wanted. She told me to listen. And then I heard the singing. As soon as I heard the singing, I knew what the hell was happening. I ran back inside and locked the door. I knew then that they'd come for me. The terms of the contract were clear." He sat back and placed his hands on the table. "The next day, I packed up and moved to Nebraska, thinking I'd go somewhere that was nowhere near any water. It took 'em about six months to find me there. Then I moved to Montana, Wyoming, down to Arkansas. Finally, back to Nashville. That was in 1985. I been here ever since."

"And they're still stalking you?"

He nodded. "Well, until I was fixin' to write this book they didn't come around all that much. Probably 'cause they know how near death I am. Dead things have a lot less interest to them. They're not buzzards, you know. The last few weeks, I've been hearing and seeing them a lot more." He inhaled slowly. "But I have my life. I keep my personal relationships loose, don't wanna endanger anyone else. I still play music, bluegrass mostly—the sirens hate bluegrass."

I thought about Nona's spirituals she'd sung to keep them at bay.

"Why bluegrass?"

He pointed at his ear. "Something about the frequency of the music. They can't abide with bluegrass—all those high-pitched fiddles playin', I reckon."

Zeke had said certain frequencies could affect the body. Could the same be true with sirens?

Wally continued. "The song they sing—that's not what gets to people. It's something about the frequency they sing in." He circled his hand around his head. "It does something to the mind. I call them the demon tones. And of course, they sing at night—in the dark—when their sound travels farther and slower. But I guess you know that." He reached behind him and grabbed his leather jacket, shook it out. "Look, honey, I gotta be going."

"Oh, of course." It would be dark soon. "Don't worry about the bill, Wally. I'll get this."

Wally shoved his arms into his jacket. "Listen, I know your friend is probably scared shitless to spill the beans about all this. I been scared about it too 'cause you know the worst thing is to tell people about it."

I nodded. "Yes, so I've heard."

"But sometimes you gotta stand up and say something. Even if it costs your life. And I know that's easy for me to say 'cause I'm old, but if we don't tell the world about what happened to us, more will go down the same path. If we can save a few others...then who knows, maybe one day someone will find a way to kill those assholes." He shook his head. "That'll be a day to celebrate. Like finding the cure for cancer."

I watched him through the window as he left. He'd survived all these years against these creatures, moving from place to place. But I worried for him like I worried for Riff. Nona had said the sirens were travelers, and all it would take would be one slip-up. One night of leaving doors unlocked or going out after midnight. In many ways, it was best to do what Riff had done. Stay in one place. If that was the case, then maybe I should return to the island, and Riff and I could figure this out together.

27

I drove home, chain-smoking cigarettes with the window down. A light rain fell, spattering my arm and the side of my face. With the radio off, the silence in the car was broken only by the bump of the windshield wipers—strangely soothing.

Was there really no way out of this contract? Was Riff doomed to live the rest of his life relegated to an island, growing old and alone with only the occasional visit from someone who cared enough to put themselves at risk?

It was dark when I arrived back at the apartment, and I was exhausted. The parking lot was deserted and the streetlights cast eerie, oblong shapes that shimmered on the wet pavement. Images Riff had created for me crept through my head—ones of women standing under such lights, waiting for him when he got home. But I was the only soul out here, which made it even creepier.

I climbed out of my car and pressed down on my fob. The telltale blip of the car locking cut through the unnerving stillness of the parking lot. Where were all the city noises that usually gave me comfort? Suddenly it was like I was back on the island with only the noise of the crickets. Holding my breath, I darted across the lot, and grasping the iron railing, slick from rain, I raced up the steps. My adrenaline pumped as I looked around, almost expecting to see someone standing in the breezeway, watching me. Inside my condo, I slammed the door shut, locked it, and slumped against the adjacent wall. I closed my eyes and pinched them. A headache pushed at the backs of my eyes. It was time for that drink and some TV. Sound.

That's what I needed to hear. People's voices, even if they were on the television.

"Hey, over here." Not the television. The voice came from inside my condo.

The shock was painful, sending a blast of cold sweat and fear through me. I craned my neck and looked over my shoulder. A shadowy figure stood at the far end of the apartment.

Like I was in a dream, the scream that I wanted to push from my throat lodged there instead. It was as though my larynx was paralyzed.

The shadow moved into the light. The man's head was higher than the top of my kitchen cabinets. Shirtless, he held his arms in arcs next to his side, his tattooed skin glistening with water. Slung low on his hips, his linen pants tapered down to bare feet, which he began to shuffle toward me.

I clutched at my throat, unable to breathe until the shriek I'd so longed to expel burst out of me and echoed in the rafters overhead. Ripping open the door, I fell into the breezeway and forced my legs to move along the landing and down the steps. My foot slid off the last one, skinning the back of my calf. And I kept running, not stopping until I reached my car.

Then, I called the police. I didn't know what else to do.

ALTHOUGH CALLING THE police felt useless, it had been a reflex—something that one would do when their life was still operating in the normal, the natural. But maybe, just maybe, this was a natural occurrence and had been a human intruder. Yes, I'd just been spooked after researching sirens for the past two weeks and learning how they'd stalked Riff and Wally.

Except what about the man's tattoos? Unless I'd imagined them, the design was unmistakable. Blue and green swirls. Ocean waves.

I waited in the car, my eyes glued to the glowing entryway to my condo. It took the police nearly ten minutes to arrive, and when they did, I led the two female officers up the stairs to my loft, explaining that I had just returned and walked in to find a man standing in my kitchen.

The officers stepped into the loft with the nonchalance of someone walking into a clothing store. "Any idea how he got in?" They ducked inside and flipped on the overhead light. A dim glow spilled across the threshold.

"No. My door was locked."

I moved inside and flipped the deadbolt, but I kept my hand on the knob in case I needed to run again. A few seconds later, the gray-haired officer reappeared from the back of my condo.

"No one here." She pointed. "But your sliding glass door is open."

"What?" I stepped inside and peered at the open door leading to my balcony. How had that happened? Had I left it unlocked? I never did that. But I had been outside on the balcony the night before drinking whiskey. Maybe I'd had a tad too much. I hadn't been myself. Maybe I'd neglected to lock it. Stupid, stupid, careless!

I didn't move. "You're sure there's no one in there."

She shook her head, eyeing me. "The place is clear."

I took a few steps away from the door, my heart fluttering as I played my eyes across the spot where the tall man had been standing. The younger officer, a dark-skinned woman whose badge read *Thakor*, scribbled on a pad of paper as she took the report.

I went through the motions and answered their questions, told them what they wanted to know.

"They didn't take anything?" asked Officer Thakor. "At least not that you know of?"

I shook my head. "Only my peace of mind." Even if I scoured my drawers, cabinets, and closets, I knew I would find everything in its place. Again, I thought of the man's extraordinary height, the designs on his arms. He had to have been one of them. If that was the case, the sirens hadn't come here to rob me. They had come to watch me, follow me, kill me. But why?

Oh come on, Callie. You know why.

Thakor nodded. Then she jerked her head toward the gray-haired officer. "Officer Willis and I will be patrolling the area for the rest of the night. We can be here in no time if you see anything suspicious."

Officer Willis eyed me with the look that a scolding mother might give her daughter. "In the meantime, keep your doors locked. All of them."

28

Instead of drinking whiskey as I'd planned, I made a pot of coffee and decided to stay awake until daylight. Sleeping was out of the question. Unconsciousness was carelessness in this situation. Each minute that passed brought me one step closer to the freedom of the light.

I turned up the television as loud as I could without disturbing my neighbors and switched on every lamp. Then I sat in the chair facing the sliding glass door, clutching my container of pepper spray.

Ten o'clock strolled to its completion.

Midnight passed with an interminable crawl.

Despite the coffee, as my adrenaline began to subside, my eyes were desperate to close. Had the man followed me after I met with Wally? Or was this a consequence of my time with Riff? I had a feeling it was the latter—because I was telling his story.

I nodded off briefly around two o'clock, my head dropping onto my chest, the sounds of voices on the television taking on a faraway cadence as if speaking from another galaxy.

The brash vibration of the doorbell brought my head up with a gasp.

"No," I whispered. Not again.

The door rattled with more pounding. Riff's tale about the women banging at his door day and night buzzed through my brain. Slowly, I rose from the chair and moved toward it, still clutching my pepper spray.

Boom-boom-boom. The panel shook with each violent strike. Someone was kicking it.

"What do you want? I'm calling the police."

"Listennnnn..." A voice from the other side of the door hissed, echoing through the breezeway.

I pressed my fingers to my temples. They were back. What should I do? What could I do? I'd been here before. *Don't open the door. They can't come through a locked door.*

The television squawked news about a local murder. People were murdered in Nashville every day—some of them on their own doorstep.

Zeke's words returned to me: "One of 'em came to the door one night. I didn't let her in though...The women that sing. They stalk you before they kill you."

My heart throbbing, I moved away from the entrance.

Then I heard it. Singing. Coming from the back of the building.

I moved to the sliding glass door and stood there, suspended, with my fingers pressed against the glass and leaving sweaty streaks. I didn't dare go out there. But I had to. I had to see what I was facing. I lifted the latch and slid the door back. As I stepped out, the cool, damp night air draped over my face like a caul. The rain still fell, splattering off the railing and dancing across my skin. I glimpsed the manmade pond that sat in the middle of the complex—a nod to green space in an urban environment, even though two large green dumpsters sat ten feet from the creation.

The exterior lighting illuminated the pond in hues of green and blue, and amid the waters—dimpled with rain—were four, five, six women clad in white, emerged up to their waists. They were singing. It was a low din—something between the sound that whales make and a Gregorian chant. It seemed impossible that humans could sing like that. It was beautiful, mesmerizing—just as it had been on the island. I stood for several minutes, unable to move, listening to the chorus. Their pale faces practically glowed in the flickering lights. Their mouths open, forming perfect ovals, like those Hummel porcelain figurines of carolers my mother used to put out at Christmas.

My fear slipped away, but an ache deep in my chest began to travel through my body. No, I couldn't allow myself to be entranced by them. Riff's voice cut through the song, almost like he was standing beside me. "Don't listen to them, Callie!"

Forcing my fingers to the side of my head, I pressed the flap of skin against the opening of my ear canal, muting the sound.

Just then, a man lumbered toward the pond. I didn't recognize him. Was he someone who lived here? Or an early morning maintenance worker? Dressed in a long-sleeved T-shirt and jeans, his dark hair slick with rain, he approached the pond as though a string were attached to his chest, pulling him.

"No!" I called out, my voice eclipsing the low hum of the sirens. "Stop! Block your ears. Run!"

Even though I pressed mine shut, a whisper of sustained pitch soared above the others like a freight train.

Wind whipped across the lawn and the pond, denting the waters and tumbling a plastic trash can. Paper towels, empty cups, bags of fast food rolled like tumbleweeds into the pool.

"Run!" I called out again.

The dumpster lids exploded open. An arm and then a leg appeared as the women emerged from the receptacles like sewer rats. With glowing red eyes and open, gaping mouths, they gathered—two, three, four of them. In slow, mechanical movements, they closed in on their prey.

"No!" I screamed.

A dark horizontal curtain hovered over the man, but he seemed not to notice at first. Then, he tilted his head and gazed at what was above him. The mass began to take shape. Legs dropped down tipped with sharp talons that sank into his shoulders. Flowing wings cut through the air, forming a canopy over the man and the other approaching women.

The man's cry pierced the barrier of my stopped ears as the shadowy, bird-like creature lifted him into the air. He kicked his legs, thrashed his arms, but the massive demon bird hoisted and carried him.

The women standing below formed a circle, their arms reaching up as they shouted and shrieked in triumph.

The flying demon hovered over the sirens and slowly deposited the man into their midst. His screams rose above all the other voices as the talons released him, and he fell into the circle.

The women stopped singing. They descended on him, bowing over him until no part of him was visible except one kicking foot.

I whirled around and fell inside, sliding the glass door across its silver tracks until it slammed shut. Then I locked it. My panicked breathing choked out all other sounds as I scrambled to my purse and, with shaking hands, pulled out the box with the earplugs Riff had given me. Pushing them into my ears, I made my way back to the sliding door, dreading what I might see. I stood on my tiptoes, my hands shaking as I pressed them against the glass, my breath fogging it.

At the far edge of the pond, the sirens moved away from each other, wiping the backs of their hands across their mouths and licking their lips. Only a dark, wet stain marked the ground where the man had been minutes before. The flying, taloned creature had also disappeared. Soon, the creatures were gone, seemingly evaporating as they moved out of view. Satiated, they'd moved on.

The world continued to turn on its axis. It was like nothing had happened. It was as if that poor man had never existed.

I pulled the curtain across the glass.

My plugged ears were filled with a low frequency, not unlike the waves of the ocean.

As I stared at the four walls of my studio, the place seemed smaller than ever and the thought came to me with an electrical burst: They had come for me. And someone else had died.

Staring into the dark and intermittently peering out the window at the empty, rippling pond, I grabbed my duffel bag from the bedroom area and pushed some clothes into it.

No, it wasn't dawn yet, but as soon as it was, I would go. I couldn't stay here. I would keep moving, just as Wally had done. I didn't understand what any of this meant, but I was too damn scared to think straight. The only place I could go where I wouldn't imperil someone else who wasn't already in danger was Invisible Island. I would go to Riff.

29

I was numb—even though I'd just seen a man killed—devoured—before my eyes and in the most horrific way I could imagine.

My hand shook as I pushed a cigarette between my lips. "That poor man. That poor, poor man."

It was four o'clock in the morning, still dark, but up ahead, traffic slowed. My GPS warned me of an accident that had spread over several lanes and backed up for miles traveling out of the city.

The users on my navigation software left comments about a small plane that had crashed near the road, scattering debris across the highway. The emergency road crew was still trying to clear the area.

I was blocked on all sides. Nothing to do but sit and wait. And by waiting, I was standing still and not on the move. Breathing in and out. Listening to the air fill and leave my lungs. Relishing the smell of smoke, car exhaust. How much longer would I be able to do that simple, physical act?

I was so tired I felt like I was hallucinating, questioning the reality of everything around me. Was I really here? Or was I dead and didn't realize it yet?

I grabbed my phone off the passenger seat and called Riff's number.

He picked up. "Hey, Callie. Sorry I didn't get your call yesterday. My phone reception has been acting up."

I hardly knew what to say. I couldn't talk about what I'd seen a few hours before, couldn't allow those images into my mind. Not yet.

"It's good to hear your voice," I said.

"Are you all right? You don't sound good."

I wiped the back of my hand under my nose before fishing through my glove compartment for a napkin. "I'm fine," I sniffed. "I'm just so glad to talk to you," I repeated. Even though I'd tried to keep an upbeat tone, my voice broke.

"Callie, what's going on? Something's wrong. I can tell. You sound scared."

I watched the police ahead motioning cars into the right lane. "I am scared."

"Where are you?"

"I'm on I-24. Sitting in traffic. There's been an accident. But I'm coming to the—"

"Are you hurt?"

"No, no." Not yet. "But I'm coming back to the island, Riff. I'm on my way to you now."

Silence.

"I just saw a man murdered."

More silence.

"Riff? Riff?"

I looked down at my phone. I'd lost him. "Damn!"

I put on my blinker, moved to the right lane, and followed the line of cars past the traffic cops diverting the route. Smoking red flares illuminated a girl with straggly blonde hair wearing jeans and a saturated peasant blouse standing next to the man in blue who waved his arms and directed us to move. The blaze lit up the dark tattoos that wound around her bare arms like wet snakes.

The girl followed me with her eyes as I drove past. I gripped the wheel harder.

A quarter of a mile up, next to the orange and white barriers erected to keep cars away from the glass and metal carnage of the accident, was the same shirtless man I'd seen in my condo. Twice the size of the police motioning cars through, he eyed me from underneath a hulkish brow, looking down on my car from a crow's nest height. I slammed on my brake, nearly plowing into the person in front of me. As I spun the wheel, my tires squealed, and I careened onto the shoulder.

Huffing out air, I righted the car's direction and turned on my blinker. Finally, someone waved me into the line, and I pulled back onto the road, following the others in a slow crawl.

"Breathe, Callie, breathe. Do not lose it. It will be dawn soon."

Another forty-five minutes and traffic rolled forward, picking up speed just as the inky sky transformed into silver—slivers of smoky gray clouds in the distance illuminated by a full moon. I was on my way.

My rearview mirror flared with headlights, and I squinted into it. Slowing, I waited for the person to pass. Instead, they drew closer, their lights disappearing as they nearly touched my bumper.

I slammed my hands against the wheel. They were following me now, trying to run me off the road.

I moved into the left lane.

So did they.

I moved back into the right lane.

So did they.

I stepped on the gas pedal and accelerated. Weaving in and out between trucks and cars, I willed myself to lose the vehicle behind me, but it stayed just a few feet away, easily maneuvering through traffic.

Then, almost as suddenly as the car had appeared, it dropped back, the headlights growing increasingly distant. Soon, more vehicles joined me on the highway, and the car's lights became indistinguishable from the others.

I breathed out. Maybe it was a drunk driver or a road rager. But I knew better. Gone were the days of me being able to chalk up strange occurrences to bad luck or bad drivers. I was a marked woman.

They stalk you before they kill you.

Up ahead, a ray of hope. The silver clouds were slowly turning a shade of pink. Above them, a ridge of orange. Daylight had come to save the day.

30

That afternoon, I took the ferry to Invisible Island. I didn't bother to contact Riff. I knew he'd be angry with me for coming back, but I was pissed at him too. I'd had a seven-hour drive to process everything that had happened. I'd moved past the terrified stage into an anger I hadn't accessed in years.

Had Riff known this would happen? Had he known that by interacting with me and asking me to write his story, I might fall victim to the same creatures that plagued him? He had to have known. Lila's absence not even a year after their marriage had most likely resulted from the same. He was like a man with a deadly infection—and I had caught it.

Sitting below deck, I watched through the salt-crusted windows as dolphins leaped rhythmically in the wake as if hearing their own music

I shouldn't even be here. I should be far away from water and on the run just as Wally had been for years. But I refused to live like that—always moving, hopping from one town to another, always looking over my shoulder. From the beginning, I had pitied Riff for his imprisonment and complete isolation. I already knew what it was to live in loneliness. Maybe that was why I was here now—a fear of living with no connection to any other living thing. I couldn't live like that. And neither could Riff.

The ferry slowed as we approached the landing, its motor churning. Once we dropped anchor and came to a standstill, I clamored on deck and onto the dock accompanied by a dozen others. With my duffel bag over one shoulder and my laptop case over the other, I began the long trek down the dock to land, where I was to catch my hired ride—an actual vehicle rather than a golf cart.

Davis, my driver, was in his early sixties and lived in Savannah but ran the business of transporting tourists in the summer. "Yeah, we get a lot of bird watchers here, people interested in Muskogee history, the Gullah culture. There's a lot going on here. It has many stories to tell."

I wanted to laugh. *You ain't kidding. This isn't my first safari.*

Davis was a retired veteran trying to live a quiet life with his wife. He wore his Army baseball cap low over mirrored sunglasses. "I saw combat three times. Don't miss that. But part of me loved the adrenaline—back in the day. Part of me still does, I guess."

He met my eyes in the rearview mirror. "How long you planning to stay?"

Maybe an hour—long enough to inform Riff he had ruined my life. Or maybe longer. "I don't really know."

"You know there's a storm blowing in?"

I shook my head. I hadn't been watching the news. I'd been too busy running from mythological creatures that wanted to kill me. "No. I hadn't heard."

"Yeah. Hurricane Matthew coming from Haiti. Supposed to be bad if it stays on its current trajectory."

Great. As usual, my timing couldn't have been worse. "I—I didn't know."

"Yeah, keep your eye on it. There's even mention of mandatory evacuation. So if you're not paying attention, you might get a knock at the door, telling you you've got an hour to get your things and go."

Mandatory evacuation? Then Riff would have to leave too.

Davis reached over to the passenger seat and riffled some papers. "You're going to Turtle Dove Way, right?"

"No, to Belle Marsh."

Again, his mirrored sunglasses flashed in the rearview. "Belle Marsh? Really?"

"Yep."

"Riff Fall's house?"

"Yes. Do you know him?"

He blew air through his teeth. "I know of him. Can't say I've ever met him. I know a guy who knows him. But I think most people around here pretty much steered clear after his wife disappeared. Lots of folks feel like... Well, it's usually the husband, isn't it?"

I said nothing.

"So, what's the connection for you? How well do you know him?"

Good question. How well *did* I know him? "I'm a friend. Plus, I'm helping him with a project."

"Oh. Are you a musician?"

"No," I said. "A writer."

"Ah." He turned down an unpaved road. "What's he like?"

I didn't quite know what to say. Because when I thought back on my week with Riff, I couldn't think of anything but how much I'd enjoyed being with him. "Riff's an unusual guy."

"I'll bet." He waved to a group passing by us in a golf cart. "Keep your eyes peeled while you're here. Hurricane like this one's nothing to mess around with."

Davis dropped me off at Belle Marsh's gate. I climbed out and slung my bags over my shoulder. "Thank you for the lift."

"Like I said, be careful."

Be careful. That would be the motto of my life now. I'd have to think about every move and every person I came in contact with.

As I walked up the path toward Belle Marsh, I looked up at the house and all its eyes. "You knew, didn't you?" I asked the structure. *All this time, you've been laughing at me, mocking me, knowing I'd end up here again.*

The archway leading to the front door opened wide, waiting to devour me.

How different it was arriving this time—unannounced, terrified, full of despair and fury at the man who had caused this earthquake in my life.

The front door opened and Riff appeared wearing a loose-fitting button-down shirt with the sleeves rolled up, his brown hair tucked behind his ears. He slumped against the doorframe as I approached. "What the hell are you doing here? There's a hurricane coming."

His dark eyes searched mine with casual curiosity and maybe a sliver of alarm. Emotion flooded me. My face burned. My fists knotted. I wanted to pummel him. "I could kill you," I said through clenched teeth. As I spoke the words, fear drilled deep into me at the intensity of my rage.

He straightened. "What's going on?"

I swept past him and slung my laptop case and duffel bag against the base of the stairwell.

The words tumbled from my mouth. "They're after me now, Riff. They're following me. You knew this would happen, didn't you?"

His forehead lined, his eyes darting side to side as if trying to comprehend what I was saying.

"They've been stalking me since I first contacted you about writing this book. And now—" I flapped my arms. "They're everywhere. And last night, I watched them devour a man." The breath caught in my throat. "It was the most horrible thing I've ever seen. How could you do this to someone else? To me? To Lila."

His eyes darkened as he stared at me, but I could tell that in his mind he saw something far away. Slowly, he turned from me and faced the mirror hanging above the hall table.

"Do you hear what I'm saying, Riff?" I barely recognized my shrill, cracking voice. "Do you understand what you've done? I mean—" I huffed out a dark laugh. "You can pretend you don't know what happened to Lila, but you *know*. I saw it happen to that man last night—right in front..." My words trailed off as my throat closed over.

He raised his eyes until he looked at himself in the mirror. His voice was thick. "I wish I'd died when I jumped from that balcony in Savannah."

"Yeah, well, I do too." The words were harsher than any blow I could have dealt him, and in that moment, I meant them.

Riff's growl was barely human as he shot out his arm and smashed his fist into the mirror, fragmenting the glass and his reflection. Grabbing the vase on the table, he flung it at the broken mirror, obliterating the object and sending shards of pottery and glass skittering across the table and onto the floor.

He spun away, kicking pieces of the shattered vase out of his path. His cries echoed in the rafters as he stalked into the great room toward the fireplace. He reached for the poker. It rattled as he pulled it from its lodgings.

I held my breath as he wielded the iron, my anger swiftly retreating into fear as he swung the poker at another vase on the banquet table. The fleeting thought that this could be how it all ended for me pushed a stream of adrenaline through my body. Except Riff never wielded it at me but seemed intent on destroying every glass item in the room. The sound of exploding porcelain and pottery filled the space. When he was done, he tossed the poker into the midst of the carnage. The finality of the iron clang against hardwood rang out like a bell.

His shoulders rising and falling, Riff cranked his neck back and turned his face toward the ceiling. The floor and banquet table were riddled with broken eggshell-shaped bits of white pottery and slivers of sparkling glass. Belle Marsh's *Kristallnacht*.

I stood riveted to the spot, not knowing whether to move or say something. I wanted to cry, but the tears wouldn't come. My shoulders hitched up and down like I'd been smashing things alongside him.

Finally, he looked at me and his eyes flared. Then he marched toward me, crunching across the bones of the objects that had once decorated his pristine great room.

I took a step back and then another. Was he coming for me next? I glanced behind me, moving backward until I reached the doorway. I held out my hand. "Riff, no."

His face changed and loosened. The fury subsided, and his eyes dulled with a deep sadness. He ceased his advance, and then, as if his legs had betrayed him, he dropped to his knees, his head bowed, his shoulders still heaving.

My anger ebbed as my scrambled brain tried to take in this moment—Riff kneeling at my feet, broken. His right hand and wrist were smeared with blood, and he transferred it to his jeans as he rested his arm against his thigh.

My muscles trembled as I forced my feet to move. I placed a shaking hand on top of his head and felt the heat emanating from his skull. Would Riff be the last person I ever touched, ever got close to?

Allowing my fingers to trail through his hair to his neck, I lifted his face to look into mine. Neither of us said anything. Only our eyes bounced a silent conversation back and forth.

Please stay.

I hate you for doing this to me.

I know.

I'll never forgive you.

I know. I'll never forgive myself. I want to die.

But I don't want you to die. I don't want to be alone in this.

I held my hand out to him and he took it. Placing one foot flat on the floor and then the other, he pulled up. I glimpsed his self-loathing and sensed his understanding that nothing he could say or do would make this okay.

Several spots of blood dotted his cheek, tiny cuts from the flying glass. I reached up and ran my thumb over it, muddling the blood with the sweat. The moment passed in silent slow motion and through the open front door, my ears picked up the sounds of the ocean as it rolled in with the afternoon tide.

Riff leaned toward me and I braced myself for the fall—the cataclysmic surrender of letting him kiss me—our lips meeting and then breaking apart, allowing all the unspoken words to flow through our open mouths as our tongues moved and touched.

He settled one hand into my hair and the other to the side of my face, and I instinctively raised my fingers to rest on his waist—then slid them up to his chest. Every touch and kiss released another wave of longing, sank me deeper into the ocean of uncertainty, and pushed me farther from shore.

Riff ran his hand down the length of my arm until he grasped my fingers. Then, he pulled away from our kiss and led me out of the destroyed room. Down the hall, past the framed generic photos of the ocean, the sky, a seabird, to his bedroom—the room that had in many ways represented the forbidden garden, the inner sanctum. Once inside, he hoisted me, pushing my back against the door as it closed behind us. I wrapped my legs around his waist and he again pressed his mouth to mine. What had started so slowly and silently quickly became feverish. A war roared inside of me. One in which I was swiftly defeated.

I clung to him as he whirled me away from the door and we fell against the adjacent wall, our mouths mashing against one another—teeth against lips, lips against teeth. This might be the last moment of pleasure I ever experienced on this earth. I grabbed the bottom of his T-shirt and yanked it over his head.

As he led me to the bed. I stared at the back of his shoulders, the tattoos that covered both—an angel on one, the kind seen in gothic graveyards, kneeling, hands pressed together, eyes closed. On the other shoulder was a woman's face—black hair and stark blue eyes—Lila. Her name was even written in cursive underneath the image.

Something ground to a halt. This didn't feel right. We shouldn't do this. I should stop him. But I didn't. I followed him to his bed, and when he turned toward me again, his hands reaching for my face, I walked into them.

We toppled onto his white bedspread. His lips found the crook of my neck, and I stared up at the white ceiling, wondering how this story would end. Because, of course, it had to end.

SOMETIME LATER, RIFF slept, and I propped myself on my elbow and stared down at him—his eyes were closed, hair was tucked under his neck, his chest slowly rising and falling. We were still here—still breathing. But we were both being hunted. Marked for death. It could come at any time.

Even so, all the rage and fight had gone out of me. It had slipped away on a tide of passion, leaving me with the darkness as it slowly closed over my head.

Riff's eyes were closed. "Why are you staring at me?" His voice rippled out of his chest as a smile pulled at his lips. "Are you plotting my death?"

"Maybe." I fell back on my pillow.

He opened his eyes. "Who could blame you? Not me."

I exhaled loudly and pulled the sheet under my arms. "What are we going to do, Riff? Before, this was just about you. Now, I'm part of the equation." A fresh wave of dread washed over me. I wasn't sure I could forgive him for pulling me into this, but on the other hand, I'd insisted on coming here to meet and interview him. "We're like walking time bombs."

Riff swiveled his head against the pillow. "I wish somehow—that if I died—it would release you from all of this. Because I gladly would."

My heart softened at the sincerity of his tone. I thought about Wally's words—that he felt the contract would be nullified only by the contracted party's death.

The sheets ruffled as Riff rolled over and pulled me against him. "I'm so sorry, Callie. There's ...no words."

He was right. There weren't.

I traced the green swirl at the base of his left shoulder, wincing as I recalled that on the other side of his body was the tattoo of Lila.

"What about Lila?" I whispered.

His brow furrowed. "She's dead."

I sat up. "How do you know?"

He stared at the ceiling. "It's been too long. She would have turned up by now. Someone would have seen her. Someone would have at least found her body."

If the sirens had taken her, nothing would have been left to find. I'd witnessed that in the final moments of the poor man by the pond.

"And I've just been biding my time ever since she disappeared." Riff's voice was flat. "Maybe it's time I start admitting what I already know—that she's gone. Really gone." He pulled me closer to his body until my lips hovered over his. "Being with you is the first time I've felt happy since she disappeared."

I lowered my mouth to his and wished my feelings for him weren't so intense. It was hard to keep my thoughts straight.

"But..." I sat up again. "What about the contract? Kirka Taylor is no longer the owner or CEO of the record label. The label no longer exists. Don't you think that should mean something? Like maybe the contract isn't even valid anymore?"

He dropped his gaze, his eyes shielded by long eyelashes as his fingers trailed over my collarbone. "Callie, I wish it worked like that, but like I said before, the sirens aren't human. They're monsters. They think like monsters. The contract is just a formality. They don't care about legalities."

"But they can be killed like humans. Their bodies are mortal."

"Yes, but once they're dead, what lived inside them just moves on to find another host. The cycle is never-ending." Pain rippled behind his gaze. "Baby, I wish I could offer you more hope. I wish my will to survive was as strong as yours. But I've lived like this for too long." He looked down at our entangled fingers.

I squeezed his hand. "Well, maybe, just maybe, I can share a little of that will to survive with you."

But in my head, I saw images of ocean waves—each washing in another brigade of water witches—never-ending and unrelenting.

31

That night, after helping Riff clear away shattered remnants of glass and ceramic from his great room, exhaustion and sweat settled over me.

"Let's go to bed," he said finally. "I'll call Esmeralda tomorrow and see if she can come in to clean up the rest of it."

Curled beside Riff, his arm slung across my body, I slept for a few hours. But sometime after three in the morning, I was wide awake and desperate for a cigarette. I sat up, staring into the darkness of an unfamiliar bedroom. Everything rushed back to me—the memory of the man lowered into the circle of sirens, the tall figure hiding in the shadows of my condo, the watchers on the side of the road as I left Nashville. Finally, what Riff and I had shared a few hours earlier melted away some of the chilling images. I wasn't sure what any of it meant or how to make sense of the horror that hung like a cobweb in my heart.

I rose stiffly and dressed, slipping my sneakers on to avoid any spare shards of glass that might have escaped the great room.

While Riff slept, I roamed Belle Marsh. I sat on the screened-in porch with all the panels rolled down and locked and smoked my cigarette, watching the room turn gray with acrid fog. Afterward, I retreated to the music room, where I settled in and wrote for an hour, using some notes I'd gathered from Riff the last time I'd visited. Sirens or no sirens, work still needed to get done. I sat back to read what I'd written.

Tap-tap-tap.

I jerked my head up. They were here. I'd tried to convince myself that maybe they wouldn't bother us anymore. My night with Riff had lulled me into a false sense of security. I pushed off the couch and went to the switch on the wall, extinguishing the light from the room. It was instinct—something my mother used to do when a horrible boyfriend would come by our house. She didn't want him to know we were home. I didn't want the night singers to know I was in here—even though they probably did.

I looked out the cathedral window onto the moonlit scene—the dunes and the beach beyond. The wind was picking up, reminding me a hurricane was on the way. The grasses swayed and flattened against the sand.

I pressed my fingers and forehead to the glass, blinking and letting my eyelashes flutter against the windowpane. Dozens of them spilled over the dunes. The gray, misty forms materialized like ghosts at first, but as they marched, the moonlight revealed their solid bodies—some clothed, some naked. I lifted my head from the glass, my open mouth fogging the pane as I counted them. At least twenty or twenty-five. So many. I'd never seen so many altogether.

They gathered in a line at the top of the dunes, their fingers lightly touching like paper dolls cut from a single sheet of paper. Unmoving, their hair whipping in the wind, they waited...and watched.

So did I, my heart pounding in time with the ticking clock in the darkened room.

After a while, their mouths dropped open, and although I couldn't hear them through the double-paned glass and the whipping wind, I knew their song had begun. This behavior was as familiar, instinctive, and unavoidable as a cricket rubbing its legs together after dark.

I observed them until the daylight began to spread across the dunes, bringing with it a gray dawn that spat rain against the windowpanes.

Finally, the night singers adjourned and turned synchronously, their eyes fixed on the horizon as they slipped into the morning.

I did not return to Riff's bed. Instead, I sat by the window—willing the demonic singers to stay away. And they would, wouldn't they? Now that daybreak was on its way?

Cracking my spine and neck, I paced the gallery of the music room and studied the faces behind the glass of the picture frames. My face reflected beside Riff's in the photo where he and Lila stood together, their arms locked as they leaned toward the camera. Where did I fit in with all this now?

I blinked. My likeness was no longer the only one in the glass. A shadow—dark and tall—forming a head, neck, shoulders—stood right behind me.

I spun around. The room was empty.

Grasping the front of my T-shirt, I breathed out. Nothing there.

Then I heard it. Humming. Low and clear. I whipped my head toward the window, my blood chilling. But the humming was not coming from outside. It was coming from inside the house. It was coming from upstairs.

32

I froze. Were the sirens *inside* Belle Marsh?

Forcing my legs to move, I crossed through the great hall, hyper-aware of every sound. Something gritty crunched under the sole of my shoe as I entered the hallway on the other side—probably a leftover piece of glass or pottery dust. The camera whirred as it followed my movement. I paused at the base of the stairwell and turned on the hall light.

The humming was not the same hypnotic wail that had sent me scrambling for earplugs previously. This was a lone female voice. The stairs creaked as I climbed. The singing swelled as I ascended. At the top of the steps, I flipped the switch that illuminated the upstairs.

A new sound—scratching, like a carving instrument whittling wood or mice inside the walls. I stopped and listened. The scratching and the humming seemed to be coming from the same place. I looked up into the corner of the ceiling. The security camera's black Cyclops eye fixed on me accusingly as I moved past it. Inexplicably, I was pulled toward the alcove at the end of the hall. The closer I drew to the blue door, the louder the voice.

A pit yawned in my gut. Someone was in that room.

I passed the spare bedrooms, the doors gaping open, and stopped in front of the chair that blocked the blue door. I stared at the antique knob, the cross hanging in the middle of the panel, slightly askew. One strip of the blue tape had started peeling away from the right side, either from the damp air or because someone had tried to remove it.

I was done with secrets and locked doors. "Hello?" I called softly.

The scratching slowed and stalled. The vocalizing faded.

I took a step closer, placing my hand on the panel. Grasping both arms of the wicker chair, I scooted it to the side. Then I stepped up to the door and pressed my ear against it. Straining to hear any sound from within, I focused on the floorboards.

A thin gray hand—little more than a shadow—slid from the narrow space between the bottom of the door and the floor. Almost as quickly, it disappeared again. What the hell had I just seen? The thing had darted so quickly—like a snake's tongue. But how could a human arm fit through such a narrow space?

I backed away, my heart galloping.

Seconds later, Riff's footsteps thundered up the steps. "Callie, what's wrong?"

I met him on the landing. "There's someone in there. Who? Who is in that room?"

Riff's face fell, his eyes trailing beyond me.

The idea that Riff had a human imprisoned in that space made him as monstrous as the creatures outside these walls. He must have been the lunatic everyone said he was, after all. What was I doing here with a man I barely knew? I'd slept with him—let into my mind, my body, and my heart.

"What's in that room, Riff?" I repeated, my voice raising.

He eyed me silently for several long seconds before his mouth opened. "Callie, I—"

The doorbell rang.

He wavered, his eyes darting between me and the stairwell. "I think that's Esmeralda. She was going to come by before going to her other job." It was like he was asking permission to let her in.

I squared my jaw. "I want to know what the hell is going on here."

The doorbell rang again.

Riff turned away from me and barreled down the steps.

I stood at the top of the landing, my gaze fixed on the alcove at the end, feeling like my mind might explode.

A few seconds later, I heard the front door creak open, and a female voice chirped. "Good morning, Mr. Riff!"

I replayed what I'd seen. I *had* seen a hand. I was sure of it. Although I couldn't explain how it had fit in the space underneath the door. It must have been the width of a popsicle stick.

My heart still hammering, my hands clammy on the banister, I made my way downstairs. A petite, dark-headed woman entered the great hall with a flurry of heavily accented words. "Oh, Mr. Riff, I hope you don't mind that I'm early, but I have to get to the other side of the island by ten to help Queenie board up the windows on the b and b, and then I'm evacuating this afternoon..." Her words trailed off as her eyes rested on me.

Riff motioned toward me. "Esperanza, this is a friend of mine, Callie."

Esperanza froze in the doorway. She nodded. "Hello."

I gave her a wave, imagining myself from her perspective. My hair was extra frizzy this morning and big as a hydrangea plant in full bloom. Esperanza showed no evidence of hiding her thoughts. Her eyes took in the situation—my disheveled appearance, still dressed in my pajamas—and her verdict quickly appeared in the quirk and purse of her lips.

My immediate thought was that she and Riff had shared a moment once. Maybe more than once.

Riff darted in front of her. "Um, we had a rather extensive situation with a few broken vases. I just wanted to clean up any remaining debris from the floor."

Now Esperanza scanned the room and took several steps inside. "Mr. Riff—where are they all? Your beautiful vases and..." She moved to the wall table. "Oh, no. The sculpture that was here."

Riff cleared his throat. "As I said, there was an incident."

Esperanza turned her eyes on me, her brows bunched together. Oh, wait. She thought I had done it.

Riff interjected. "I think we cleaned up most of the glass and pottery."

Esperanza sighed. "I see." She waved her hands. "I don't judge. None of my business. So, I will sweep, vacuum, make sure there are no pieces left behind."

Riff smiled. "Thank you."

Esperanza motioned at his T-shirt and pajama bottoms. "You should get dressed, Mr. Riff."

And I took that to mean I should as well.

I started for the bedroom but Esperanza skirted in front of me, opened the door to the hall closet, and bent inside, blocking my way.

She spoke into the closet rather than to me or Riff. "I'm surprised you don't have the television on. And why haven't you boarded up any windows yet? You know, Mr. Riff, this storm is supposed to be bad. Most of us are leaving."

She finally dragged the vacuum out and closed the door, her gaze venomous as she glanced at me. I smiled at her as I turned sideways to edge past. She whipped the cord around her hand, her dark eyes following me with a suspicious squint. "You should be packing to go, you know. I don't judge, but I wouldn't be worrying about vacuuming right now." Then she rolled the vacuum toward the great room. "I just do what he tells me."

All my things were in Riff's bedroom anyway. I entered his room and then the ensuite, where water pattered against the shower tile and the mirrors were fogged with steam. I shut the door behind me.

"Tell me, Riff," I said to the white shower curtain, my voice echoing. "I need to know what is going on in that room upstairs."

For a long moment, he didn't answer. When he did, his voice was low, muffled. "Give me until the afternoon, Callie." He spat out water. "Zeke will be here soon. Once he's gone, I'll tell you everything."

In the meantime, something or someone was behind that blue door. I wanted to strip off all the tape and fling it open. But too much had happened—too much I didn't understand. To be honest, I was scared to open that door. I was scared to know what was behind it.

"Will you give me that, please?" Riff asked. "Give me a few hours."

I caught a glimpse of myself in the fogged mirror—sleep-deprived, out of place, and lost.

My eyes seemed to ask, "What are you doing to yourself?" They also said I needed another cigarette.

Still in my pajama bottoms and T-shirt, I carried my phone as I moved through the screened-in porch and outside onto the beach.

After lighting my cigarette, I walked to the front of the house and looked up at the attic window. The sun glared against the glass, obscuring the view of anything behind it.

I pulled up a browser on my phone and tried to get enough reception to read news about the weather. It took forever to bring up articles, let alone videos of weather forecasts, but I managed to glimpse a few headlines. Hurricane Matthew was lashing the Bahamas with winds over 100 miles per hour. It was expected to head toward Florida next.

"Oh, look! Lady Friend is back!"

I raised my head. Zeke was jogging across the sand, toting a guitar case.

My hand flew up to the loose-fitting neckline of my T-shirt. "Zeke. Hi."

He nodded, a big smile stretching across his face. "You came back. Just in time for the storm."

"That's what it seems like."

"Mom says we'll all have to evacuate by tomorrow. Governor's going to issue the order this afternoon." Zeke's eyes remained fixed on me. "Are you going to leave if there's an evacuation?"

"Yes." And maybe even before, with the way things were going.

"Will you take Riff with you?"

I shot a glance toward the house. "I don't know, Zeke."

Zeke gave me his usual unfazed, good-natured smile. "Well, I'm going in. Don't want to be late. Come listen to the lesson if you want."

I watched him trek in through the screened-in porch. No, today I wouldn't sit in.

I finished my cigarette and returned inside, where the vacuum and the electric guitars competed for maximum volume. As I approached the great room, Esmeralda sailed by the door pushing her roaring apparatus. I darted into the security monitoring area.

Black and white images flashed, showing one corner of the house and then the other. I focused on the upstairs monitor as it displayed the black runner carpet and the perfectly set wall tables decorated with stacks of old nautical books and vases like the ones Riff had destroyed the previous day. The upstairs hallway camera captured one side of the hall with its open guest room doors and then rotated toward the other. Another camera remained on the blue door. One strip of blue tape curled on the floor like a dead snake—the piece peeling from the right side this morning. Now it had come off completely.

The vacuum's hum ended. I needed to move. I pulled myself away from my security watch and lurched toward the stairwell.

The hum of rolling wheels across hardwood invaded the hall. With my hand on the banister, I climbed the first step as Esmeralda came through, driving the vacuum back to its stall. She stopped when she saw me, her eyes widening.

I gave her a brief smile and continued up the next few steps.

"I don't go up there," she announced.

I paused. "You don't clean upstairs?"

"Never," she said, her voice echoing a little too loudly. "Mr. Riff says no one uses the upstairs. No need to go up there."

She seemed to challenge me with her eyes as if to imply she was the keeper of the upstairs—or maybe to warn me that she would alert Riff.

I jabbed my finger toward the sky. "I left something up there and need to grab it."

"Hello?" Zeke's voice echoed down the hall. "Hey, Callie, come listen to this."

Esmeralda blinked and shoved the vacuum toward the hall closet.

I hesitated.

"Please," Zeke said. "Just for a minute. I want you to hear this new song Riff taught me."

Although I couldn't see his face from where I stood, Zeke's request was enough to erode my resolve. I exhaled. I'd lost my opportunity. The door would have to wait.

THE LESSON WAS FINALLY over. Not that I hadn't enjoyed listening to Zeke and Riff play together, but the *sturm und drang* in my brain drowned out much of the music. Riff was the first man I'd cared about in years, but caring about him came with a lot of baggage. And questions. And fears. I knew much of what he'd told me was true. After all, I was living in the wake of the sins he'd confessed. But now that my life was on the line, I needed to know everything, starting with what was in that room. I couldn't ignore it any longer.

Zeke looked back and forth between Riff and me. "Is she going to be your new girlfriend?"

My face burned. Red bloomed in Riff's cheeks as well.

Zeke balanced on one foot and attempted to whisper to Riff. "Hey, when we evacuate tomorrow, I think you should go with her."

Riff half-suppressed a smile, then prodded Zeke with his pointer finger, prompting him to move toward the exit.

Zeke resumed his balance on two feet and edged toward the door. "My mother says it's high time you moved on and found someone new."

"You tell your mama to mind her own business." Riff again poked Zeke in the back.

"I tell her that all the time." Zeke stopped beside me in the doorway. He leaned over and whispered, "Guess what I got?"

"What?" I whispered back.

"I got that Rife machine." His eyes sparkled. My mind reeled back to the discussion we'd had about his mother's cancer and his desire to acquire a machine that he felt had a chance of curing it.

I gasped. "You did? How did you manage that?"

He beamed. "Ordered it online. My grandpa gave me the money. He's real old, but he actually thinks it's worth a shot. He doesn't want my mom to die—especially not before he does."

A rare current of tenderness flowed through me at the combined efforts of an old man and his grandson trying to save their respective daughter and mother.

The old Callie would never have believed Zeke's machine would cure his mother's cancer, but now, with all that had happened, I was willing to believe—like Zeke's grandfather—that it was worth a shot. Zeke was a determined young man—filled with hope—and innocent enough to believe anything was possible. So who was I to deny him his dream?

He leaned toward me again. "And you know what else?"

"What?" I whispered again, smiling.

"Since I've been using this machine, I haven't had any visitations from the night singers."

Now he had my attention. "Really?"

He nodded, dimples appearing in his cheeks. "Last night, I saw one of them coming up the beach toward our house." He brought his hand up quickly like he was flipping a switch. "And something just told me to turn my machine on—let's see what they'll do when I blast them with 300,000 hertz."

"What happened?"

His cheeks stretched, followed by his shoulders shaking with giggles. "She doubled over, grabbed her ears, and freaking ran back down the sidewalk, away from my house. I was playing the sound from inside and she could still hear it."

My brain churned. Hadn't Wally Lux said something similar? Yes, something about the sirens' power wasn't in their song but in the frequencies at which they sang.

If what Zeke was saying was true and there were frequencies that could repel them, then maybe *I* needed to get a Rife machine.

Zeke's eyes shifted to the side. "The research I've read says cancer cells begin to disintegrate at between 100,000 and 300,000 hertz. And these creatures—well, they're kind of like cancer. So, what if I hit them with 500,000 hertz? Would they just blow up?"

33

I followed Zeke and Riff outside through the screened-in porch and waved him on his way. Once he was gone, I reached into one of my cargo pants pockets and pulled out my lighter and pack of cigarettes.

Riff crossed his arms. "When are you going to quit those things?"

Squinting up at him, I held the flame to the end of the cigarette, got my drag, and blew it out again. "When are you going to tell me what's in that upstairs room?"

A muscle in his cheek twitched. Without answering, he shifted his gaze toward the water. "Abbot's here."

Another distraction.

Riff moved past me, walking long strides toward the dock. I followed.

As we approached, Abbot unloaded a large cooler with a handle on either side. His eyes met mine, and his smile melted away. Of course he wasn't happy to see me. I'd defied his recommendation that I not come here again.

Riff called out to him. "You're late."

Abbot shifted his gaze back to Riff. "I had a few things to take care of. There's a hurricane comin'...or hadn't you heard?"

"I heard," Riff said.

"It's torn up the Bahamas. Governor just issued the evacuation order—people need to get out of the low country."

Riff nodded. "Mm-hm."

Abbot fixed his eyes on me again. "It's not safe to be here."

I set my jaw.

Riff glanced in my direction. "I'll make sure she's out of here before it hits."

I narrowed my eyes at Riff. How could he talk about me leaving and not him too?

Abbot didn't move. "I can wait. Grab your stuff. Let's go now."

I was ready to leave if Riff was. I had no idea where we would go—the two of us on the run from death. But I didn't want to leave without him.

Riff anchored a hand against the dock post. "You go on, Callie. It'll be better if you go now."

"Yeah, don't want to wait too long," Abbot said. "There comes a point when no boats can come in or out of these waters. And that time is coming soon."

I was torn. I didn't especially want to ride out a hurricane that had the potential to kill us, but even on the mainland, I still wouldn't be safe. "I'll wait for Riff."

Abbot shook his head. "You might be waiting forever then." He pivoted and pulled the anchoring rope from the dock's post. "I'll be back tomorrow if I can navigate the waters. I'd advise you both to get your bags packed."

I grabbed one handle of the cooler, Riff grabbed the other, and the two of us made our way back to the house, struggling to balance the weight of the container.

Once inside, we carried the cooler into the kitchen and set it on the floor.

Esmeralda had left sometime during Zeke's lesson, and the smell of cleaning fluid hung in the air.

I rested against the counter. "What are you going to do? You can't stay here."

Riff popped open the top of the cooler. "Island folks don't just go 'cause they're told to," Riff said. "Most of us will ride out this storm just like all the other ones."

I stared at him. Was he actually planning to stay through a Category 4 hurricane? Belle Marsh would be wiped out. "This sounds like this could be a really bad storm."

He shot me a dark look. "Hurricane's not going to blow away the sirens."

I reached out, grabbed his wrist. He flinched.

"What if there are hundred-mile-per-hour winds? They're saying the island may be underwater."

Riff set his mouth in a line as he unloaded a roll of butter, a loaf of bread, and several brown-wrapped packages from the ice. "Callie, I'm going to make sure you get to safety, and that's all you need to worry about."

I shot my fingers into my hair and dug my nails into my scalp. "I don't understand, Riff. We're still standing—alive. Breathing. Isn't it worth a shot? I mean, are you just going to give up? 'Cause I'm not." The thread of rage I'd felt yesterday weaved through my veins. Hot blood rose into my cheeks. "Look, you got me into this mess. Staying with me through this seems like the least you could do."

He raised his eyes from beneath dark brows.

I'd hit a nerve.

Thump. Thump-thump. The sound came from upstairs followed by a wail. Male? Female? It was hard to tell, but it reverberated through the house as though amplified through a speaker.

"Let me out."

A chill hung in the air.

Riff's face loosened, and his pupils dilated in high alert. "No. Callie? It's not what you think."

Why did people say that? The phrase itself insinuated that, in fact, it was exactly as you thought. Someone was locked upstairs.

Then came the sickening possibility: Was Lila locked in that room? Had she been up there all this time?

"*Someone* is upstairs." My voice was cautious, and I spoke the words more to myself than to anyone. A replay of Riff destroying every piece of art in his great room replayed in my brain.

His voice was low, rough. "No, there's no one."

The lie was so big it was hard not to believe it.

Thump.

Pivoting, I rushed from the kitchen, my sneakers squeaking against the tile. Riff grabbed for my arm. "Callie, no. Wait."

In the hall, I grasped the banister railing and shot up the steps, taking two at a time.

Riff followed, inches behind me.

At the top, I darted forward, stopping only once I reached the alcove, my eyes riveted to the blue strip on the floor. That door was a symbol of all that needed to be protected in Riff's life. In some ways, it was symbolic of Riff himself, who hurtled down the hall like a crazed bull.

I knew he would do whatever he had to do—even if that meant tackling me to the ground—to keep whatever was behind that door inside.

The painted panel rattled, visibly pulsing in its frame.

"Let me out! I'm dying in here!" the voice rang out.

I backed against the opposite wall. "Who. The hell. Is behind that door?"

Panting, Riff reached out for me. "Callie, I—"

"Is it Lila?" I spat out the words. If they came from his mouth, it would be too horrible. At least if I said it first, it might lessen the blow.

His face sagged in disbelief. "What? No, of course it's not Lila."

The door jolted again.

I jutted out my chin. "Riff, open it."

He shook his head, his voice breathy. "Not a chance."

I'd read this guy all wrong. I'd fallen for the innocent act, the charm. I'd trusted him. And now, here was the truth. I shot my gaze toward the end of the hallway. The stairs were a good five yards away. How could I skirt past him and get out of here? Where would I go?

I flinched as Riff reached toward me, expecting him to strike me. Instead, he pulled open the drawer of the small table under the window and took out a roll of blue freezer tape. The adhesive squawked as he yanked out a yard. Then he clamped his teeth down on it, tore off a strip, and immediately smoothed it along the untaped side of the door.

Stepping back, he released his defensive stance. "It's not Lila." He rubbed his hands up and down his face. "It's Kirka."

Transcript of Full Verbatim Interview With Riff Fall
10/6/16
4:30 p.m.
Callie: Are you sure you want me to record this?
Riff: Yes. All of it. I'm not holding anything back anymore. I'm ready to face the consequences.
Callie: Okay. The recorder is on.
Riff: I just want to say one thing before I start because what I'm about to tell you will no doubt change your opinion of me. I mean, I really can't believe you're still sitting here in front of me. I never expected us to get this far in the process.
Callie: What did you think was going to happen?
Riff: [pause] I didn't expect to see you again after you left the first time. Damn sure didn't expect everything that's gone on between us. Now I'm sure you wish it hadn't.
Callie: Tell me what happened.
Riff: [clears throat] Lila and I had only been married about a year. And now I had this hanger-on with Silla. She was around all the time, sitting up on the dunes watching. Or sometimes I'd roll up to the grocery store on the other side of the island and she'd be sitting there waiting for me. She wasn't the only one. There were others following me around the island, watching me from the woods. It was just like it had been in LA, except I was here.

Lila kept asking me what was wrong 'cause she didn't know, of course, and I kept telling her it was nothing. I was getting more and more irritated with her because she kept asking. And then, I went on a bender. For two, maybe three days, I drank. I started in the morning, and I drank all day.

On the last night, Lila asked me who was the girl hanging around on the beach and around the house; she asked me if I was screwing around—what was wrong and... [yells] I just couldn't take it anymore. [groans] I don't remember anything after that. Callie, honestly, I don't even remember it. But I think...I might have killed her.

Callie: You think you killed Lila?

Riff: I don't remember.

Callie: How did you kill her?

Riff: I said I don't remember.

Callie: [pause] Um...

Riff: Maybe I, uh, maybe I strangled her? I don't know.

Callie: If you killed her, what did you do with her body?

Riff: Maybe I dumped her in the marsh.

Callie: *Did* you dump her in the marsh?

Riff: I don't remember.

Callie: If you don't remember, then why do you think you killed her?

Riff: I remember calling Abbot. He came right away. I remember what he said to me. "She's gone." He said, "You gotta let her go."

Callie: Did Abbot see a body? He must know something. Did you tell the police this?

Riff: [barely audible] Callie, that's all I remember. I was blacked out. Abbot and I never spoke of it. Lila was just gone. That's all I knew. And yes, I called the police after she'd been gone a few days, after I'd sobered up and come back to my senses. They came in, searched the house—searched the whole damn island. They didn't find her. [pause] Didn't find any sign of blood or anything.

Riff: [pause] I can see it in your face, Callie. You think I'm a monster.

Callie: What does this have to do with Kirka? How did she end up in your attic?

Riff: [sighs] After Lila disappeared, I stayed drunk for a couple of weeks. Then one night, Kirka showed up at the door. I hadn't seen her since the band broke up. And I couldn't believe she was standing there in the doorway. Like she belonged here or something. I had to ask her in, but as soon as I did, I felt this...like, a shift in the air. I knew I shouldn't have let her in.

Callie: What did she want?

Riff: She knew Lila was gone, had left, whatever. She wanted to talk to me about a different project—separate from Cry of Crows. A solo project. Just me. She pitched a lineup of session musicians for the album. She wanted me to come back to LA with her, work on a few songs, do some recording. [pause] She wanted me to sign a new contract. I told her no way. Told her to get out. I didn't want anything else to do with her. I said, "I'm never going back to that life again—and I'm sick of you sending out your minions to watch me every second and track me all over the place." I told her, "I moved to Invisible Island to get the hell away from you and your people." She laughed then. She was like, "You don't get it, Robert. My 'people,' as you call them, are everywhere. You should know that by now. You think you came to this island to get away from us, but you were drawn here because I'm in your mind, still seducing you, still telling you what to do and where to go." That's when I realized I couldn't get away from her. I was in this secluded place, cut off from the rest of the world. Anyway, she said, "You've never paid for breaching the first contract. I'm offering you a chance—forgiveness from the old contract's terms. We can start a new one, draw it up together. I'd take it if I were you."

Callie: Why would she offer you forgiveness?

Riff: She wanted me to forget Lila. She said if I left with her that night, she'd forgive everything, including what I owed her. I'd paid her for breaching the contract. My lawyer had handled all that. At least, he'd handled the monetary payment, but that wasn't enough for her.

Callie: What else was there?

Riff: She brought a copy of the contract with her. She rolled it out on the banquet table and pointed out the indemnity clause.

The language was cryptic, but as she read it out to me, it became very clear what she was saying. Losing me as lead singer of the band would cost her money, but her remuneration would be acquired through punitive actions, not compensatory ones. These were to include familial, nuptial, and personal ties to people, places, and certain freedoms—all of which could and would be restricted if a breach of contract occurred. These actions would be at the discretion of the label.

Callie: What did that mean?

Riff: You're looking at it. The terms of my punishment were couched in legalese: I could never leave this property, and I would never see Lila again. Whether that was by my own hand or Kirka's.

Callie: What did you say?

Riff: I told her I wasn't going to sign her new contract, and I told her to get out. She was pissed. She told me I'd never be free of her—that I'd be stuck here on this island, spending the rest of my life alone, washed up, and eventually killed and eaten by sirens. The last thing she said was, "And remember, your final condition, as outlined in your contract, is silence. The non-disclosure clause is firm. You will never tell a soul about any of this. Ever. And if you do, your death will follow." I just wanted to kill her then. I didn't care what happened to me. I wasn't going to allow her to rule my life. I told her that. I said, "I'm going to kill you." After that, she got this weird look on her face. She just sort of smiled and said, "Robert, you can't kill us. We are as old as time. Even if you kill this body, we'll just get another. We've occupied many bodies and stolen many souls."

That's when I really got it—that I was dealing with something that wasn't human—that all those things I'd learned in church when I was a kid—hellfire and brimstone, demons and witches—it was all true. I was looking right into the face of evil. [pause] Anyway, I snapped. I lunged at her, grabbed her by the throat, slung her to the ground. But all the while, I could hear this laughing—this maniacal sound—like three people laughing at once. I just wanted to crush her throat. Stop her from singing or laughing.

I came at her again, and she got up and ran. But she didn't go outside like I would have expected. She ran upstairs, all the way up to the attic, laughing the whole time—like we were playing a damn game.

Once I got up there, something just overtook me. I shut the door. I knew only one of us was leaving that attic...I barely remember what happened next except that I cornered her. She was standing there saying, "Come on, Robert. Kill me. You know you want to kill me. Then you really will never be free of me."

I could've killed her with my bare hands, but instead, I went for the baseball bat—the one I'd hit my stepfather with when I was a kid—it was up there, leaning against the wall like it had been waiting for me all this time. I grabbed it, and I swung. [pause] And kept swinging until she was dead. At least, until the physical body was dead.

Callie: [audible shudder] Shit, Riff.

Riff: I'm not finished yet, Callie.

Callie: Okay.

Riff: Afterward, I was covered in blood. So I closed up the attic and locked the door. Then, I took a shower in one of the upstairs bathrooms. But the whole time, I felt like someone was watching me, breathing in my face. I thought it was just my conscience. I was in shock. I'd killed someone. I was just rinsing off like, now what? What do I do now? But I went downstairs, sat up all night wondering what to do, wondering if I should just kill myself. I guess I should have. [long pause]

The next day, I started hearing them. The footsteps. Like someone was upstairs and moving around in the attic. But I knew that couldn't have been Kirka moving around. Then, the voices started calling my name. "Robert. Robert." Driving me insane.

I just kept thinking, I've got a dead body in my attic. So, I taped up the door, pushed a chair against it, and that was that.

Callie: You didn't consider getting rid of the body.

Riff: I knew her demon was in there too. I wasn't going to risk letting it out.

Callie: And no one ever came looking for her?

Riff: No one ever came looking for her. I didn't even care if they did. I was ready to end it all. A few weeks after that, I stopped hearing the footsteps. Everything upstairs was quiet again. It was like nothing had happened. For a long time, I convinced myself that it hadn't happened. Except Lila was gone. And she never came back.

Callie: I'd like to stop the recording now.

MY HAND SHOOK AS I pushed the recorder into my purse.

We sat across from each other at the banquet table in the great room, now void of all its decorations. Sound seemed to echo louder than before, our breathing reverberating off the table and traveling into the rafters.

Now that I knew the truth, horror replaced my anger. His story had changed. My trust was wounded.

Riff sat at the table, his eyes downcast, his fingers locked together. A man who had just confessed to murder. But murder of what? Of whom, exactly?

"So, Kirka's remains are still up there?"

Riff nodded. "As far as I know. Along with the demon or demons that used to live in that body. Like I said, I've kept that room sealed off since the night it happened."

I let out a long stream of air. "Riff, I don't think you killed Lila."

"You don't know that."

"You've just told me every detail of how you killed Kirka Taylor. You would've remembered—some part of it. And you said the police never found any trace of her—no blood, nothing." I shook my head. "They would have found something."

Even so, Riff had killed a woman. Maybe I could rationalize that Kirka hadn't really been a woman, wasn't human anyway, but he was still capable of that violence—still dangerous.

Yet as I looked at him now—broken and more alone than ever—his eyes dark and dilated, I felt things for him I shouldn't have. How could I still ache for a man who'd confessed to murder?

"Should be a bestseller for you," he said in a low voice. "Publish every word. It won't matter by then. I'll be long gone."

Was this the way things were going to go? Was all of this for nothing? Because now I wasn't even sure I could publish this book with Riff's ultimate confession at the end.

A rock formed in my throat. "Riff, look, you've made some terrible choices, and on top of that, you've been a victim of some pretty horrific circumstances."

"I'm scum," he said. "Just like the detective said. A coward. Too worried about dying to tell the truth." He raised his eyes and met mine. "But not anymore."

"What about me?" I said bitterly. "You think these things will just stop following me when you're gone?"

He blinked.

"Don't you want to help me? You can't do that if you're dead."

I pushed my chair back and went around to his side of the table. Then I lowered myself before him and forced him to look at me. "The thing is..." I tried to keep my voice steady while scanning my mind for the ramifications of what I was about to say—the vulnerable position I would be putting myself in. "I've been thinking about it—about where we could go—to be safe. I thought about my grandparents' house in the mountains. It's landlocked. Harder for them to get to us. Zeke says his machine is keeping the sirens at bay. We could get one of those. We'll figure it out as we go along. But we should go."

The hard edges of his face softened. That's right. He hadn't known that the sirens were stalking Zeke too. I was surprised they hadn't visited Elijah—maybe they were too scared of Nona.

The rock in my throat expanded to what felt like a boulder, threatening to choke me. "I don't even care if you don't feel the same. But I care about you. I want you to live."

He slid his hand under my jaw, and I leaned my head against his palm.

"We have to find a way out of this," I said. "We *will* find a way."

We stood. He leaned forward and put his forehead against mine.

I could tell he wasn't convinced, but I kept talking. "When Abbot returns for us tomorrow, you'll come with me. If you're not worried about your life anymore and don't care if they find Kirka's body in the attic, then what does it matter if you die on the boat, on the mainland, or in the mountains."

"Or in prison?"

"Riff. You've already been in prison for years." I motioned toward the walls. "Maybe there aren't any bars on the windows, but there might as well be."

He nodded.

Maybe I was getting through to him.

"When I came back here, I was enraged at you for dragging me into this. I know you didn't mean to, but I'm a part of this now. We're tethered together through whatever this is. I'm scared—really scared. But none of us are safe. Not really. None of us are getting out of this life alive. So shouldn't we live while we have the chance? Shouldn't we at least try?"

"Yes."

"I don't want one of these sirens to kill me, but I've lived through a lot of tornadoes and outrun a lot of them too. I really don't want to die in a hurricane. Do you?"

He worked his mouth back and forth.

I put my hand against the rough skin of his cheek. "Riff, please, please come with me."

His voice was a low exhalation. "I'll come with you."

Relief overwhelmed me. "Great."

He stepped past me, his shoulder brushing mine. "Let's get out of this tomb."

34

The following day, we kept the television on news and weather as we worked to secure the house. Abbot was coming. Hearing that Riff had finally agreed to leave, he'd promised to brave hell and high water to get us to the mainland. Riff warned that we should expect a lecture for waiting until the last minute.

I only prayed we hadn't waited too long. Abbot had said Calibogue Sound would soon be impassable.

The news cycle was clogged with warnings about Hurricane Matthew, now rampaging through Florida. The storm was breaking records, and the weather commentators speculated that by the time it hit coastal Carolina, it would still be a Category 3. Winds of 100 miles per hour were expected—storm surges of seven feet. The governor warned this was the last chance to get out. Anyone living on the coast should get 100 miles away, at least. The National Guard had been called in. Roadblocks would direct traffic away from the coast.

Before placing one of his prized guitars in its case, Riff sat in the chair by the window in the music room, the instrument across his lap, his fingers interwoven in the strings. As he played, he drowned out the television with slow, crushing chords—the minor descending scale interrupted by his voice.

Trying to stay above the surface line
I'm doing what I can to find
The answers and what lies ahead
But I'm drowning in the surf instead.

This soft opening gave way to the chorus in which Riff's full-throated cry bounced off the ceiling and crested through the eaves above our heads. A voice breaking with pain.

I've been waiting for this day
To give everything away
So if you want to know who I am
This is your one chance.

He slowed the strumming and ended the song with a final chord. I waited for the lingering overtones to fade before speaking. "When did you write that?"

He shrugged, whisked the guitar off his lap, and settled it back into its case. "Yesterday, today, I don't know." He stood and began to unfold a mud-brown tarp. "Here, help me with this."

I grabbed one end of the tarp and helped him stretch it across the top of the baby grand. We covered and secured the instruments as best we could. Guitars in cases stacked in closets. The framed albums were removed from the walls, wrapped, and placed in suitcases.

Riff's phone sang out a Cry of Crows song, and he pulled it from his pocket and walked with it into the other room.

On the TV, a reporter interviewed people boarding windows and packing their vans with belongings. Invisible Island, she stated, would soon be underwater. Still, others said they wouldn't leave. They would ride out the storm—no matter what that meant.

Riff returned, speaking into his phone. "No, Ben, sorry. I haven't seen him today...Yeah... I see. I understand. I'll let you know if I hear from him." He clicked off his phone. "Zeke's missing."

No. Not Zeke.

"His dad said they were packing up too, trying to get out of here today, but he wasn't in his bed this morning. They've got people out looking for him."

"Police, or—"

"I think just volunteers." He looked up at me. "Why would he run off when he knew his family was leaving? Where could he be?"

But we both knew where he could be. I shuddered at the thought.

Riff paced the room, hooked his hands around the back of his neck. "Shit. And I've seen a bunch of them around the property's perimeter today."

"Sirens? You have?"

He nodded.

"Why didn't you tell me?"

"Didn't want to freak you out any more than you already are."

Another wave of dread assaulted me. "Do you think this storm is stirring them up? Making them more active?"

"I don't know." He scrubbed his hands over his face. "I just wish I could be out there helping them look for Zeke. But I wouldn't even know where to start."

"And we're leaving within the hour," I reminded him. I was anxious to find Zeke too, but we couldn't stay. Abbot would be here soon, and there couldn't be anything keeping Riff from escaping.

My chigger bites still hadn't healed from the last time I was here, and I raised the hem of my cargo pants to scratch them. My eyes trailed over the bags sitting by the front door. Riff's was there, along with mine. The bottle of holy water Nona had given me sat on the table. I'd take it with us. Just in case.

Upstairs, the banging had started again. Every so often I heard the voice shrieking, "Let me out!" Even though I knew who it was, it unnerved me. There was something nearly human in the cries, and under other circumstances—if I knew nothing about sirens—I would have broken down the door to free the person on the other side.

Instead, I steeled myself against the sounds, hoisted my duffel bag, and carried it outside. Riff followed me with his own and dropped it on the front porch before going back for another.

"I'll carry these down to the dock," I called through the open door.

Despite my nervousness about what we were doing, my heart was light. We were getting out of here. Riff was coming with me. Who knew what this meant for our future, or if there even would be a future, but for now, there was this—whatever this was. I dropped the bags on the dock and looked out over the sea. It was beginning to get rough, the waters rising to foaming peaks and the trees bowing in the wind. As it neared the day's end, the sky was a watercolor painting of gray and charcoal, a white-tipped boat on the horizon.

Abbot. He was nearly here.

I jogged back to the house, where the front door stood open. "Abbot's coming. I just saw his boat."

When I didn't hear an answer, I wandered into the great room. "Riff?"

No, not Riff. A woman stood by the banquet table, her long, caramel-colored hair draped over her shoulders, covering most of her white T-shirt. Her arms were decorated with the familiar symbols of the sirens.

"Riff!" The scream died on my lips as the siren drilled her stare deep into me with eyes like the ocean. The front door had been left open, and she had easily walked inside—a leaf blown in with the wind.

We'd been distracted and careless. The creatures had probably known that we'd let our guard down in our haste to evacuate.

Riff's footsteps shuffled at the entrance and continued into the great room. "Hey, Callie, I think there may be a few things..." His voice trailed off.

Should we run? Or back away slowly as one would under the sights of a wild and dangerous animal? The siren lunged forward and stomped her foot with an exhaled "ah!" A vocalization one might hear from an opera singer warming up. Her cheeks bloomed with what looked like sunburn, and her eyes blazed with fury.

"Callie, get out!" Riff waved his arm like he was shooing me from the room. "Get out now!"

I couldn't move. My feet wouldn't step to the left or the right. I couldn't even turn my head, couldn't look at Riff.

The siren took another step toward me. "Ah-ah!" That familiar chromatic descent.

I felt Riff's fingers wrap around my bicep. "Callie, go now!" He swung forward and grabbed the plastic bottle of Nona's holy water from the wall table with his other hand. Squeezing the bottle, he sent a stream into the demon's face.

Her throat wrenched, transforming her melodic vocalizing into shrieks of anguish. Holding her face, she stumbled toward the door. Riff followed her, continuing his onslaught, slinging his arm forward and dousing her head, back, and bare legs with the water as steam rose from her tattoos. She crossed the door's threshold, but Riff emptied the bottle on her back. The rest splattered across the porch, washing bugs, leaves, and debris down the front steps behind her. Then, he slammed the door shut and tossed the plastic container. It rebounded off the wall, bounced, and rolled to its final resting place in the corner.

Shoulders heaving, he reached for me and folded me into his arms. "Sorry, Callie. I should've been paying better attention."

I shivered, afraid to close my arms around him; instead, I held my hands palms up as breath puffed from my mouth.

Yes, we'd been too complacent and allowed ourselves to breathe too freely. Despite the incoming hurricane, the day had almost felt normal. Two people securing a house before a storm. I'd permitted myself the tiniest bit of excitement, thinking maybe if we left before dark, we might escape unscathed.

"It's getting dark," I whispered against his neck. "The storm is blowing in. Abbot should be at the dock by now. We have to go."

But were there more outside waiting for us? My fears had been confirmed. The incoming storm made them more active, bringing on a false night, a chaotic atmosphere where these beings thrived.

Our breathing echoed in the rafters. Then, another sound—footsteps, shuffling—like someone was climbing the stairwell barefooted. Riff pulled away, grasped my hand, and led me to the tiny space containing the security system.

We stood in front of the monitors as they flashed grainy, black-and-white images of the great room, the music room, the screened-in porch, the front door. As the upstairs hallway appeared, so did the shoulders, then the sinewy back of a man with hair the color of lime-green icing on a birthday cake. His tattoos were black bands interwoven like the pattern of a basket. He seemed to know exactly where he was going as he marched straight toward the attic door.

"Oh, shit," Riff breathed.

Seemingly paralyzed, we watched as the man grasped the top of the loose tape on the left side of the door. With a downward jerk of his arm, he stripped away the blue freezer adhesive. As though he knew the camera was on him, he held up the dangling strip—a fisherman with his prized catch of the day.

"No!" Riff ran headlong for the stairs.

I followed him, reaching the steps as his feet disappeared onto the second floor.

"Riff, wait!"

Riff had no weapons, and the man was at least twice his size. What was he planning to do? How could he fight this creature?

As I crested the stairs, the thumping from inside the attic door increased. Riff hurtled toward the siren, arriving just as the man pulled the last of the blue tape away. With a wild cry, Riff launched, tackling the siren from behind. He clung to the creature's back as it slung him left and right, barely hampered by Riff's grip on its shoulders.

I looked around for something that could be used as a weapon. A boat oar made of old dry wood hung horizontally on the wall. My heart pulsing in my ears, I lifted it from its hooks. Wielding it over my shoulder, I advanced toward the wrestling match. Then, aiming for the siren's head, I swung it like a baseball bat, slamming it into his skull. The oar splintered, bits of dead wood sprinkling his emerald hair like confetti. The creature wheezed, raising one hand to his head as he shoved Riff in the chest with the other. Riff staggered backward, colliding with the opposite wall of the alcove.

From the other side of the door, a voice whispered, "Help me. I'm still here."

Clutching his head with one hand, the siren shot out his arm, grasped the doorknob, and twisted it. Splintering and cracking preceded spears of wood breaking free from the panel, jutting out from around the doorknob like exposed broken bones.

My eyes trailed to the bronze object the siren held in his hand. He had pulled the entire knob and lock from its lodging.

"No!" Riff's voice broke with a yell.

With a scream of rusted hinges, the door burst open. Cold water sprayed my face, followed by a blast of wind through the corridor that whipped my hair back. I clung to the wall, my gaze fixed on the now-open attic. A set of wooden steps led up. Seconds later—the smell of something rancid and decaying entered my nostrils—the stench of death.

Riff grabbed my hand. "Come on."

We bolted for the stairs. I tried to match Riff's pace until my hand was wrenched from his. Something gripped my ankles and the world tipped around me. My shirt rolled under my arms, and my skin burned as I was dragged along the hall's carpet runner, past Riff, and toward the stairs. Completely unable to control my movement, I reached out, my fingers curling for anything that might stop me from going down the wooden steps.

But I only grabbed a handful of air. I went down. One, two, three, my head bashing and my spine scraping against the hardwood. My hand brushed the banister, and I wrapped my fingers around the rail. My body jerked, then elevated like a human kite.

Riff tripped down the steps behind me. "Callie!"

His voice was eclipsed by the same sound I'd heard just before the man by the pond was murdered. A freight train seemed to howl through the house, blowing pieces of debris down the stairwell. The walls rattled like a pressure cooker at full boil.

Riff clutched my ankles, his voice raking the ceiling. "Let go of her, you bitch!"

My fingers ached and began to slip from the railing. Finally, unable to hold on any longer, my hands slid away, and with Riff still grasping my legs, I crashed, cracking the back of my head against the sharp corner of a step. My vision fuzzed, the edges of my sight blurring with white static. Riff grabbed my hand and pulled. With starry explosions going off in both eyes, I scrambled to my feet. Barely aware of what I was doing, I barreled down the steps behind him, missing one or two at the bottom.

The house grew dark as though black clouds had moved into the interior. Another gale-force gust ripped down the stairwell, sending Riff headfirst against the far wall. Again, I grabbed for the banister, but my hand closed around nothing, and I catapulted across the room, tumbling on top of the banquet table, skidding across it and off the other side. Riff fought to get to his feet, his head down as though trying to move a boulder against the wind. The table shifted, and its chairs toppled like soldiers falling in battle as the heavy oak inched across the floor toward the wall, closing in on us.

The table began to act as a battering ram, pressing us to the wall and butting us. Then, it scooted back and shot forward again, ramming me just below my ribs. I doubled over the flat surface, attempting to wedge my palms between the table and my collapsing midsection. Riff clamped his fingers around the edge of it, trying to keep the furniture from crushing us. We pushed, managing to hold it long enough for me to drop to my knees and crawl out from under it, but that left Riff to fend on his own. The table anchored him against the wall, threatening to cut him in two. His face contorted as he labored to move it away from his body, his shoulders heaving. Then, the possessed furniture shot back and prepared to ram him again, giving him just enough time to stagger from its path.

Clawing our way toward the front door, we made it as far as the entry hall, where a blast of foul, hot air pressed us against the wall again, disabling any movement or even the ability to open our eyes.

Would it ever end? Or would this be how we both died? The hurricane seemed to be taking place inside Belle Marsh, all at once.

After a few minutes, the wind lessened, and the whirling air grew still. I looked over at Riff. Trembling, he wrapped his arm around me. His eyes glimmered in the darkened room—the breath whistling in and out of his throat.

Creaking. Popping. Someone was moving above. And music—sounds of choral singing—voices from the ocean's depths.

"No, no, no," Riff whispered. The front of his shirt was covered in blood that ran from his nose and continued to collect in the space over his lip, his chin, the hollow of his neck. His voice was a rasp. "Come on, Callie. Let's go."

The sensation washed over me suddenly and without warning: I no longer felt the need to go. The music was haunting—voices raised in hypnotic singing—seeming to come from another dimension. I was reminded of a time when I was younger and had my tonsils removed. As the anesthesia worked its way through my bloodstream, I'd been powerless to fight it. The lack of control over my own body had been both frightening and euphoric as I'd dropped off to sleep.

Now, I honed in all my focus on the stairs. Something was coming down. One step, then another, then another. The flutter of wings. The scrape and scratch of claws. From the darkened stairwell, something stepped awkwardly out of the shadows. Long, spindly legs with taloned toes. At a quick glance, it had the appearance of a shadow woman wearing a flowing gown. But it couldn't be a woman, for the legs were like a bird's, stork-like and tipped with claws. Large, gray-black wings sprouted from her shoulders, and red hair hung down, covering the front of her feathery body. Arms, too long for a human, ended in three scaled fingers moving like antennae.

"Come on." Riff tugged me toward the door. But my hand seemed to act of its own volition, reaching out to grasp the edge of the wall. I could feel my body being anesthetized by the music, the need to hear more.

"Where are your earplugs?" Riff yelled. "Put them in now."

Earplugs? I didn't know where they were. In my duffel bag, maybe? No. "In my pocket." Riff unsnapped each pocket of my cargo pants one by one, patting me down until he found what he was looking for. Straightening, he jammed the plugs into my ears.

The sound of a waterfall filled my senses. The music muted; the euphoria slipped away. Terror returned.

Clutching my arm, Riff guided me toward the open door. We plunged into a world with dark skies and winds as wild as they had been inside Belle Marsh. Our feet whipped through the seagrass toward the rolling tide of the ocean—and the dock.

Was Abbot still there? Or had he seen what was happening and turned around?

Bird wings fluttered. Wait. There were no birds. They'd moved on in preparation for the storm. I tilted my head back. An enormous flying creature swooped over us. I felt the tendrils of her hair brushing my face, the breeze from her wings. She sang loudest of all. Even through the earplugs, I could still hear strains from the song of the demons that had lived in the body of Kirka Taylor—until Riff killed her. Then they'd been contained in his attic, but now they were free, angry, and ready to feed.

The creature dove again, flying so low that one of her claws grazed my face. Hot blood ran down my cheek.

A scream tore from my throat, and I ducked as my sneakers hit the flat-packed sand, now blowing across the beach in dusty, whirling clouds. My hand was sweaty, but I held on to Riff's wrist and the two of us barreled toward the dock.

In the distance, Abbot. He stood at the water's edge, fighting the wind and holding his baseball cap to his head.

"Come on!" he yelled. "These winds are beating the boat all to hell." Obviously, he didn't see the black demon dipping through the sky.

My eyes flickered past him. Out of the crashing ocean tide, three, four, five, six sirens waded toward him, wearing flowing peasant blouses and cut-off jean shorts, the green and blue swirls darkening their skin.

Abbot's eyes widened as he glimpsed them. Then he turned and took a few slow steps before running for his boat.

We were almost there. Riff and I leaped in sync onto the dock just as Abbot dropped into the boat, yanked the rope from the post, and fired up the motor.

But Riff stopped running a few paces in, and my arm stretched out behind me until my fingers lost touch with his.

I spun to face him, walking backward. "Riff, what are you doing?"

"Come on!" Abbot yelled. "Get in the boat!"

"What are you doing?" I screamed.

The army of freaks marched through the water, their feet cutting through the breaking waves. They seemed to draw more and more of their kind with every step. Several yards out, a few were swimming toward the beach like a school of sharks. They moved with unbelievable speed, their arms cutting through the waves. They sang as they swam, but with my plugs secured in my ear canal, I could only hear a buzz of watery noise that wasn't unlike the hum of bees.

Overtop of them, a dark figure flew with wings like a giant raven. They were all coming for us now.

Abbot gunned the motor.

I waved my arms. "Hurry, Riff!"

He took a few steps forward and wrapped his arm around my waist. We moved toward the boat, where Abbot held his arm out to me, his face red, eyes bulging.

"Go on." Riff nudged me forward. "Get in."

Wait. What was he doing? I hung onto the dock's post.

"Let's go!" Abbot called out, flapping his hands.

Riff put his fingers to his ears and removed his plugs.

Suddenly, I understood what was happening, and I ripped out one of my earplugs. I wanted to hear Riff say the words to me—that he was coming, that my instincts were wrong.

"Take care of her, Abbot." His voice was just a whisper in the wind

Grabbing handfuls of his shirt, I attempted to pull him into the boat. "You're coming with us. I'm not leaving you here."

"They've come for me, Callie," he said. "It's time."

"No. It is not time."

He jimmied his fingers underneath mine, prying them from his shirt. "I'm not coming, Callie. If I do, they'll follow us. Get in the boat. Now."

"Why are you doing this?" My voice broke.

"You're a survivor, Callie." He took one of his earplugs and held it to my ear. "Don't watch, okay? I—" He pushed the plug into place, drowning out the rest of his words.

Riff half-pushed and half-handed me into the vessel. My foot hit the cushioned seat hard before I stumbled onto the boat's floor.

My heart felt like it was exploding.

I spun around and reached for his hand, but he stepped back.

The winds picked up speed and the lights on the dock flickered.

Riff's gaze rested on Abbot and his lips formed the words, "Get her out of here."

"No!" I leaned over the side, grasped for the dock, for him, but Abbot was already backing the boat away from the wooden structure. "You can't. You can't."

Down the beach, the night singers were coming, moving slowly but drawing closer with every step. Overhead, the flying creature swooped low, creating her own wind.

Abbot steered the boat out into the rough waters until we no longer faced the shore.

I scrambled to the back of the boat, my palms sliding against the wet railing. "Riff!"

But Riff was running back to Belle Marsh.

35

Abbot gunned the motor.

I fell against the seat of the boat, shaking with devastation and released adrenaline. Riff was gone. And what a terrible, terrible death. Just like Lila.

The boat pitched in the rough waters, the bow and stern moving like a hobby horse—and my stomach rose to meet my throat.

Abbot yelled something, but I couldn't hear it and was beyond caring. He stood at the wheel, his cheeks wet with what looked like tears. Or maybe they were damp from the rain.

He signaled for me to remove my earplugs.

I took one out.

"I gotta slow down," he said. "These winds are getting harder to navigate. Already thirty to thirty-five-mile-per-hour gusts and rough-as-hell waters. This isn't going to get any better. It's going to get a lot worse. It was crazy to wait so late to leave."

If we hadn't waited so late, maybe Riff would still be alive. Maybe we'd be in the mountains, nowhere near the ocean and the night singers. Rage swelled in me like the waves around us. Anger at Riff, at myself.

Abbot swung his arm, gesturing broadly. "Go to the back of the boat."

Clutching the front of my life jacket, I moved from my seat behind Abbot to the seat farthest from him. Then I clung to the side and watched the black waters crest in the distance. The storm was blowing in fast.

To our right was the abandoned resort—the siren house. Through one of the broken upstairs windows, a white curtain fluttered like a flag of surrender.

The boat tilted sharply toward the port side. A leg, then an arm, then another leg appeared as a man crept with surprising agility over the side. With water streaming from his naked body, his black tattoos gleaming and contrasting with the neon color of his hair, the male siren embarked wild-eyed, smiling...and singing.

I replaced the plug in my ear and grabbed the boat's railing as it rode the back of a wave and crashed on the other side, nearly unseating me.

The unnaturally tall creature appeared unshaken by the tumultuous conditions. He licked his arrowhead-shaped teeth and steadily advanced despite the boat's rocking. I felt like I was falling from the top of a skyscraper, the pain and horror increasing with every floor I plummeted past. Riff was dead—and now this thing—this mockery of a human—was going to kill us.

Abandoning the wheel, Abbot flipped down a compartment in the cockpit and fumbled with a long pole that ended in a spear—the sort of instrument that might be used when deep sea fishing. In one movement, he reared back and thrust the weapon into the creature's chest.

The boat pitched again.

The siren's scream pierced the wind and the protection of my earplugs.

Abbot's arm and body jerked as he yanked out the harpoon and fell backward against the wheel, jerking it to one side. The siren's face contorted, his features compressed as he looked down at his chest and the gory hole in his sternum spewing black, tarry blood. He dropped to his knees, then to all fours.

The boat climbed another wave and dropped on the other side, jarring my back and pelvis. My hand slid against the railing, its surface as slick as if slathered with oil.

Abbot raised the spear again and plunged it into the siren's spine. The being stopped flopping and his body flattened out in the walkway like a dead fish.

Abbot dropped the weapon into the floorboard and turned back to the wheel. But we had changed directions, and the boat was battered by waves coming at us from the sides. Not only were we in danger from the sirens, but the weather was worsening by the minute. The winds swept over the waters, turning them into sharp, lashing tongues. The boat tipped from side to side. Still, I kept my eyes on the body of the night singer, the blood pooling beneath it.

A black, shadowy texture began to form over the siren's bloody skin. It was as if I were watching computer graphics in a movie as the dark spirit separated from the corpse. It looked much like the thing that had emerged from the attic. Bird's legs with talons, shadow-like undulations with every movement. Yellow eyes glared at me, full of venom and radiating evil.

The demon leaned down and sank its teeth into Abbot's arm, tearing away a chunk of flesh.

Abbot's face twisted, his voice breaking in a cry.

"Stop!" I screamed.

The thing pivoted and faced me with glowing, birdlike eyes as Abbot's blood dripped in strings from its lips. Slowly, it drew onto its knees, bringing one leg up and then the other until it stood to its full height—probably close to seven feet tall.

It came for me one step at a time as I backed away. Then, its mouth dropped open, revealing its fangs—flashes of silver smeared with human blood. With a waving tongue, the creature produced its song—a hawk's cry—a shriek of war and assured victory—the sound muted by my earplugs, the din of the boat, and the wind.

Abbot jerked the wheel, trying to right the boat's course, but the water overwhelmed the vessel, smacking against the side, tilting and nearly flipping us. My equilibrium altered, I toppled and my head contacted something hard. But it didn't shake the stalwart balance of the night singer.

Hanging onto the back of a seat, I pulled to my feet, despair and abject terror colliding in my brain. There was no way out of this. Jumping into the water would ensure my death by these creatures. Staying on the boat meant this thing would devour me. But the choice wasn't mine to make. The boat rose upon the water's swell as if hoisted by a crane, and the black bird-like creature pushed off and flew into the stormy skies.

My vantage point tilted sideways. And water closed over my head.

36

Buoyed by my life jacket, I swam. I had no idea what had happened to Abbot or the boat, but the shore lay in front of me, the abandoned resort rising above the beach—a ransacked monument to an unheeded warning and curse. Were sirens swimming below, waiting to drown me or eat me alive? I kicked harder and thrust out my arm. A wave washed over my head, pushing me forward and leaving me gasping for air.

It was strange—the things you thought of when faced with death. Riff should have been foremost in my mind. Instead, I thought of surviving. That was all I could think of—getting to shore.

Water filled my mouth and as I surfaced, my sinuses stung and acidic bile rose in my throat. I spat and coughed. The sand bar rose up under my feet and I clawed at the waves as if I could push them behind me.

The wind howled, and from somewhere nearby, a tree branch cracked. Gusts of bark and leaves flurried overhead. I glanced behind me once more at the dark crests rising and falling. No sign of a boat. No sign of Abbot. I turned back toward the resort and trudged along through the wet sand. What could I do? There was no way I was getting out of here now. I would have to find a place to weather the storm.

I picked my way through a hole in what had once been a retaining wall but now looked like a graveyard of wood and cement. Digging my fingers into the soft earth, I scrambled up the embankment onto the saturated seagrass and spotted the old, weathered gazebo standing like a gatekeeper in the dark. Erosion had removed a chunk of land that had once separated the wedding pavilion from the beach. The structure might slide off the sandbank and into the ocean at any moment.

Keep walking. I glanced up at the hulking structure. Wait. Were there lights on inside? Yes, the broken-out windows and those still containing panes glowed with orange illumination.

I stopped. I couldn't go in there. I'd been here before and I knew what was inside. Yet behind me were the raging waters that had taken Abbot and his boat.

Choose your death.

A set of arms closed around me and I was lifted off the ground. My scream sailed through the air and blew away as I thrashed, slamming my head back until I heard the crack of bone. But the tree-branch-like arms kept me locked against a human body.

Panic and desperation fueled my fight as we approached the rear of the resort, which looked even more ominous under darkened skies. I kicked harder, my feet tangling with vines that grabbed for my ankles. We were moving toward a metal door, and I screamed again, but as before, my cries were carried out to Calibogue Sound to drown. No one would find me here.

My captor jutted out a leg that was the circumference of an oak tree, kicked the door open, and carried me into the darkened service entrance.

I twisted my body, wrenching my back. My cries for help reverberated off the ceiling as the door to the outside slammed shut. The creature chuckled, a low, melodic rumble that echoed through the hallway like a requiem. I kicked out at the walls, the air. The timbre of his laughter intensified as we moved along a basement corridor, passing plastic-wrapped refrigerators and industrial-sized ovens. Everything seemed draped in a sepia fog. Humidity increased with every step. An open door in front of us revealed the indoor pool—we were headed right for it.

Was this how he would kill me—by drowning me?

The green, rancid water smelled of mold and rot and undulated slightly as though someone had been swimming in it.

Inches away from the pool's edge, the siren released his hold and I slid down his body. As my feet contacted the floor, I whirled around to face him. Like all the other male sirens, this one was a giant with wispy purple hair that reminded me of a troll doll I used to have.

He stared at me, his face creased with amusement. But suddenly, the lines around his mouth turned down and his eyes narrowed. Something was happening to him.

The siren crossed his arms over his chest and doubled, pressing his hands against his temples. A terrible scream began in his throat and burst forth with agonizing force—a metal music singer's cry—and a wake-up call that my earplugs must have fallen out in the water.

The being dropped to his knees and dove headlong into the murky pool. Ripples broke the surface, followed by bubbling. An underwater explosion caused vibrations beneath my feet and turned the pool into a fountain. I stepped away from the edge as the geyser spewed into the air and deepened into a dark red. Seconds later, the water settled and the ripples dissipated. Where the siren had entered the pool, there was only placid water, stained with a crimson cloud and bits of debris on the bottom.

Schools of fish swarmed under the surface, circled, and then retreated, disappearing through a wide underwater tunnel at the deep end.

I was alone.

The sound of my breathing hung heavily in the damp air. Across the room, an open door beckoned, and I skirted around the edge of the rippling pool and hurried toward it, keeping my eyes fixed on the water lest something burst from the surface. I had no idea where it would lead, but I plunged through it.

A hallway. The hardwood floors looked as though someone had taken a sledgehammer to them. Shards of wood littered my path, along with plastic bags, discarded cartons of milk, and an empty wine bottle. This place had been nice once. Expensive. Now, it had become the sirens' refuge. Stepping over the chunks of wood and garbage, I noted how the gold brocade wallpaper hung in strips. Whole swaths had been torn away. Graffiti—strange symbols and words—decorated the ruined walls. Jagged holes gaped at me.

I put one foot in front of the other and kept moving. Down one hallway, then another. How did I get out of this place? It was like a maze. At the end of one corridor next to a stairwell, bright orange spray paint warned, TURN AROUND.

At the words' suggestion, I wrenched my neck and looked behind me. The wall sconces—once grand, now a mockery of wealth amongst all the ruin—flickered. The place could lose power at any moment. Then I would be in the dark—at the mercy of whatever was in here with me. What I would give to have my cell phone. But it was lost with all the rest of my things. It hardly mattered now. No one could help me.

The shuffling of feet. Whispers. I froze.

A dim light strobed over the form of a female siren. The woman's cheeks raised in a vacant, unnatural smile that didn't reach her icy eyes.

She advanced, hissing, "Shhh."

The only place I could run was up the steps. I climbed a flight and emerged in what looked like a lobby. Destroyed floor tiles lay before me, the ceramic pulverized into dust, creating craters in the floor. Overturned armchairs and side tables were now fit for kindling. Fish bones and rotting entrails littered one corner and filled the room with the stench of decay.

I rushed across the lobby, splinters of wood and tile crunching under my soaked sneakers. Then I jogged down another hallway lined with doors, most of them opening to ransacked guest rooms. White feathers and stuffing from sliced-open pillows and sheets were strewn on the floor. Paintings that had once hung over the beds were defaced with blue and green spray paint.

To my right, a black hole in the wall gawped. The size of a tractor trailer's tire, the opening seemed constructed of black PVC pipe. I placed my hand on the inside of the tube and brought my fingers away damp with oily droplets.

Vibrations shook the floor under my feet. Splashes, gurgles from inside the pipe.

But my attention was drawn away by an explosive crash. Glass breaking followed by shrieking wind. Probably a tree falling through a window.

"Ah-ah."

Oh no. I knew the sound too well. The siren's prelude.

I pivoted. Standing a few feet behind me was a female siren dressed in the signature cut-off denim shorts and a midriff peasant blouse, revealing the telltale spirals and swirls upon her skin. Water dripped down the front of her blouse from her dark hair.

From behind me, someone whistled the same two notes.

I spun again. Another male siren with bright orange hair pointing up like a flame stood at the other end of the hall, his head nearly touching the ceiling. His arms hung well past his hips as if they'd been stretched, and where his hands should've been were flipper-like apparatuses—the fingers like fins. His catfish lips attempted a vacant smile.

He marched forward with purpose, confidence, intent.

I caught my breath, bracing myself, ready to fight for my life. But he interrupted his assassin's march when he sidestepped into a room at the end of the hall.

"Ah-ah."

I whipped around in the opposite direction in time to see the female siren in the peasant blouse scamper away.

Now, the head of a different siren, one with blonde corkscrew hair, poked out of one of the doorways. "Ah-ah." She too darted back into the room again.

They were playing with me. Toying with the mouse before they killed it. Was this how Lila had died too?

A floorboard creaked behind me and again I turned. Two more tattooed beings advanced like wolves who'd cornered their prey.

Water dropped onto my forehead.

"Sssssssss..." The sound hissed above me as a tendril of what looked like black hair brushed my cheek.

I tilted my head and stared into the green eyes of a woman as she crawled above me, her neck angled unnaturally like a contortionist. As though her hands and knees were attached to the ceiling, she hung upside down, her dark hair dangling like ropes. Wearing the denim and peasant blouse as the other women, her arms and legs had all the same marks, except her tattoos looked more like scales.

A shriek ripped from my throat. Instantly, the others began to scream, matching my pitch, mimicking my terror.

I hurtled into the closest open room and slammed the door behind me, flipping the brass lock just above the doorknob. *They can't pass through a locked door.*

The door rattled, the lever flapped, and the panel jolted. They must have been kicking it. They might not have been able to pass through a locked door, but they were doing their best to break it down.

I surveyed the windowless room, which had probably once been a conference room. Three huge aquariums spanned the length of the walls and seemed to disappear into cut-outs in the drywall, suggesting the tanks expanded beyond the one room. Although they contained murky water like the pool, the remnants of aquatic life that gathered in stagnant ponds still swam among the green algae.

The door continued to pulse, and from the hall, hissing sounds intermingled with harmonic "ahs." How many of them were on the other side of the door? They'd all congregated at Belle Marsh to kill Riff. Maybe they were filtering home now—just in time for their second meal. I was trapped. I couldn't stay in here. But I couldn't go out there.

The door rattled again, this time so violently I thought it might splinter.

And then the sirens began to scream.

Oh, how I wished I still had my earplugs. They hadn't drowned out all the sound but muffled most of it. The screaming went on for a minute, maybe a little longer. Then another explosion shook the room, sending ash and debris raining from the ceiling and billowing under the door.

Everything stopped. The banging ended. The screaming ceased.

A glug sounded from the tanks followed by a swish of water. I swiveled toward the aquariums as a multitude of bubbles invaded the space. On all three walls, the same occurrence was happening. Sets of arms reaching forward and then pulling back. Swimmers—one in each—all of them naked men. They might not have been able to come through a locked door, but they could travel through the aquariums.

The three figures synchronously crested the water and shifted the massive lids just enough to exit. Hands grasped the edge, a leg bent and raised, a foot braced against the glass, and then they were up and over the side, dropping to the ground as water poured from their muscular bodies.

Fear crushed my throat, sending my heart into spasms. All three of the men were aroused. They raised a finger to their lips.

"Shhhh."

Vibrations of terror jackhammered through me as I backed toward the door. The male sirens' glistening feet shifted slowly toward me in a marching rhythm.

"Shhh. Shhh. Shhh." Strange, fixed smiles tipped their lips, accompanied by emotionless eyes.

Suddenly, as had happened with the siren in the pool room, all of them doubled over, holding their ears, their screams forming a unison thread of sound. Another blast rocked the room, followed by the shattering of the windows in the hall. Pieces of glass skittered under the door.

What was exploding? The floor shook as though bombs were going off. Would the whole place blow up?

I braced my back against the wall, squatted down, and threw my arms over my head.

When I looked up again, the men in front of me seemed to come apart. Limb from limb, sinew from sinew, cell from cell. A red explosion that left only pieces of ash fluttering in the air—all that was left of my assailants.

Gasping, I reached a sweaty hand for the lock on the door behind me. I quickly flipped it, gripped the knob, flung the door open, and ran down the hall.

Crunching over broken glass, I tried to remember which way I'd come. Left or right? The left, yes, it must have been left. Several staring sirens lined the walls. As I skirted past, they reached out but with no great effort to grab me. They laughed, mimicked my pants and gasps, some of them drawing their hands up to their mouths and widening their eyes to act out fake terror.

I careened down another hallway. I must have been getting close to the stairwell now. Up ahead, the mouth of the great black tube waited for me. I needed to get past that. The stairs weren't far beyond. A foot emerged from the hole, and then a leg, arms.

Another naked night singer emerged from the pipe. His black eyes fastened on mine. I smelled the algae on his skin and the pungent scent of dank water as I attempted to dart past him, but a second later, he, too, dropped to the ground, writhing as if in pain. A loud pop sounded. What looked like red paint splattered the wall where he'd stood only moments before.

Simultaneously, the window behind me shattered, blowing slivers of glass along the floor.

Ducking, I turned sharply and took the stairs to the basement. That was the way I'd come in; it had to be my way out.

"Callie!"

I squinted to the end of the corridor through a haze of floating ash.

A man with curly red hair smiled at me from behind a rolling cart, upon which sat a thin glowing tube set horizontally atop some sort of transmitter. A laptop and a box with knobs and various cords running from it completed the setup.

Zeke? My mind reeled. What was happening? Was he a mirage?

"Zeke!" I stumbled forward until I reached him, opened my arms, and pulled him into an embrace. Not a mirage. He was flesh and bone. Zeke had survived. But how? "Everyone's been looking for you," I panted. Even saying the words seared my heart. Just a few hours ago, Riff and I had talked about going out to look for Zeke. It seemed like months ago now. "I was so worried they'd gotten you."

Zeke smiled. "No, I'm getting *them*." He pointed to his machine. "It's just like I thought, Callie. They can't tolerate this frequency—this level of hertz. They break up into particles and disintegrate." He rubbed his chin. "I haven't quite figured out why. The sound is safe enough for us to hear. But I think it must have something to do with the machine disrupting their energy's vibrating frequency. The supernatural part of them is more like a microorganism than a human—like a parasite. Their bodies just burst apart. You know, like, how an opera singer can shatter glass with their voice?"

How was he so calm, like he was in his private laboratory testing scientific theories? Meanwhile, I craned my neck, scanning the hall behind me.

As thankful as I was for Zeke's machine, this was no time to stand around talking about his paranormal breakthrough.

"We can kill them all, Callie," Zeke said. "They're not very smart. I've been rolling through the resort, taking a few out at a time." His voice shook with excitement. "I'm using a battery pack, so if we lose power, don't worry. We're still covered." Zeke pointed. "You want to see something really cool? Go into the pool room."

The only thing I wanted to see was a door to get us out of here. "Zeke, we should go. It might not be too late to get you back to your parents' place before the worst of the storm hits."

Zeke's eyebrows knit together. "Not yet. Not until I've killed every last one of these assholes." There was something in Zeke's eyes I hadn't seen before. A determination, a fury. He viewed these creatures through the same lens as his mother's cancer. Something to be eradicated. He rolled the cart ahead of me and opened the metal door that led to the pool room.

The pool was filled with sirens. They stood waist-deep, fifteen of them at least, all staring at us like we were gazelles that had wandered into the lion's den.

The wheels of Zeke's cart squealed as he rolled it into the room. It was the only sound.

He motioned me forward. "Come on in, Callie." As if he had all the time in the world, he stepped on the brake that held the cart stationary, then typed something into the keyboard and adjusted a knob on his machine that sat on the second shelf of the cart. "One thing I've learned is that the corporal form of sirens—they actually move pretty slow. It's the non-body part of them that's fast-moving."

Thunk. Something plastic rebounded off the side of my head. A multicolored beach ball bounced across my path. The sirens scooped water out of the pool, attempting to splash us. One of the female sirens pulled herself onto the side. Naked and leaving a trail of wet footprints on the concrete behind her, she strode across the concrete to the other end of the room. The blue and green designs covered her arms and legs and wound their way across her chest, abdomen, buttocks, and back. She appeared reptilian. In the corner sat an apparatus resembling a boom box from the 80s or 90s. As she bent over it, making sure her buttocks were within view in full-moon fashion, she turned her head toward us and stared with eyes that resembled a lizard's. Yellow, divided by a slit of a pupil.

A foam pool toy bounced off my back as music blasted from the boom box in the corner. Death metal, complete with a Cookie Monster singer. The sirens in the pool thrashed their heads, the women slinging their long, wet hair so it slapped the water's surface. It was like being at a heavy metal pool party.

"Now watch this," Zeke said.

The horizontal tube on the machine flared and glowed bright orange.

The pool water began to bubble as though it were boiling. It spilled over the sides like molten lava. The sirens clutched their ears, shrieking and screaming, some of them sinking into the water while others popped like balloons, sending puffs of ash and debris into the bubbling flood. With every vanishing siren, a little thrill—a temporary satisfaction filled the holes in my heart, fueled by the violence of the thrashing music.

For all those whose lives had been ruined, destroyed, or cut short. For Riff.

As the last night singer turned to ash, I dropped to the ground and finally allowed myself to cry.

37

Zeke and I emerged the next morning from the basement of the Invisible Island Resort.

The storm had hit hard and raged through the night with one lull in the early morning before banging on, shaking the heavens above us. Sometime during the worst of it, the power had gone, and we'd been immersed in darkness—all except for the glow of Zeke's machine, which continued to illuminate and protect us throughout the storm, thanks to his multiple battery packs.

It was Saturday, and the landscape was strewn with fallen trees and mounds of debris—both organic and synthetic. Items that had been outside were now inside the building. The reverse was true as well. Pillows, plastic, old pages from magazines, and even several items of clothing were scattered across the lawn. With my foot, I nudged what looked like a chef's coat.

The gazebo was no longer there—only part of the concrete platform where it once sat and an empty cliff that promised a severe drop onto the beach below.

Zeke trailed me, carrying his equipment, several waterproof carry cases, and a fold-up cart he rolled along at his side like a walker.

We picked our way through the sodden lawn to the front of the resort, where tree limbs and branches cluttered our surroundings, obscuring the paved path. Zeke gave a running narrative, pointing out all the damage.

"Look, those trees are blocking the roads. No carts will be able to get through there." He gestured at a relatively unscathed stable, the top of the stall doors opened and horses' heads peering out. "Looks like the Thwaite's horses all made it, but they'll have to clear that paddock."

My goal was to get Zeke to the island's station that served for police and medical emergencies—if it was still standing. As we walked along the obstacle course of carnage, we avoided the tangles of electrical wires and spears of tree trunks.

I had not told Zeke about Riff. He would find out soon enough. Anyway, I couldn't yet acknowledge what had happened. My insides felt heavy with exhaustion and grief, and I wasn't ready to share that with anyone else.

For the most part, the island was deserted, but as we continued, people began surfacing. The whine of chainsaws cut through the silence, and we passed several survivors who stood in their yards, assessing flooded paddocks, damaged roofs, lost docks.

I caught snippets of their conversations. "...fifty to sixty-mile-per-hour sustained winds...gusts up to 130. Thought the roof was going to come off."

When we reached the station, no one was there, so we kept going, moving toward Bloodreed Point. We passed marshes that had the eerie appearance of early romantic-era paintings. Old boats had slipped under, weighted down by the rainwater, and now only one end or the other split the surface.

Despite the officials' warnings that the island would be submerged, the storm hadn't been as bad as feared. Most casualties consisted of trees, docks, and a few homes. As we reached the other side of the island and drew closer to Belle Marsh, we saw more people, some starting up generators. Groups of folks worked together to drag trees from the road. They waved as we passed, asking if we had fared all right during the storm.

"I don't know about my house," Zeke called back. "We're on our way there to see the damage."

It took us an hour to walk to Zeke's house, which was still standing. It was a large two-story on the beach elevated on stilts, looking out at the water that now rolled underneath it.

"It's flooded," Zeke announced, pulling ahead of me. "But it's still here."

Holding his equipment close to his sides, Zeke waded through the water and climbed the stairs to go inside.

While I waited for him, I stared down the length of the beach. If I walked just a little farther, I'd come to Belle Marsh. But what would I find? An empty house. The thought of it turned my stomach. No, I wouldn't go there.

Somewhere on the other side of Zeke's house, a chainsaw buzzed. Then it stopped. Voices, cries, whoops, yells. All happy sounds. I assumed Zeke's parents had seen their son. Inhaling slowly, I waded into the standing water, feeling the debris from trees rolling under my feet as I crossed the front of the house. A group of five or six people stood beside a huge tree that had uprooted from the soft sand and fallen, crushing the deck. The couple, who I assumed were Zeke's parents, had wrapped their arms around their son so that only the top of his curly head was visible.

A man began to climb down from a ladder buried in the tree limbs, holding a chainsaw at his thigh. As he descended, I blinked at the tattoos on his forearm, his bicep. He dropped to the bottom of the ladder, his tousled brown hair replete with leaves and twigs from the tree he'd been cutting.

Dark eyes settled on mine as he put down the chainsaw.

Riff.

38

It was a little like waking from a nightmare, but the processing and acceptance happened slowly over the course of the day. Riff was alive. I was alive. The sirens—at least the ones we knew of on the island—were gone.

That night, Riff and I returned to Belle Marsh, now more like a boat than ever, with standing water surrounding it and trees fallen on all sides like a frame.

My sneakers had been completely soaked through as we'd helped Zeke's family cut up the fallen tree and remove debris from the road that led away from the beach. We hadn't said anything to each other about what had happened or how either of us had come to this moment. I finally removed my soggy shoes and waded through the shallow waters that nearly met the swimming pool. The cover had blown off, and the pristine blue waters were clouded with sticks, branches, and one lawn chair we'd neglected to pull inside.

Part of me wished it had all washed away into the ocean, leaving the property swept clean as though no one had ever occupied it. I could convince myself that my time there had only been a nightmare. Except there was Riff.

Standing at the pool's edge, we were finally alone—two people back from the dead with no idea what life would look like in the future. We turned to one another and walked into an embrace. I buried my face into his damp neck, smelling layers of salt, sweat, and fear.

"I can't believe you're alive," I breathed against his skin.

"I barricaded myself in my bedroom," he said. "Locked the door, waited, and prayed the windows would hold against the wind. And after a while, everything stopped. They stopped knocking on the panes and rattling the door. When I came out in the morning, they were all gone."

I pulled away from him enough to look up at his face, the sunburn showing through his stubble, his eyes shining and so very alive.

"You left your property, and you didn't die."

He stared down at me, his arms around me tightening. His mouth twitched. "I don't know, I can't explain it, but I just felt like I could leave and I'd be okay. I knew the neighbors would need help and figured if ever I was going to take a chance—after surviving everything else—this was the time." He pushed a frizzy clump of hair out of my eyes. "But what about you? Where were you? How did you end up back here?"

In a breathless stream, I told him everything that had happened—about the boat capsizing, swimming to the resort, and finding Zeke there with his siren-slaying machine. "When he cranked this thing up, the sirens just exploded—like zombies in a video game."

Riff's face was somber. "What about Abbot?"

I bit my lip. I felt sure Abbot was gone, but I didn't want to say it. "I'm not sure, Riff. Once I started swimming, I couldn't see him or the boat."

Riff dropped his gaze and breathed out. It was too much to take in. There would be time to talk about it later.

We entered through the screened-in porch and surveyed the damage, flashlights in hand.

Inside, we found the wreckage of Kirka's tirade. Furniture overturned. Scattered glass from a broken window. Unlike my lost duffel bag, which had blown away in the storm, I located my laptop under a chair and my purse in a corner, my cell phone still inside.

Upstairs was worse than downstairs. In the guest rooms, bed linens were strewn on the ground, mixed with broken glass. Smashed frames and artwork littered the floor, the walls still dripping with water. It looked a lot like the abandoned resort. It seemed the sirens' chosen décor was vandalism-inspired.

At the end of the hall, the blue door lay on its side. The arched opening—the mausoleum—awaited.

Riff reached for my hand. I clasped his and squeezed. We would go in together. Whatever was up there, we'd deal with it. We entered and climbed the steps. The space was a holding cell of smells—a musty, earthy dampness mixed with rotten eggs and decomposing organic matter. As we crested the top step, Riff shined the flashlight along the floor. The light bounced off glass from a broken window. The shards intermingled with leaves, vines, and twigs. A few boxes sat in the back corner. A lamp, several cans of paint.

And nothing else.

There was no dead body, no bones. It was just an attic, nothing more.

Riff stalked the room, shining the light in every corner, shoving the boxes aside with his foot.

The remains we'd both expected to see weren't there.

WHAT HAD HAPPENED TO Kirka's remains? Did they blow away in the storm? Were they somehow destroyed along with the other sirens? Or had there ever been a human body to dispose of? We had no answers.

It was several days before travel to and from the island was possible, and during that time Riff and I joined with other survivors to help with the clean-up—cutting trees away from powerlines and dragging debris out of the roads. We helped Nona and the others serve food to the community at the café and cleared spoiled food from the refrigerators. There was no power and wouldn't be any for several weeks, but there were generators and generous hearts.

Through it all, I never spotted a siren.

During the day, helicopter blades pulsed overhead. News crews filmed footage of the carnage and those who had stayed to clean it up. At night, Riff and I sat outside by the firepit, still wary and watching as the daylight hours ebbed and the darkness flowed, our ears peeled for the first echoing note on the wind.

I'd run out of cigarettes several days before but had bummed a couple from one of the locals, one of whom had also donated a pack of nicotine gum. Then, I limped through withdrawal with what I had.

"I'm proud of you," Riff said as we sat staring into the firepit's flames. "Something good came out of this for you after all. Maybe you'll quit smoking for good."

I laughed. "Maybe." Although if someone offered me one right then, I would've gladly lit up and puffed away. "I'm going soon. Back to Nashville. Back to finish your book and back to my real life."

Riff nodded, caught his tongue between his lips, and turned his face toward the flames. "Yeah, I know."

It was a long shot, but I aimed anyway. "Why not come with me?"

He closed his eyes. "I knew we were going to come to this point." He sighed. "My real life is here, Callie. Belle Marsh is my home. This is my community, and I want to help them rebuild."

I couldn't begrudge him that. Now able to leave his property and move through the island like everyone else, he could finally join his own life; I couldn't expect him to join mine.

"And," he added. "I've got a solo career to rebuild."

"I understand." I looked into the flames and let the heat dry my eyes.

39

It only took two weeks to finish writing Riff's book. The chapters came together like I was a conduit through which to channel his voice. My short time with him allowed me to get to know him in a way I hadn't known anyone. We'd shared our secrets. And that had changed me.

Back in Nashville, I thumbtacked photos of Riff and Cry of Crows to the wall around my computer. When I needed a little inspiration, I'd look at the pictures and hear his voice in my head. I'd kept in close contact with him after cell phone service was restored to the island, and read him whole chapters over the phone. Sometimes he commented or asked me to change something. Sometimes his silence told me everything I needed to know.

One night, as I scavenged in the kitchen for something to eat—a box of cheese crackers, a jug of milk on its way to Sourville, and a couple of rubbery strawberries—my phone buzzed with an incoming text.

Hey, doll. It's your old dad again. Just checking in to find out if you've made up your mind about seeing me.

I'd almost forgotten about Dad. I'd been stringing him along for a couple of months but hadn't made a decision. Maybe it was time I met with him, saw what he wanted, and hopefully got the answers I needed. If he was willing to come to Nashville to see me, who was I to say no?

QUINCY CALLED ME THE following morning.

"I read it," he said.

I sat on the swivel chair at my desk, coffee in hand. "And?"

Quincy blew out air, creating static over the line. "What can I say, Callie? It's staggering. But I mean, the publisher's a little concerned about the material. I'm a little concerned, to be honest. A few weeks ago, you told me you believed Riff's story."

"I believe him. All of it." I filled my mouth with coffee and swallowed hard. "I believed Wally Lux too."

"I never took you for someone who bought into the supernatural."

I tapped my fingers against my mug. It would be impossible to explain to Quincy what had changed my mind. He'd have to hear it to hear the singing to understand, and that wasn't anything I ever wanted him to experience. "Let's just say that the island is a magical place. It made me a believer."

He sighed. "Anyway, for what it's worth, the book is really good. It's like Riff wrote it."

"That was the idea."

"Yeah, but I mean, there's something else to it. Usually, I can still hear your voice in the writing. There's none of that here."

"Thanks."

Quincy laughed. "It was kind of creepy, actually. I just hope the publisher doesn't, you know, think the subject matter is a little too weird with the supernatural stuff and all. Makes it sound like Riff's confirming everyone's suspicions about him."

"He's not crazy."

Quincy paused. "Hey, how are you doing? With everything?"

Quincy didn't know everything. He didn't know about Riff and me, and I'd decided not to tell him. Everyone didn't need to know everything.

"Fine," I said. "I'm just fine. Oh, and I'm meeting with Trace at the end of the week."

"What? Shut up. You're joking."

"Nope."

"You going to bury the hatchet?"

"Hm, don't know about that." Quincy still didn't know what "the hatchet" was. Maybe one day I'd tell him.

"Well, look, I'm sending the final draft to the publisher today," he said. "I'll get back to you as soon as I hear from them, but I think they'll want it. I mean, delusional or not, the guy's got a following."

IT WAS IMPORTANT THAT I see my father on my turf, so I asked him to meet me at a bookstore in Brentwood, where I'd met with Abe Brion earlier in the day. Now that Riff's project was over, I could start Abe's, which was pretty much like every other musician. Even so, this time, there was something refreshing about the normalcy of a story about sex, drugs, and rock and roll.

I sat at the table in the bookstore coffee shop, alternating between nervously licking the icing off a chocolate cupcake and inhaling the coffee aroma from my paper cup.

What would Dad look like now? It had been so long since I'd glimpsed an online photo of him. I remembered him with long, straight, dirty-blond hair and icy blue eyes that always seemed to look right through me—or past me. I remembered leather jackets and fringed boots and skull rings. I remembered dagger earrings and combat boots and—

"Callie?"

I looked up. The man standing at the table's edge might have been a stranger. Gone were the leather jacket and dangling earrings. His face was older and thinner, lined and road-worn with several days' stubble. The tan windbreaker he wore hung from his frame, making him appear frail—like an older person whose blood had thinned and who needed to wear a jacket even inside.

I set down my cupcake. "Hi."

"Hi." He smiled and motioned to the chair opposite me. "Do you mind if I..."

"No, go ahead."

He braced his hands on the table and settled into the chair, wincing as if sitting was painful. "I would have known you anywhere."

I couldn't say the same, but I nodded.

He coughed out a prolonged hack, then plucked a handkerchief from his pocket and swiped it across his mouth. "Do you live here in Brentwood, or—"

"No, I live in the city. I was with a client earlier, so meeting you here made sense."

As a kid, I remembered Dad's teeth as blindingly white. Now, they were yellow, the grooves stained brown.

"I hear you're doing well," he said. "Really successful. I'm proud of you."

I took a beat, processing. I touched my cup of coffee. Still too hot to drink. He was proud of me? That might have meant more if he'd called me on occasion over the years.

I bit my lip and nodded. "Thanks." I pinched off a piece of the cupcake and popped it in my mouth. How was this conversation going to go? Was he going to toss out platitudes, and would I simply acknowledge them? How did I breach the subject of what I really wanted to know? Could I even do it?

"Are you married?" he asked.

I shook my head. "Nope. Not married. No kids. You?"

He looked off into the store. "I've been married a few times. I'm divorced now. No kids other than you."

Surprising. "Are you still playing music?"

He shook his head. "Not anymore. I've been sick for a while." He held up his hand and wriggled his fingers. "These don't work so well anymore."

My heart squeezed. That he was unable to do what he'd always loved was sad. I'd feel bad for anyone in that situation. "I'm sorry to hear that."

His eyes were clear now, and a hard line divided his gray eyebrows. "Callie, I wanted to see you—I really wanted to see you. Thank you for meeting me."

I sat up a little straighter.

He placed his fingertips to his forehead. "I'm starting to remember bits and pieces. Things I wish I didn't." He dropped his gaze to his hands. "But once you remember, you can't *unremember*, if you understand what I mean."

I compressed my mouth.

"And it's not that I haven't thought about you over the years. I have. But it hurt too much to think about it—about you." He lowered his chin. "About what happened to you. About what I let happen to you."

I wiped my hands on my napkin and settled them into my lap, balling them into fists.

"I was using drugs pretty heavily when you were young—and that's no excuse." He held up his hands. The fingers were bent, gnarled. "I don't want you to think I'm letting myself off the hook here because I'm not. I take full responsibility. I should have protected you, Callie, and I didn't. I should've killed Frankie for even thinking about touching you." His eyes watered. "Instead, I was a stupid asshole without a molecule of integrity. I wanted to keep my band. If I'd admitted to myself that Frankie took advantage of you..." He shook his head. "I'd have had to break up the band. I was a selfish bastard. I didn't want that."

I sipped my coffee and swallowed, letting it scorch the back of my throat. Focusing on the burn kept me from feeling. With every word Trace spoke, I fell deeper into the past, rolling back the years until I was fourteen. I didn't want to be that girl again.

"Do you want some coffee?" I shot my eyes toward the counter.

Trace shook his head. "No, thanks." He rubbed the back of his hand under his nose. "I just wanted to say I'm sorry, Callie. I know you must hate me, and I don't blame you. Look, I know what I did. I know what Frankie did. The regret I feel now—about what that must have done to you all these years—" He broke off, covered his eyes. "Once a few years had gone by, even after Frankie died, I was too embarrassed to contact you. So I buried the whole thing."

I took another sip.

"When I think of all the years we've missed when we could've had a relationship..." He took his hands away and wiped at the tears collecting under his eyes. "I always loved you. I just didn't know how to show you."

I exhaled air through my nostrils. "So why now?"

He cleared his throat. "I'm dying, Callie. Stage four lung cancer. Years of smoking finally caught up to me."

I flinched, my gaze shifting to customers coming and going.

"I'm not telling you that for sympathy, but I thought you should know all this—before I'm gone."

I blew over the top of my coffee cup and sipped again. It had cooled off and didn't burn when I swallowed it. After all this time, the hatred I'd felt for my father wasn't there anymore. I couldn't find it. The man I'd imagined as a self-important rocker was now just a broken-down old man dying of cancer.

"I forgive you," I said, the words surprising even me.

Trace jerked his head up, his eyes round. "Thank you, but I didn't expect you to forgive me."

"Still, I do. I forgive you."

He chewed at the side of his mouth, apparently out of words.

I cleared my throat. "Tell me about your illness. Are you still being treated?"

He shook his head. "Nothing else they can do. I've got a few months. If that. No more treatments."

I didn't know if it was unburdening myself of the anger I'd held onto all of these years or if it was my burning throat or memories or what, but I suddenly felt like being a part of my dad's life—even if only for a few weeks or months. I wanted to help.

I folded my hands and leaned forward. "So, I know someone you should talk to. His name is Zeke."

A Final Note

I saw her a year and a half later at the publicity gathering for Riff's memoir *Fallen Star*. She stood by the wall near the open bar, holding a glass of wine and staring at me. The conference center was teeming with events and people who slid past her like running water. I caught glimpses of her gold dress and burnished auburn hair.

She looked exactly like the photos I'd seen online, shapely in an almost cartoonish way, with hypnotic green eyes that shimmered even under the crappy fluorescent lighting. It couldn't be her, not really. Could it? Yet the way she stared at me made me believe she knew me too.

I looked around for Riff. *Kirka Taylor isn't dead. She's here.*

But when I finally located him, a circle of reporters swarmed around him, and by the time I hurried back to the bar area, I only saw the back of her as she walked away on the arm of some guy in a sports coat.

When I told Riff later, he said it was probably just someone who looked like her. "I mistake women all the time for Lila too, but of course it's not her."

I felt sure it had been her. I'd seen the siren, the demon in her eyes. Maybe she'd gone on to occupy the body of another woman who could reflect the same predatory vibrations.

Like Lila and all the other victims, Abbot's body was never found. Only parts of his boat were located in the marshes—some twenty-five miles away. The most vicious trait of a siren was how they left so little to the survivors. No remains to identify, not even a shred of clothing or a hat—nothing to bring closure. Instead, loved ones were left with the mystery, the wondering, the agony of not knowing.

Sometimes, I still think I hear them. At night, just before I sleep, I imagine a voice in the breezeway singing notes human vocal cords couldn't possibly create. But then, I realize it's a drunk man or woman stumbling up the stairs to their condo. Other times, just like the night of Riff's publicity junket, I'm sure I see one of them—when I'm standing in a crowd or visiting friends at the beach. The vacuous stare of a tattooed girl standing on the threshold of Souvenir Palace or Cotton Candy Cradle. Then she turns and joins her boyfriend, and they walk off toward the Ferris wheel hand in hand.

Trace finally passed away a month ago after a valiant fight, including several consultations with Zeke and his machine. My father later told me that he found someone in LA who boasted a similar apparatus, and he felt he had received some benefit. At least, he thought it had bought him an extra year of life in which we enjoyed frequent talks. I was at his bedside in LA when he passed. He may not have been around for me during my beginnings, but I considered it a privilege to be there for him at his end.

Zeke is at Georgetown now. He received a scholarship through the university and multiple organizations based on his paper on innovative technology. He still extensively researches the power of frequencies and says he wants to find a permanent cure for cancer. I have no doubt that he will.

Riff and I maintain separate lives but still see each other often. He comes to Nashville, or I go to Invisible Island, and we have become a part of that community. His solo album was released shortly after his book and is doing very well. But with his busy tour schedule, it doesn't make sense for us to stay in one place. At least not now.

So, I've settled into my cigarette-free life in Nashville with my new mutt from the local shelter—Robert. My new goldfish proudly bears the name Lila, and the two already have a love affair. Robert sits in front of the bowl every day and watches Lila move, whining a little as though he wishes he could swim alongside her. In turn, Lila doesn't seem to want to be on dry land, but she does watch him with interest. I send Riff pictures of them daily.

And I have begun my own project, entitled *I'm Sort of With the Band: My Life Not Quite Living With Trace Rowe*. Beckett House has already contracted it. It should be on the shelves sometime next year.

Author's Note

I have always loved music.

I confess that I was a bit of a groupie as a teenager, majored in music as a college student, and, as an adult, still enjoy a live concert with a great band.

Riff Fall is an amalgamation of several lead singers over whom I fangirled throughout the years. Who am I kidding? I'm still a fangirl!

Invisible Island was inspired by a real place called Daufuskie, a remote island off the southernmost coast of South Carolina. There is no bridge for access—only ferries and boats. Therefore, it has retained a primitive flavor with dirt roads, golf cart transportation, and around 400 full-time residents. The island is rich in Muskogee and Gullah history, which I could only hint at in this story. I had the privilege of visiting Daufuskie twice in the past year, and I never encountered a siren. However, the abandoned resort is real and many say the Gullah curse is real as well. Built in 1986, the Melrose Resort at Daufuskie Island began as a high-class spa and convention center with a world-class golf course. A series of scandals, bankruptcies, and Ponzi schemes resulted in the resort shutting its doors around 2011. Hurricane Matthew did a number on the place in 2016, and since then, vandals have completely ransacked it. Recently, an international hotel developer bought the resort, golf course, and accompanying property, so we shall see if the place can be resurrected after all.

The island is truly a magical place, and if you don't mind some potholes, limited eating options, and a much slower pace, I highly recommend Daufuskie for total relaxation and a unique experience.

Royal Rife and his machine are real, and if you do a little research, you may find yourself on an interesting journey with electromagnetic frequencies and their healing powers.

Most people know about Homer and his epic poem *The Odyssey*, but I did not realize that Pliny the Elder and others had also addressed sirens in their writings. Their descriptions did not depict the creatures as mermaid-like but as evil, half-human, half-bird beings. I chose to use these historians' accounts with a dash of Homer's seductresses in the mix. Even though I didn't set out to write a story about sirens, Circe and the music business seemed to go together like peanut butter and jelly, so the story grew into something different as I went along.

To strike a final chord, every book is an interesting path for me—one filled with research, travel, and questions. This book has left me with more than I started with—about Daufuskie, electromagnetic frequencies, and Gullah heritage. I will no doubt be plumbing the depths of those questions for some time to come.

Acknowledgments

Many thanks go out to the initial readers of this book: The members of the South Carolina Writers Association Greenville Group, Lisa Godfrey, and Deborah Harris.

Thanks also to those who offered plot lifelines when I was literally drowning: Stephen Lee and Christie Mangelsen. I know neither of you will ever read this book, but your suggestions were pivotal to the storyline.

Thanks to all the wonderful folks on Daufuskie Island who answered my crazy questions. A special thanks to Sallie Ann Robinson, whose wonderful Gullah Heritage Tour taught me so much about the area. I still have a lot to learn, but I can't thank Sallie Ann enough for her warmth, jovial personality, and willingness to answer all my questions. This was especially true with some facts I'd gotten wrong, such as haint blue isn't widely used on Daufuskie and Gullahs don't always put their graveyards next to water. And I was thrilled to learn that Spanish moss is edible and has health benefits.

I am grateful to the bands Creed and Evanescence for providing me with the music I listened to and was inspired by throughout the writing of this book.

As always, thanks to family and friends who put up with me, listen to all my wild ideas, and continue to encourage me. Thanks to the Good Lord above for allowing me to write these crazy stories.

Thanks to Lisa Godfrey for your skills in the developmental and editing phases. Thank you, Lisa Hollowell and Deborah Harris, for your eagle-eye proofreads.

Finally, readers, I could not do this without you. Thank you, thank you for your continued support. Much love to you all.

Did you love *The Night Singers*? Then you should read *Until Death* by London Clarke!

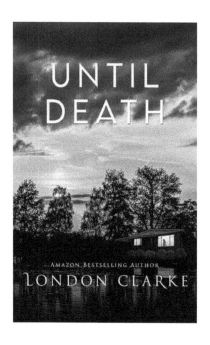

In this haunting tale of supernatural suspense, love will be tested, secrets will unravel, and the dead will speak.

Hope Hendriks thought she had hit rock bottom when her husband took his own life, leaving her broke and homeless. Hoping for a fresh start, she takes a new job in Tennessee, moving into a run-down rental property in a lake community. Still mourning the loss of a man she seemingly never knew, Hope is confronted by a host of alarming and inexplicable occurrences that suggest her deceased husband may still be with her.

Down on his luck and living with a volatile girlfriend, Reed Sewall finds his new neighbor intriguing. More than once, she's asked him to check the house for home invaders, and although he has no expectations beyond friendship, his attachment to her grows.

Even so, she's a grieving widow, and he's a battered boyfriend—not a great recipe for a relationship.

As Hope seeks to uncover the mystery of her husband's life and death, the supernatural activity within her home intensifies, and neighbors whisper tales of a family who met tragic ends within its walls. Reed soon finds himself pulled into Hope's perilous quest for answers, and a horrifying force set in motion long ago threatens to pull both down in death's grip.

Until Death is a haunting exploration of the ties that bind us even in death and questions whether love can conquer all when faced with unspeakable evil.

Read more at https://www.londonclarke.com.

Also by London Clarke

Dunmoor
Dunmoor
House of Brutes and Angels

Legacy of Darkness
The Meadows
Whickering Place
Nocturne House
Pearse

Standalone
Wildfell
The Neighbor
Until Death
The Night Singers

Watch for more at https://www.londonclarke.com.

About the Author

London Clarke is the author of nine novels, which have repeatedly reached #1 Amazon bestseller status in ghost thriller, horror suspense, and vampire suspense categories. When she's not exploring remote islands, abandoned houses, or Spanish moss-riddled woods, she can be found sitting at her computer, planning her next scary book. Clarke lives in South Carolina with her husband and two Italian greyhounds.

Read more at https://www.londonclarke.com.